Gettysburg by Morning

Randy O'Brien

Gettysburg
by Morning

Addison & Highsmith

Addison & Highsmith Publishers

Las Vegas ◊ Chicago ◊ Palm Beach

Published in the United States of America by
Histria Books
7181 N. Hualapai Way, Ste. 130-86
Las Vegas, NV 89166 USA
HistriaBooks.com

Addison & Highsmith is an imprint of Histria Books. Titles published under the imprints of Histria Books are distributed worldwide.

This work of fiction contains graphic language, violence, gore, brutality, and sexual violence, including racial epithets used in historical context.

Library of Congress Control Number: 2021945384

ISBN 978-1-59211-101-5 (hardcover)
ISBN 978-1-59211-207-4 (paperback)
ISBN 978-1-59211-274-6 (eBook)

Dedication

Thanks to my editor Kurt for support and for keeping the history accurate. Thank you to every teacher and employer who challenged me and supported my effort to find my voice. Thanks to every librarian who guided me toward the inspirational books for which I am thankful. Thanks to Steven Womack for his guidance and friendship. Thank you to my grandmother, the strong, loving, quiet poet who inspired me. Thanks to my mother and father for their reassurance and support and my sister Cindy's backing and love. Thanks to my daughter Molly for being the shining light in my life and to my darling wife, Beth, who brings joy and laughter into my life.

Chapter 1

July 4, 1861

Eloise clutched the sheaf of papers to her heart. They moved, almost fell. She glared down at them. She paused for a moment and found a new grip. She had spent most of last night and much of this morning poring over one history book after another in hopes of making this a memorable speech. She wanted it to be the best speech ever at an Independence Day celebration.

"Not today," she whispered, "not this most important day."

A brilliant yellow sun beamed down on her as her new shoes skipped along the cobblestones of downtown Concord, Massachusetts. A single bead of sweat ran down the side of her face. She brushed it away but did not stop moving. She passed the storefronts and homes of the locals, recognizing that most of them were likely already at the park, waiting for the celebration to begin. She saw her reflection in the windows. She was thin and raven-haired, with a tiny waist and small breasts. Her eyes were her best feature, dark blue and large with thick lashes and shapely brows. Her eyes were just like her mother's. Eyes just like her brother, come to think of it. In the distance, she heard a band start playing "Yankee Doodle Dandy."

"Oh, no," she gasped.

She redoubled her efforts and pushed on. The edge of her dress brushed the ground, and she worried that somehow the brilliant red fabric might have a dusty covering by the time she reached the gazebo. She decided that it was better to have a dirty skirt than to drop her notes. She turned a corner at Front Street. The General Store was already closed. Sacks labeled Rice and Beans, a roll of cotton, and single-shot rifles filled the windows. She stepped around a large pile of horse dung, hoping against hope that the edge of her skirt would miss it. It did. She blew out a gasp of relief. Concord was a thriving town with plenty of opportunities for young people to find their place in the world unless there was war. If there were a war between the states, the young men would enlist, and the government would draft them into the Army. The women would have to stay home and do their best to keep the home fires burning.

The music grew louder as Eloise rounded a street corner, and she knew that her introduction would soon follow.

She began practicing her opening line in her mind. The speech ran well over ten minutes, but she knew the opening line was the most important. It would be the one line everyone would remember. It would likely be the one line that the newspaper would quote in the next morning's article. She hoped it would be an article that would likely lead the news with a "hopefully" attractive drawing of her next to the columns of print.

She slowed her pace a bit, not wanting to appear wholly winded and frazzled as she passed the crowd sitting on blankets and enjoying their picnic lunches. First, she strode past the Spiegel family, who had lived next door for over ten years. Next, she passed the Spurlock family with three brothers, each equally handsome and robust – a whole flock of eligible bachelors, as her mother would often remind her. Near them was Minister Hemlock's small family. Finally, Eloise nodded and waved at the mayor's large family of thirteen.

Sitting in front was her family, small though it was; Jeremiah, her father, and her brother Edward. They had dressed as Minutemen in celebration of the holiday. Her father wore a single ribbon of red, white, and blue on his lapel. He was proud of his grandfather's service, but he never handed down any stories about what happened in the war. It had been presented by General George Washington, and Eloise's father wore it rarely. This was one of those special occasions.

Eloise's mother had passed the previous year, and while they had found a way to go on, it had been a difficult transition. There was more than one occasion that she had seen her father sitting on the back steps of their home by himself, staring into the distance. Her brother, Edward, had been hard hit by the loss, but his reaction was more directed at spending time in the woods by himself.

The band continued to play. Eloise stepped to the back of the gazebo and shook hands with Jason. He was the emcee of the program. He was as tall as Eloise but was fair with brown eyes and a thick beard. She had enjoyed school with him as they grew up together, but his interests had become farming and hunting. She had worked in her father's livery and enjoyed the horses as much as dealing with the people.

"Eloise, where have you been?"

"Just adding a few last-minute touches to my speech."

"We were close to having the mayor speak."

Eloise handed Jason her notes and smoothed her skirt. She widened her eyes, swiping at the corners. She pinched her cheeks, hoping against hope that her race to get there hadn't caused her to glow and distract from the words she was to deliver.

"That would not have been a complete tragedy, but he can be quite boring when he speaks off the cuff."

Jason smiled sheepishly and looked down at Eloise's notes.

"He's right behind me, isn't he?"

The Mayor of Concord had pulled on a waist jacket and a small red tie. He adjusted his tricorn hat and tugged at his ruffled sleeves.

"Hot enough for you, Miss Eloise?" His Honor asked.

Eloise dipped her gaze at the ground and blushed unwittingly, giving her cheeks the desired effect of youthful beauty.

"It will soon be hotter still after I give this speech," she replied.

"You're hoping to rile the crowd into a mob?"

"No, Sir," she said as she looked him in the eye, "merely righteous indignation over what has happened."

The mayor clasped his hands in front of his massive belly. He smiled and reached into his pocket for a cigar. "Righteous indignation, indeed," he said.

The band, a mixture of old and new players, fiddlers, and brass players, moved to the last song on the playlist. Jason handed Eloise her notes and tugged on his waistcoat and black tricorn hat. The Independence Day celebrations had become more elaborate each year, this time ending in fireworks coordinated with the playing of music by the town's brass band.

Eloise let the music wash over her. She closed her eyes and tried to think of different ways she might deliver the opening line of her speech. Should it be a whisper, drawing the people into her spell? Should it be a shout of emotion and a rallying cry? Should it be delivered in a conversational tone, with the simplicity of two people talking over the back fence of the news that was on everyone's lips?

Would there be war? Moreover, what would Massachusetts' place be except at the very front of the line? This was the seat of freedom. This was the place where it had all begun. America came into being because of what happened at Concord just eighty-five years before.

The final notes of the song echoed through the small outdoor amphitheater. Jason adjusted his collar and strode up the steps behind the band. Band members clutched their instruments and moved their chairs to the back of the gazebo. They exited, looking at Eloise and giving her words and nods of encouragement.

Eloise closed her eyes again and said a small prayer for strength and courage.

Jason tugged the podium from off-stage and dragged it to the center of the platform.

"We are proud to have one of our own with us today. She is a recent graduate of Concord school with an emphasis on history and writing. She has read the classics and has mentioned reading the law one day in hopes of becoming a lawyer."

A murmur moved through the crowd. A family to the right of the stage closed their picnic basket and passed around a small jug. The brilliant sun had several in the group unbuttoning collar buttons and taking off coats. A breeze moved through the amphitheater, and several people gave visible sighs of relief.

Eloise wished Jason would move past all the flowery words of his introduction. She had grown up in this community and knew most of the people in the audience, as well as she knew her brother and father. She turned her head and gazed at the sea of people waiting to hear what she would have to say. Her stomach did a flip, and she felt another bead of sweat move down the side of her face. She quickly brushed it away.

What could she say to people anxious about the recent happenings in South Carolina? What could she say that might allay their fears and inspire them to feel good about the country and the new president?

Jason turned from the podium, walked across the stage, and held out his hand to Eloise. She took it and walked up the steps. Her notes were clutched in her right hand as she stood behind the podium. She looked down at her scribblings. The yellow pages seemed filled with useless words and phrases. It was all wrong. There was no emotion. It was all head, no heart—facts, figures, and dates that had little to do with the actual reason for today's celebration.

"*No heart*," she thought. Now, it made no sense to her. She took the notes and put them on a small shelf under the podium.

The crowd was growing restless, and some people had averted their eyes in embarrassment for her.

She gazed down at the eyes looking up to her. It was as if she could feel their anxiety about the future. It was as if she could feel what was in their hearts. She would speak from her heart to theirs.

She raised her chin and slapped the top of the podium.

Chapter 2

"Four score and three years ago, the men of this town engaged in a battle that would lead to America's independence, creating a new nation, conceived in liberty and dedicated to the proposition that all men, black or white, are created equal. On April 12th of this year, Confederate soldiers fired on Fort Sumter in South Carolina in a vicious and unnecessary attack on those of us who believe in the Union."

She felt the blood rise in her cheeks again. This time she knew her heart was pure and filled with emotion.

"The question we have to ask is, do the words of the Declaration of Independence encompass the Negro? Our forefathers created the United States of America, not two separate nations. I am a simple person who, deep in her heart, believes in those sacred words that proclaim all men are created equal. Our future depends on that belief, and it is only with that assurance that we will progress and fulfill our destiny."

Eloise scanned the crowd, looking for signs of interest or approval. There were several faces upturned and eyes fixed on her. Several faces dipped down toward their meals or children as they played on the soft pallets. A few were already asleep. She would ignore those who didn't pay attention.

"The question we have to ask is, does the Negro not bleed when he is cut? Does he not wish to have a family and that his children should someday have a better life than his own? We are not so different, but as long as Negroes are seen only as property and farm implements, our Southern brethren will not yield to the inevitable—that this country is and always will be the United States of America."

Eloise saw some of those sleeping, still sleeping. Others sat wide-eyed, hanging on every word. Others again looked in horror, not believing the words and images she was using. She continued.

"My subject, then, fellow citizens, is 'American Slavery.' I shall see this day and its popular characteristics from the slave's point of view. Standing here, identified with the American bondsman, making his wrongs mine, I do not hesitate to declare, with all my soul, that the character and conduct of this nation have never looked blacker to me than on this Fourth of July.

"Whether we turn to the declarations of the past or the professions of the present, the conduct of the nation seems equally hideous and revolting. America is false to the past, false to the present, and solemnly binds herself to be false to the future. Standing with God and the crushed and bleeding slave on this occasion, I will, in the name of humanity, which is outraged, in the name of liberty, which is fettered, in the name of the Constitution and the Bible, which the Rebels disregard and trample upon, dare to call in question and to denounce, with all the emphasis I can command, everything that serves to perpetuate slavery — the great sin and shame of America! I will not equivocate — I will not excuse — I will not rest until we grind this terrible abomination into dust. I will use the severest language I can command. Yet, not one word shall escape me that any man whose judgment is not blinded by prejudice or who is not at heart a slaveholder shall not confess to be right and just."

She paused a second and found a small jar of water on the shelf inside the podium. She picked up the glass and took a sip. She cleared her throat and soldiered on toward the end.

"But I fancy I hear some of my audience say it is just in this circumstance that you and your brother Abolitionists fail to make a favorable impression on the public mind. Would you argue more and denounce less, would you persuade more and rebuke less, would your cause be much more likely to succeed? What is this but the acknowledgment that the slave is a moral, intellectual, and responsible being?"

With that exclamation, several of the faces in the crowd that were dozing or preoccupied with something on the ground turned to Eloise as she banged her fist again on the podium.

"For the present, it is enough to affirm the equal manhood of the Negro race. Would you have me argue that man is entitled to liberty? That he is the rightful owner of his own body? You have already declared it. Must I argue the wrongfulness of slavery? Is that a question for Republicans? Is it to be settled by the rules of logic and argumentation, as a matter beset with great difficulty, involving a doubtful application of the principle of justice, hard to understand? How should I look today in the presence of Americans, dividing and subdividing a discourse to show that men have a natural right to freedom, speaking of it relatively and positively, negatively, and affirmatively? To do so would be to make myself ridiculous and to offer an insult to your understanding. There is not a man beneath the canopy of heaven who does not know that slavery is wrong for him. This is a government of the people, by the people, for the people, and it shall not perish from the earth. It is time for real Americans to stand up and say, No More."

She stepped from behind the podium and searched the faces of the crowd.

"I say, slavery is wrong, and war is right!"

She raised her arms and led the chant.

"Union, Union, Union!"

The crowd also rose and joined her.

"Union, Union, Union," reverberated through the amphitheater.

She looked down at her brother and saw his eyes shining with tears. His face contorted, his mouth shaping the words, "Union, UNION, UNION!"

Chapter 3

Eloise took a step down from the gazebo and rushed to her brother.

"I did it," she said, smiling.

"Yes, you did," he agreed. He took her in his arms and hugged her. "I am so proud of you."

"I think it's going to be in the paper," she said. She glanced over at the reporter from the Observer.

The young man was writing furiously on his papers. He wore a simple brown suit and a white shirt. He wore glasses, and his hair was black and oily. As if he knew someone was observing him, he glanced up, looked around the park, and returned to his scribbling. Yet, even from that distance, she could see a sketch of a young woman, mouth open, arm raised, with wide eyes. It was the moment she led the crowd in the chant for "Union."

"I think you've given him some grist for the mill," her brother said. He lifted her, spun her around, and put her back on the ground.

"You shouldn't do that." She blushed again. "We're not kids anymore."

He turned up his nose and said, "Just because we've grown older doesn't mean we can't still play like we used to."

Eloise straightened her skirt and her high neck collar. "It's undignified."

Edward bowed and swept this three-cornered hat at the ground. "Your wish is my command, my lady."

Eloise blushed and moved to the pallet where her father sat. She looked down at him.

"Father, how did you like the speech?"

He looked up. His eyes were tired and downturned at the corners. "The speech wasn't for me. It was for the young men who may soon give up their lives for their country."

"Pish posh," she said as she lowered herself down to his level.

"War isn't all patriotism and flying flags." He swept his hand across the top of the grass at the edge of the blanket.

"I know that," she said. "But with a show of might, the South will surely give up their foolhardy and treasonous behavior."

"I have read of great arguments in the halls of Congress," he said with a resigned air. "Beer halls filled with men fighting over the petty ideas of politics, duels, for God's sake."

She said, "I really don't think a full-scale war will be necessary to prosecute the ones who lead this lost cause."

"I remember the arguments for and against the revolution against King George. The words inspired and angered but meant little when standing in a line; musket raised, awaiting the order to fire and end the life of another human being." He took a deep breath. "I hope you are right."

Eloise sprang to her feet, still feeling the elation brought on by her success.

"Let's go home, Father," she said as she lowered her hand.

He reached up. A sense of pride and dread filled his mind.

They bundled up the picnic basket and blanket and moved through the crowd of well-wishers and supporters. She overheard some as they pointed out how Eloise would make a great politician's wife. Others regretted their inability to vote for her in the upcoming elections.

"One day, "Eloise said as she led the two men in her life through the threshold that designated the beginning of Freedom Park.

"Yes," she continued, "one day, the government will affirm that all men and women are created equal in this country."

"Equal rights for all," Edward said as he juggled the picnic basket and his pipe.

***

The next day, Eloise's speech filled the left column of the newspaper's front page. There was no drawing of her, but another column reported the reaction to her speech from people who had observed it.

"Rousing," one man said.

"Patriotic," said another.

The writer made a point of indicating where the speech had been interrupted by cheering and applause.

Eloise read both articles twice.

She wished there were something more she might do to support the effort to put those Rebels in their places. She knew she could roll bandages, sort supplies, and sew uniforms. That had already been proposed and was recognized by society as acceptable professions for Union women supporters. But Eloise wanted to do more.

She thought she might want someday to rewrite her speech. They would need to raise money to finance the war. She would go on tour and speak to groups, women's groups more likely, that might support the government's efforts and the new President.

She plucked her broom from the closet in the kitchen. She swung the head up to her face and then back down to the floor. She began to sweep and hum a jaunty tune.

She swept toward the back door, allowing the dust to settle a bit between strokes. She spun the broom again and bowed to the head as if it were a young gentleman caller.

"Why don't mind if I do," she said to the broom.

Still humming, she tapped the end of the broom on the floor and began a slow waltz. Her skirt spun around her legs as she quickstepped with agility and perfect rhythm.

"Thank you very much for the compliment," she said as she nodded to the broom. "I don't have much time to practice, so I'm very pleased that you like what you see."

Edward appeared at the back door and watched her as she spun, face gleaming, eyes shining, and a wide grin stretching her lips.

She bowed again to the broom.

"Bravo," Edward said. "A fine dance."

"Edward!" she screamed. "You startled me."

As he leaned against the door jamb, he asked, "And what about your dance partner, was he startled, too?"

"He is the perfect partner. He never asks rude questions. He's always on tempo, and he never steps on my toes."

"And he never eats," Edward said.

Eloise spun the broom around and began sweeping again.

"And he's always handy when it's time to clean up."

They both laughed. He walked across the room, picked up the newspaper, and read the headline.

"Congratulations on your success." His heart filled with pride, and he believed everything she'd said.

"My only hope is that my words might someday inspire people to take action."

He glanced up at her and smiled. "Your words already have," he said as he pulled a slip of paper from his coat pocket. "I've just been to the county seat, and I've placed my name on the roster for serving in the Army."

Eloise's face jerked up. She caught Edward's eyes in her gaze.

"No, Edward, not you, that's not what I want. We need you here."

"I will do our family proud. I'm joining the Massachusetts 20th. I'm awaiting orders for training, and then I'll likely be sent South."

Eloise pulled a chair from under the table. She folded her hands in front of her and nodded for Edward to sit with her. He obliged.

"Let me remind you that our mother has just died. That our house is still in turmoil because of that."

Edward raised his hand, but she would not stop.

"Our father is still grieving the loss of his soul mate. To have a child, his favorite child, leave and place himself in mortal danger is too much for the family to bear, for him to bear."

"I would debate you on your thinking that I am the favorite child, but there is no question that the current state of affairs requires that someone take action. You said it yourself."

"But, Edward," she pleaded.

"I'm sure you and Father will get along swimmingly without me. And as you say, time and time again, the South will surely see the error of secession and capitulate within weeks, if not months."

Edward took Eloise's hands in his across the table. "I'll be fine. I'll be back home before you even realize that I'm gone."

"But —"

"No buts. And think of the adventure, the opportunity for the display of valor and courage. Times like these spawn great men."

Eloise began crying, and her nose ran. Edward produced a handkerchief.

"Dry your eyes, dear sister. Your words have inspired me to take up arms and defend our freedom and home. There can be no greater pride."

Edward's words failed to stop Eloise's tears, but deep down, there was a spark of confidence in her brother's decision and how her words had encouraged the spark into a flame.

Chapter 4

Eloise tied her horse to the hitching post in front of the courthouse. She patted the horse's neck and looked up and down the busy street. "You'll be fine right here, Junebug."

She adjusted her hat and looked across the street to the clerk's office. A bright sun was just beginning to dry the mud left behind by the morning rain. She marveled at how her tiny little town was growing into a bustling metropolis. She surmised there must be over two thousand people in the city limits and half as many outside. "*Where will we put all these people?*" she thought.

She tugged at her sleeves, picked up her bag from the wagon seat, and took a step around a mud puddle. A series of broad, wooden planks had been placed through the middle of the street. Eloise gathered up her skirts and leaped toward the center of the dry wood. Her foot slipped, but she caught herself before going headfirst into a puddle.

Horses and wagons bustled around her as she dodged potholes and piles of horse dung. She touched her handkerchief to her nose as she tried to hold her breath.

A horse reared, startling Eloise, and forcing her to take a step back. The rider yanked at the reins and settled the animal down. He pulled the edge of his hat down at Eloise as he turned the horse north. "*Outrageous,*" she thought. "*I could be killed in the streets of my county seat.*"

She hurried across the street and stood for a moment at the door that read "Department of the Army." She paced for a moment. She pulled a small note from her bag and studied the page. Satisfied, she knocked and waited.

"Yes, come in." The voice was gruff and angry in tone.

She opened the door and waited for a moment for her eyes to adjust.

"Hello, is anybody here?" Eloise asked.

A uniformed officer stood at the window. He was tall with a shock of black hair. He gazed out the window but seemed unfocused and lost in thought. He raised a coffee cup to his lips and took a sip.

"Too hot," he complained.

Eloise grasped her bag with both hands. "If I might have a moment of your time."

The man turned. He wore a large handlebar mustache, a white cotton shirt, a dark blue uniform, and black boots. "Young woman. Can I help you?"

"I'm Eloise Jacobson."

"Oliver Wendell Holmes," he said.

"Pleased to meet you." She nodded but didn't offer her hand.

He waved her to move closer. The office had a large bookcase filled with books against one wall. A giant hearth with a dying fire sat behind Oliver. In the corner, a reading lamp sat on a small end table. A small stove with a cooking surface rested next to the fireplace.

She sat across the desk in the center of the room. She placed her bag on the floor next to the chair and removed her hat.

"My brother, Edward, has decided to join the effort to protect our Union."

"Just a few days ago, yes, I remember," Oliver said as he smoothed his mustache. "Please forgive me. Are you warm enough? I can poke the fire a bit if you are cold."

She glanced at the young man and then back down at her papers. "No, I'm fine. Yes, I'm very proud of him, but I wanted to know if there is something I can do to help."

Oliver steepled his fingers in front of his face. He looked at her over the "roof" of the church his hands had formed. He leaned back in his chair.

"As you know, there will be a great need for military support here in Massa —"

"I know all about rolling bandages and raising money with bake sales," she said. Her frustration was barely contained. "I am young, healthy, and intelligent. I am ready to fight."

"How old are you, if I may ask?"

She felt a muscle in her cheek twitch. It sometimes happened when she lied. "I am eighteen, sir."

"And you have experience in shooting, bayoneting, knife-fighting. You feel you are strong enough to march the required twenty miles a day and be prepared for battle." Oliver had affected a biting tone to his voice and even allowed a sneer to play at the edge of his mouth.

"Of course not. You are mocking me, sir," she huffed. "I will not have it." Her eyes grew large, and her breath was shallow. She would not allow tears to form in the corners of her eyes. She redoubled her efforts to keep herself in check.

"I'm sorry, Eloise. I didn't mean to be rude." He was taken aback by her reaction. He had never seen a woman react in such a way. "I have rules and laws to follow, young lady. I am constrained by those and others as to the kinds of skills you can contribute to the effort."

She slowed her breathing. She took out her handkerchief and wiped the end of her nose. "There must be something substantial I can do?"

"Again—"

"My family at one time owned a livery. We now operate the telegraph office. My brother and I are both skilled operators."

Oliver's eyes widened, and he let his hands relax. "There is now and will be a need for that skill in the future, no doubt. I will keep this in mind for, you said his name is — "

"Edward. Yes, we are not here to talk about him, though, Mr. Holmes. I would like to contribute."

"You want to fight?"

She moved about in her chair, looked down at the floor that needed sweeping, and said, "Yes."

"Again, let me remind you, I am constrained by the laws of our country and the norms of society that that is not your place."

She realized she was overplaying her hand and that a more lady-like tone might be more efficient. "I understand. I get excited at times. Maybe I've overstepped."

Oliver stifled a grin. "Yes, you definitely have. I will mention this telegraph operating skill to Edward—"

"Morse code," Eloise said.

"Yes, and ask if he wishes to help with communications. He was very riled up when he came in."

She blushed, but a slight twinge of pride swelled in her heart. She said, "For better or worse, that can be attributed to me." She opened her bag and pulled out a copy of the newspaper article of her speech on Independence Day. She smiled as she handed it across the desk to him.

Holmes unfolded the paper and glanced at the top of the page. "Yes," he said, "I remember reading this. You wrote the speech?"

She blushed even more, hated herself for doing so, and said, "I had written the outline before stepping on the stage, but much of what is here was spoken extemporaneously."

He looked at her from the top of the newsprint. "That is remarkable."

Her eyes flashed as she said, "It's remarkable that a woman could speak in patriotic terms and cogently express herself?"

Oliver took a quick breath and pulled in his chin. "Of course you can. That's not what I meant."

"So, what did you mean?" she asked, barely holding in her ire.

He shuffled his feet under the desk. "I meant that — are you a reader?"

"I have read the classics."

"And your favorites?" he asked.

"I was most engaged with Plato, Socrates, Aristotle, and Marcus Aurelius — *The happiness of your life depends upon the quality of your thoughts: therefore, guard accordingly, and take care that you entertain no notions unsuitable to virtue and reasonable nature.*"

Eloise grinned. "How about this one? *It is not death that a man should fear, but he should fear never beginning to live.*"

Smiling, Oliver said, "Amazing. A fellow traveler."

"I have ambitions to read the law someday."

Oliver's eyes widened, and he sat forward. "Clearly, you would be a great addition to the bar."

Eloise tried to suppress a smile, but she was not successful. "If I am ever allowed to practice."

"I predict that many changes are coming. One will be women lawyers."

"And women voting."

He leaned back in his chair and said, "Eventually. Let me give this some thought."

Satisfied, Eloise glanced at Oliver and began to assemble her things. "You will inform me of how I might best serve the defense of the Union." She said, "I will compose a letter to that subject within five days."

"Make that three," she added, smiling.

Amused, the corners of his lips moved up and down quickly. Finally, he said, "I will try my best to make that happen."

He stood and bowed from the waist. "I am thrilled to make your acquaintance, Miss Jacobson."

She stood and nodded. "I am pleased to meet you also. My brother was very complimentary of you."

Eloise closed the door, took a handkerchief from her pocket, and dabbed at her cheek. It was as if the sun had grown brighter and was warming her face alone, to the absence of everyone else. She smiled as she stepped off the porch and into a small puddle.

"Gracious me!" she exclaimed. She looked to see if anyone had heard her and was satisfied that she was the only one.

She pulled her foot from the muck and shook it as daintily as possible. She took two steps to the right and leaped toward the plank bridge across the street.

Chapter 5

I felt my shoe touch the plank and slip just a tad. I took a quick breath, glad that for the moment that I may have saved myself from the embarrassment of landing face-first into a mud puddle, or worse.

I adjusted my skirt and looked over my shoulder.

Oliver Wendell Holmes was standing at the window of his office. He was holding his coffee cup and watching me. I saw a wave of panic cross his face and then a sly smile as if surprised by my athletic ability.

Would that I could prove to him and all the others that I have value in this fight against the traitors of the South.

I rested my foot on the wagon step and cleaned some of the mud from the side of my shoe. I pulled myself up to the seat and grabbed the reins. I sat, turned the horse's head, and urged her away. I clicked her into a canter just because I wanted to feel the wind on my face. I pulled off my hat and put it next to my bag at my feet.

I'd show them, that's for sure. I could be a nurse, maybe even a doctor. I could be a spy. I could be a telegraph operator. There would be some value in that.

Junebug and I trotted through the countryside. We soon found the farms at the edge of our hometown and passed many wheat and cornfields.

The streets through town were slowly drying from the morning rain, but some ruts caused the wagon to shift left and right. I enjoyed the gentle sway. It had the same rhythm as music.

I nodded at Mrs. Swinburg as she passed in her covered surrey. I really like her hat. I have the perfect dress to go with it.

Who is felling that tree? Ah, that very handsome Harry Smith and his brother. Why hasn't he asked me to the dance tonight? I'm just as pretty as that woman. What is her name, and why can't I remember? Sharon Macher. That's a name that you would think would be hard to forget.

I'll just give them a glance and maybe bat my eyelashes a bit. Should I pinch my cheeks or lick my lips? Oh, never mind.

"Hello, boys, don't get too hot," I yelled over the sound of their chopping and Junebug's clopping.

"*Why did I say that?*" I thought. "*What's wrong with me?*"

I regained my composure and said, "Harry, come see my father. We're going to need some wood for the winter."

Harry nodded and doffed his hat.

I snapped the reins just a bit too hard. Junebug lurched in her traces.

"Junebug, slow down before we take a tumble! Whoa, whoa, slow down now! Good girl."

That man, Holmes, he was certainly condescending. It would seem to me if you're preparing for war, you'd welcome any form of help that anyone would make available. He'll never be much of an officer. I could see that just by looking into his eyes.

He was quite handsome, though. That mustache should go. Way too much. I can't imagine his men would find that encouraging. How could they? He needed to be clean-shaven with his hair slicked back and neat along the neck. That would make him look both professional and inspirational.

Just how inspirational does an officer have to be these days, given the attack in South Carolina? I hope our good President Lincoln has the backbone to stand up to the rowdies.

My goodness, it is hot and humid today. I shouldn't be surprised, given the rain this morning and the bright sun.

Oh my, where is my hat? It makes me wish I had brought a jar of water with me. I had no idea that it would take so long to get here. I guess I should have asked Edward.

Should I go to that dance tonight unescorted? What a scandal. Just imagine the talk. But truthfully, I feel I've become something of a symbol for women who wished to be seen as strong and independent. So how can I let social mores keep me from having a good time?

I'll wear my blue dress.

Later, I fixed dinner for the men, and with much consternation on their part, I went to the dance.

I love Fall. It is the best time of the year. I especially enjoyed the smells of the first frost. The leaves burning, and the sky at sundown was such a beautiful shade of orange.

The barn was decorated with the colors of the season. There was Harry and his brother. They cleaned up nicely. I'm glad they're here. Which will ask me to dance?

After a moment of hesitation, I made eye contact with Harry. Soon after, he sauntered across the room.

"Miss Eloise," he said, "you look lovely tonight."

"Thank you," I replied.

"The blue really brings out the color of your eyes."

"I made the choice just for that reason."

The band started a new song. Harry offered his hand, and I took it. He led me to the center of the stage, and we danced with great joy and enthusiasm.

We were winded after, so Harry escorted me to the refreshments table and poured me a cup of cider.

"Your speech the other day was really marvelous, Miss Eloise," he said.

"Thank you for your attention. I worked hard on writing it, and then put away my notes and just spoke from the heart."

He seemed surprised by the admission. Was his attitude the same at that rascal, Oliver Wendell Holmes? Regaining his composure, he said, "I could tell you were well prepared."

I took a sip of cider. It was strong and pungent, just the way I liked it.

"So, you think that war with the South is inevitable."

"I see no way of avoiding it, do you agree?"

"I'm afraid you are right. It will be a horrible conflict."

"But we will prevail, and I believe rather quickly. The South is underfunded and has no access to the munitions plant that they will require."

Harry nodded his head and took a sip of cider. "I hope you are right."

I'm jogged out of my thoughts about myself for a moment and realized just how many lives would be changed by the war.

Edward appeared at the large barn door. He scanned the room. His gaze rested upon me, and he sprinted across the room.

"We must go! Father has taken ill."

I handed Harry my cup, and I joined Edward as he rushed toward the horse and wagon.

"Be easy with Junebug," I said. "She's had a long day."

Edward said as he leaped into the buggy's seat. "I've already contacted the doctor, and he'll meet us there."

"Who is with Father now?"

"I asked Mrs. Macher to stay with him until we can get back home."

Edward flipped the reins and urged Junebug onward.

"I'll pray that he will be all right."

"I'll join you," Edward said.

We pulled up to the house and hitched Junebug to the post. Miss Macher stood next to the lantern hanging next to the front door.

"The doctor is with him," she said.

"Does the doctor know what happened?"

"He said from the symptoms described, your father has had a heart attack."

I put my handkerchief to my mouth and gasped. "Father must survive. Without him and Mother —"

Edward put his arm around me. "Doctor Grant will do all that he can."

"Yes, of that, we can be assured."

A half an hour later, Doctor Grant came out to talk with us. Father was resting, he said, but his breathing was labored and uneven. He said we should visit him.

I stood in the lamplight and watched Edward kneel next to his father's bed. He took his father's hand and patted the back of it. Father's face registered no reaction.

"Eloise," Edward said and looked up with tears in his eyes. "What are we going to do?"

"We will be brave and do for Father something that he can't do for himself. We'll pray together."

"Yes," Edward said, "we'll pray together."

I knelt next to Edward, and we both folded our hands. We recited the Lord's Prayer together; then, we were silent until morning light glowed through the bedroom window.

Father died later in the morning. We are alone now, Edward and me. We knew Father was in heaven with Mother, but we were both unsettled and uneasy about our future.

Chapter 6

Edward stood holding his cloth bag. A wave of anger crossed his features, something like Eloise had never seen before.

"Please, let's have a cup of tea and talk about this," she said.

"I need to leave at dusk."

"You need to stay here," she said.

"I'm sorry, but I cannot wait," he said.

"Why, Edward?"

He set his jaw. "You wouldn't understand. You're so much stronger than me."

"I'm your sister. Of course, I can understand whatever you feel."

He rubbed his hands over his face. She looked carefully and believed she saw tears.

She said, "It has only been a week since Father's passing, Edward. You are still upset."

He moved toward her as she blocked the front door. Dust motes swirled as the light of the setting sun enveloped her.

"It is because of our father's passing that I have decided this."

"But you will become a criminal, hunted for desertion."

He hunched his shoulders forward as if preparing for a fight. "So be it."

"What about our family's name?"

Edward stifled a chuckle. "Our family's name will survive, as will the world, but if I join the Army, I may not."

Eloise glared at him. She tried to think of something else to say to try and stop him. She had already expressed the consequences of his actions. She knew that she might never see him again if he was imprisoned or, even worse, executed for his decision.

"Is there nothing more I can say?" she asked.

Edward stood, looking at her for a very long moment. "As always, you have made all the proper, logical arguments. But you have forgotten the most important argument; life is too short to waste it in such an effort. Why should I care if the people of the South wish to become a separate nation? It matters to me not one whit. Why should I care if they keep their Negroes or set them free? I have no stake in the matter. What I *do* have a stake in is my life. I'm heading west. I may go to Canada. I haven't decided yet. If I can contact you in the future, I will."

Eloise was taken aback by Edward's argument. "If you leave, this will be our last sighting of each other."

Edward's eyes dipped to the floor. "If that is the case, goodbye."

He brushed past her and through the door. He strode across the front porch and into the front yard. A low fog engulfed the lot, and his outline soon disappeared in the mist. He never looked back.

Eloise placed the back of her hand to her mouth. She stifled a thought to run after him, to try and re-engage him in a logical argument, appeal to his patriotism or his obligation. Still, if there was one thing she knew about her brother, it was that when he had made up his mind about something, there was nothing that would change it.

She stepped back from the door, closed it, and sat in the chair at the end of the dining room table. She picked up a stack of notes, her notes from her Independence Day speech.

"*What have I done?*" she thought.

She shuffled through the pages, wondering what would have happened if she'd stuck to her text and not spoken from her heart. Many of the points she talked about were touched on in the speech.

She looked over her shoulder at the dying fire in the hearth. She considered tossing the papers into the blaze to destroy them.

"*What am I going to do now?*" she asked herself.

She put her hands over her face and vowed not to cry. It was a time to act and not falter, but what steps could she take?

She stood, picked up her papers, and spread them over the tabletop. She tried to see any part she could have removed. What should I have not said? Was there anything she could have said that would have discouraged Edward from enlisting?

She realized the madness of her thinking. She realized she had no more control over what other people did than a kite had over the wind. She paced in front of the hearth.

She would focus on running the telegraph office. She was confident in her abilities there. She knew everything there was to know about the code and how vital precision was in the execution. She knew how to run the family business, even if there was no family left.

She brushed a tear from the corner of her eye. She would not allow herself to cry, to feel sorry for herself.

She swept the papers off the table and mashed them into a ball. Then, she tossed them into the fire. The blaze illuminated the darkening room.

Eloise looked up at the mirror over the fireplace. A thought raced through her mind.

"*How hard would it be?*"

She could cut her hair. She could wear loose-fitting clothes. For the first time in her life, she felt thankful for her lack of bosom and slender hips and legs.

"*Madness*," she thought.

She glanced over at her writing desk. She knew her place in the world, and while her brother would be seen as a traitor to the effort to keep the Union together, she would redouble her efforts to speak the truth to power. She would begin an editorial that would inspire more to join in the preservation of the Union.

She sat at her desk and put pen to paper.

She wrote: We must agree with the President that a house divided against itself cannot stand. We must make the words put forth in the Constitution that all men are created equal more than just empty words.

She stopped writing and said to herself, "Why would anyone believe anything that I write? My own brother chose to flee from his responsibilities. I have no credibility. Any member of my future family and I will be shamed."

She balled up the paper and threw it on the floor.

She would keep a diary of her efforts. She would organize her thoughts and continue to support the efforts of those who spoke out against slavery. She would use her words to save herself and her family from the shame her brother had brought on them.

She thought about her father. How proud he was of his home and his business and how important it was to keep Concord connected with the rest of the world.

She looked in the mirror again and sighed.

"Madness," she said.

She thought, "*There is nothing I can do. I am helpless.*"

Chapter 7

The brim of her hat kept flopping over her left eye. She pushed it up, but it continued to obscure her vision. She frowned, knowing that it was just a nuisance she could quickly remedy. She should pull the wagon off the side of the road and deal with it. She pushed it up again, this time with more force. She cursed softly under her breath. Not so that anyone could hear, thank goodness. However, she should pull the wagon to the side of the road just to be safe. The horse wouldn't care. She would probably appreciate the chance to catch her breath. Junebug was young now, but she would grow older, and Eloise knew she would die soon, just like everything and everyone else in the world. The world was a horrible, stinking place, and soon everyone and everything would be dead. She snatched the hat from her head and tossed it into the ditch. She screamed.

She knew it was futile, ridiculous. She pulled the wagon to the side of the road. She tied the reins to the brake and stepped from the cart. Head down, she stomped back to where she'd thrown her hat. She bent down and picked it up. She dusted the brim, wet her fingers, ran them along the area that kept flopping over her eye, and put it back on her head.

"There," she said, "Perfect."

She was glad no one had heard her outburst. She was glad no one would ask her what was bothering her and what could be done to fix her problems.

Eloise hitched Junebug to the post in front of the telegraph office and fetched her bag from the wagon seat. She looked up and saw how low clouds covered the morning sky. She pulled the edges of her shawl tighter over her shoulders. It was early in the fall, but there was already a chill in the air. She turned.

It was as if she could feel the eyes of the people in the town watching her walk. Of course, she knew that wasn't the case, and yet the feeling was still there.

The sale of the livery to invest in a telegraph had been a considerable gamble for the family. Everyone had a vote, but she and Edward were the most forceful in the argument. His point was that communication was always needed. Providing a service faster than the mails would be a sound investment, even with the current limitations. Mother and Father eventually came around, and within months the telegraph office was a success.

She looked up at the big sign over the door and unlocked the door. It was cold and dark, with a single shaft of morning light cutting across the floor. The fire had gone out, but several embers continued to glow. Eloise considered poking the leftovers but decided there were more pressing issues to deal with.

She found Verdell leaning back in the office chair, his hand still resting near the telegraph key.

"Verdell," she whispered.

He failed to stir. She took off her shawl and put it on a hook next to the front door.

"Verdell, wake up," she said.

His handlebar mustache twitched, but his eyes stayed shut. Eloise knew he would awaken if the telegraph key started transmitting a message. Still, he was oblivious to anything else going on in the office.

She moved behind the desk and touched Verdell on the shoulder.

He started awake. "Miss Eloise!"

"Wake up."

"I'm awake," he said. "Just resting my eyes."

He straightened his coat and glanced at the telegraph key. It was still, as it had been for much of the night. He straightened up in his chair, and his left foot moved in reflex. It kicked an empty whiskey bottle that rolled from under the desk.

Eloise dipped close to Verdell's face and sniffed. There was a sour, rancid smell drifting around his face. She knew the aroma came from the whiskey, but the putrid smell bothered her. Was he getting sick?

"I only took a sip. There was a chill in the air, and I needed warming up." She gave him a skeptical look.

"I was agitated." He came up with another excuse.

"And you needed to relax while you were working. This is unacceptable, Verdell."

"I know. I know. It won't happen again." He crossed his heart. "I promise."

"I've heard that too many times in the past."

"This time, I mean it." He looked sheepishly at the telegraph key.

"If you weren't my father's little brother—"

"I know, I know," he said, nodding.

She put her hands on her hips and stood over him. "Are there any overnight messages to deliver?"

He yawned, covering his mouth with the back of his hand. "I can't believe I fell asleep. I am so sorry."

"Overnight messages?"

"There is only one, Ma'am. Should I engage young Stuart to take it?"

"Yes," she said. She took Verdell's place behind the key as he vacated the seat.

She pulled a sheaf of papers from a drawer and opened the inkwell. She took a book from her bag and opened the page to the bookmark.

"Will Mr. Edward be taking the afternoon shift?" Verdell asked.

"We're going to need to bring in Stuart full-time. Have you talked to him about that?"

"Yes, of course. We talked about it when we first learned Mr. Edward would be joining the Army. He's still learning code, but he'll pick it up quickly when put him behind the key."

She said, "We're going to need more help here."

"Along with Stuart?"

She gave him a quick, sharp glance.

"Well, John Durbin expressed an interest in learning the craft the last time I spoke with him at the store."

"Is he capable?" she asked.

"He seems trainable. He is of draft age, so there's that."

She glanced up from her writing. "We will wait to cross that bridge when we come to it."

Verdell sat across from the hearth, pulled an apple from his coat pocket, and polished it on his vest. "War is going to disrupt many lives," he said. He pulled a pocket knife from his trousers and began to peel his breakfast. He started at the top and quickly moved around the fruit in a single peel.

"Tis cold in here," remarked Eloise

"I'll get on that," he said.

She turned a page of her book and said without looking at him, "When you have a moment." She tugged her sleeves over her wrists and turned the text into the shaft of light.

Verdell peeled the apple, humming to himself as he worked.

"Isn't that a song your group played at the dance the other night? What's it called?"

"*Gentle Annie*, a right smart little ditty, if I do say so my —" He stopped talking, realizing that the dance was the night his brother had died. He returned to his apple.

"You can speak of it if you need to. Your brother's passing, I mean."

He took a deep breath and sighed. "I should have stayed longer."

"It was a long night. There was nothing any of us could have done. You needed your rest. You would not have known he would pass that morning."

"I was exhausted."

"It's fine," she said. She didn't look up.

"Do you think he knew I was there?"

Now, she looked at him. She had never seen him look so old and so sad. She thought for a moment and tried to put herself in his place. The guilt of being the last of the three brothers would weigh heavily on his heart. Finally, she decided to say, "I think so."

"Good," Verdell said. He took a bite of the apple. "You can't ask for much more than that when you're dying."

She took a sharp breath and turned a page she hadn't fully finished reading.

"Is Edward going to come by and say goodbye to me?"

She debated whether she should share the family shame with her uncle. "I'm not sure. He was packing as I left this morning," she lied.

"I would certainly like to at least be given a fond farewell."

Eloise took a deep breath and turned a page. She blinked her eyes. A tear crept down the side of her cheek and dropped on the paper with a fat "plop." Verdell looked up at the sound. "Oh, dear girl."

"It's fine," she sniffed.

"You ain't alone, Eloise. You have a family here, and we all love you."

"I know. It's just that so much has happened so quickly."

She closed the book and looked out the window.

Verdell sat his apple on a plate on a table near the opposing window. He picked up some kindling and leaves and tossed them into the hearth.

"We'll have you all warmed up before you know it."

He picked up a poker and jammed it at the ashes. A flame ignited and began to engulf the leaves. Verdell picked up some sticks and tossed them into the fireplace.

"That's gettin' it started," he said as he put a couple of small logs onto the fire.

"Yes," she said, sniffing, "it's better already."

"I'll take Junebug over to the livery and go see what that boy's up to." He turned and walked toward the door.

"Yes," she said, "good idea."

She felt tears come to her eyes again as he closed the door. She was correct; too much had happened too quickly. There were too many things happening that were out of her control. She looked at the floppy hat hanging next to her shawl. She would need to learn that there were times when she could do nothing and let it go.

Chapter 8

I looked at my hands. Once skilled as a telegraph operator and carpenter, now they were torn and covered with scabs from catching them on thorns and brambles. I ran through the forest by the river but not on the road. I knew there could be lawmen or soldiers looking for me, knowing that my induction date had long since passed. So I had to be careful until I reached the Mississippi. Once I crossed that, I would be able to take one long, deep breath.

I know this is wrong. But I also know this is my only chance to find a safe place in the world. I'll cross the river and start a new life, maybe with a work crew that will ask no questions about my background and why I've chosen not to fight in the war.

There was a part of me that had this nagging question; why was this my fight? I knew the president said that the Union should be preserved, but why should I shed blood to make that happen? Why not just let the South go its own way? Their argument did make some sense. Why shouldn't states have the right to determine how their people would hold property or sell the same? Maybe my small contribution would have made a difference, but it is more likely that I would be just another corpse.

Thinking of this made my head hurt. I looked to my right, and there was a flat, dusty road that would transport me perfectly. I had tried following that path, but I riders had come upon me too quickly for me to hide in these hills. My fingers that had once brought news to people as the telegraph operator and entertained them with music shook in fear and trepidation.

There were times I wished to my soul that I was back home, caressing the keys of my piano, knowing that the sound would carry me away to a place where all my worries would subside. Have I made a mistake? Should I have served in the Army and ended the South's rebellion?

Up ahead, two riders shook me from my thoughts. Their steeds fought against their bits and stamped as they moved along the roadway. I stumbled behind a bush and waited, holding my breath as they rode past. One of the horses stopped and laid a massive pile of dung next to my hiding place. My mind immediately went to my present state and how, in many ways, my life was lower than this steaming metaphor.

"*Don't look up. Keep your head down, Edward,*" I thought. It was not the time to reveal yourself and let yourself be captured. I remembered reading how the war would likely only last a few months and that the North, better equipped and manned, would easily overcome the rebels. I felt a pang of hope as it crept into my heart.

Would it be possible for me to return home someday under a presidential amnesty? No, that was asking too much. Instead, I should focus on heading west and making a new life for myself there.

The riders moved their steeds close to the water and let them drink. They pulled flasks from their coats and took long swigs. I felt my mouth watering as I remembered the taste of whiskey and that warm feeling as it made its way through my chest. "*Focus, Edward,*" I thought. Now was not the time to reminisce about the good times I'd had. One of the horses turned his head and looked right at me. Did he recognize me as a threat or some kind of curiosity?

Here I was, on hands and knees, trembling at the thought that a horse might alert his master that I hid from him. How pitiful I had become. I should have just stood up, took my responsibility, and knew that I had done the right thing.

Who was I to judge that the South had not struck their own blow for freedom just as we did with England just decades ago? Why shouldn't they have the right to self-determination? Who were we to force them to accept a way of life they reject?

The horse moved closer to the water. I could feel the sweat dampen my arms, and a single bead of water ran from my hairline to my chin. Is the smell enough to make the horse turn his head again? I believe they are some of the most intelligent creatures on earth. What modes of detection were they capable of, given the right circumstance?

The rider pulled on the reigns and moved his horse back toward the road. The clomping of their hooves rung in my ears, and the creak of their leather saddles reminded me once again how far away from civilization I had run.

My belly made a noise, reminding me just how long it had been since last I ate. I looked around the thicket of brambles and noticed some ripening blackberries. I thrust my already-wounded hands into the thorns and pulled loose some berries. They tasted bitter but brought some moisture to my lips and solace to my belly.

I looked at the setting sun and checked the coins in my pocket. I hoped I was near a ferry that would take me across the river and to freedom. It was my only hope.

"Ho, there, boy. Get up with your hands in the air," the deep voice said, startling me.

I turned and looked at the barrel of a rifle. The man stood behind me and squinted his one good eye.

"I give up."

The bounty hunter wore a flop hat, a canvas shirt, and dungarees. There was a sheen of dust on his clothes, and a neckerchief rested on his chest. He snarled. "Is you a runner?"

I pleaded. "Yes, I'm on the run."

He cocked his rifle. "Most of the rewards these days are dead or alive. Give me a reason to shoot you, and I will."

I dipped my gaze to the ground and said, "I will give you no reason, sir."

"Now, denounce your running away from your obligation to serve and pledge allegiance to the South and our 'bellion against the Northern intruders."

I thought for a moment of the irony. "I pledge."

"What's your name?"

"Edward, sir," I thought for a second and said, "Edward Corrigan."

Chapter 9

The idea came to her that night like a bolt of lightning. Eloise bolted straight upright out of her sleep. She took a moment to find her bearings.

She got out of bed and sat on her chamber pot. She sighed and relieved herself.

She walked to the mirror. She pulled up her hair and studied the sharp cheekbones and shadows placed on her face by the full moon. Impossible. And yet, she knew she would have to try.

"It is decided."

She felt the hard wooden planks as she walked. She picked up a glass from the kitchen table and took a sip of water.

She returned to bed and pulled her covers around her. She fell into a deep sleep.

***

Was this really the only way?

There had to be another way.

She picked up the scissors and stared at herself in the mirror.

This was how she would save her family, her country, and Edward's life.

She grabbed a lock of hair and held the scissors.

She hesitated for a moment. The weight of what she was contemplating engulfed her mind.

"Off with you," she said as she cut her hair.

The lock came loose in her hand. She placed it in the basin and grabbed another.

"Off with you," she said, but this time there was a tinge of anger in her voice.

She let the second lock of hair fall into the basin.

"Off with you," she said between clenched teeth.

More hair in the basin.

"Off with you," she screamed.

Soon, she was shaping the sides of her hair, cutting them close and parting it on the left side. She noticed for the first time how much she resembled Edward with his new haircut.

"You bastard," she said as she snipped the last lock of hair that rudely fell over her eye.

She picked up her floppy hat and plopped it on her head.

***

She packed the last of Edward's clothes into her bag. She'd washed and ironed the shirts and pants so many times. She'd been a good sister, and this was her thanks. *Damn you, Edward*, she thought.

She put the bag next to the door.

She sat at her writing table. She began her instructions to her uncle with a simple list of things he would need to do to secure the house and the business. She paused as she began to fabricate a story for her absence.

She wrote, "I'm going to Maine for the season. I will return as soon as I feel myself again. The last few months have been too much, and the only solution is a change of scenery. I trust you will secure the homestead and our business. I love you, Uncle."

She folded the papers and put them in an envelope. She put the letter in the bag, on top of the boots, and cinched it tight.

She went to the stable, saddled Junebug, and rode toward town without looking over her shoulder.

The morning air was crisp. She soaked in all the smells as she rode. She took delight in the aroma of apples as they sat in boxes waiting to be picked up and taken to market. She caught the scent of a wood stove and cooking for the workers at a farm. All she knew already, she would miss—unless she was discovered.

She left the letter with Stuart at the livery and wished him well in his work at the telegraph office.

"Where you headed, Miss?"

"Out of this place for a bit," she said as she clucked her tongue and moved the reins over Junebug's neck.

The horse turned and loped out of town. Eloise pulled her hat even lower.

After several days of riding, she drew close to the city. She found a quiet place off the main road and continued her transformation. She pulled on Edward's clothes and hung her old hat on a tree limb. She smiled and thought, "*A gift to an overheated rider.*"

She put Edward's old hat on and tugged at the man's shirt, undoubtedly too large for her, but it was comfortable. She would make it work. Finally, she pulled on Edward's boots, staring at the shine for a moment before she stood.

Junebug didn't register any change in her owner. She nuzzled Eloise as she buttoned her coat. "Not now, girl," she said.

She would need to figure out how to change her voice. To merely deepen the tone wouldn't be enough. She needed to make it sound raspier somehow. She would begin smoking, something a young woman would be forbidden to take up. She pulled a small pack of tobacco from her bag, Edward's bag, a pipe, and a match. She cleaned the bowl, just as she had for Edward and her father, stuffed the black leaves in, and put the stem to her mouth. She drew in as the match touched the tobacco. She coughed, spit, and resolutely took another draw from the pipe. She coughed again but with less violence. She took another drag and soon found herself feeling comfortable with the smell and the irritation.

She took a last drag on the pipe, letting the smoke envelop her face and head.

She knew she would need the smell to permeate her clothes and body.

"The transformation is complete," she said, only altering her voice slightly as she put away the pipe.

Junebug looked up from her grazing, and a puzzled look flickered in her eyes. Eloise patted her on the neck and put her foot in the stirrup. Then, she launched herself over the saddle and tied the bag to a loose strap.

"We're in the thick of it now, Junebug."

She turned the horse toward the setting sun and urged Junebug toward Boston. She would need to find a place to make camp soon and break out her provisions. She knew someday she would be at a place where there would be no turning back. A shiver of excitement and dread ran down her spine.

Chapter 10

I looked down at my hands as they clutched the drumsticks and waited for the countdown for the beginning of "Battle Hymn of the Republic." It was a song I knew from the earliest time in my uncle's band. We'd traveled the country for as long as I could remember. I couldn't remember my parents, but I loved my free uncle as I loved this song, but I grew so tired of playing it for every rally and political speech. I wanted these hands to grab a rifle or a bayonet and help end this horrible rebellion. I wanted to feel the shudder of the explosion and smell the gunpowder.

My Black hands were not so different in this effort. Is my color the only thing that held me back from being a soldier?

Or was it my name, Mordecai Smith? A slave name and not my secret African name, Adebowale that was only known to my family.

I thought of my brothers and sister, who didn't get away and still labored under the yoke of slavery. I thought how lucky I was to be in the North and in uniform for this effort, but how under-used I was!

And so, I stood there in the long line. We'd practiced marching and playing for so long the act became second nature. I looked at the dais as the politicians sat and looked over their papers. Another boring rally with the hope that more people would join the fight. White people, of course.

The man in the stovepipe hat slumped in the chair next to the podium. His face was craggy with scars, but I could see an intensity in his gaze that showed his intelligence and emotional connection to the crowd.

I responded to the band leader's nod and began the drum roll. The national anthem rang through the small amphitheater as everyone stood.

I watched them as they turned toward the flag and put their hands over their hearts.

At the end of the song, we turned in unison and marched from the area left of the stage. We moved to the back of the crowd in a roped-off area so that we wouldn't be a distraction from the speeches.

I couldn't hear the words being spoken, but I watched as the crowd reacted to the ideas expressed. I felt the emotion in the group, but I knew I would still be separated from thoroughly enjoying the freedom they spoke of until the war was over.

Chapter 11

I thought my face and body would have hindered my entrance into the Massachusetts 20th. Still, the biggest problem was a mistake discovered by the clerk in my, or should I say, Edward's, induction letter. There was great consternation on the part of the representatives of the bureaucracy. Still, I was finally signed off, assigned a bunk, and scheduled for thirty days of instruction to fire a rifle, march, and, most importantly, take orders. I kept to myself and refrained from talking with the others as much as possible. There were others in the 20th that were shy and scared, and while I was neither, it was a part I played so that I would not be detected.

There were several instances where I had some difficulty with running and jumping. Still, I surprised myself and my instructor with my ability with the rifle. There was extensive loading, aiming, and target practice. I became comfortable with the noise, and my scores were near the top of the class. I realized it was not unlike the rifles Edward and Father used for hunting. I had accompanied them on several occasions but had only a few opportunities to shoot.

While provisions were sufficient, we found ourselves in need of game. It was on one of those expeditions that I was suddenly overcome with a longing for home. I don't know if the surroundings looked so much like Concord, or maybe it was the smell of chimney smoke or cooking from the small cabins there in the woods that sparked such melancholy. I separated myself from the hunting party, hid behind a clump of bushes, and cried. After a while, one of the other soldiers came looking for me, and I managed to compose myself before he came upon me. I assured him that I was just feeling a bit homesick, and he convinced me that many in the camp were sharing those feelings.

I found that entries here in my diary were very helpful in controlling these feelings. If I could reflect on the events of the day and put those emotions in separate chambers of my heart, I would be able to function with as much effectiveness as the other "men."

Making these entries led to some jesting from the others, but I didn't mind. They also found it strange that I found solace and joy in reading. I was still working my way through the camp bookshelf and found several about Napoleon and Alexander the Great.

I was surprised that others were not as interested in becoming educated about the "ways" of war. They were more interested in writing letters to their sweethearts, smoking, and spitting dip. I found myself helping some of the men who wished to write home to their women and made some pocket change for the task. My abilities in operating a telegraph key never came up, and I didn't volunteer the information. I didn't want to draw attention to myself in any way.

Soon, the days fell into a dull routine with only a few additions and subtractions. If anyone suspected my deception, no one let on. Except for the apparent problems with latrine visits, I found that I could fake shaving without detection. Many of the soldiers were very young and had very light beards. I fit in well with them. My biggest problem involved my voice. I became accustomed to lowering my register and sharpening my vowels. When I found myself sounding too feminine, I would cough, act as if I was choking on some spit, and begin again. Many of the other enlistees had very few years between when their voices had changed and now.

On a Thursday, we found out our first assignment was to march to the Capital and participate in security for the transportation of goods. It seemed a simple task, but we all knew the importance of the continued support of the war effort and took our assignment seriously.

With Junebug still with me, I improved myself as a rider. I was soon listed as a possible scout for future operations. I didn't volunteer for this duty and felt some consternation about the potential assignment. I didn't like the idea of being separated from the safety of the troop.

Being with Junebug also helped me deal with my feelings of loneliness and homesickness. Caring for her had always been part of my chores at home, but now she was the only one with whom I felt comfortable using my "real" voice. I was always careful, of course, but dropping that mask, even if it was only for a few minutes a day, was so helpful.

We again fell into a routine with minor alterations in duties. I unexpectedly thrived in the service of my country. Of course, we all knew that this simple assignment of jiggling locks and checking that workers who had access to facilities were not pilfering from the stockpiles would eventually change. The reports from the effort to quell the Southern uprising were not going well. We knew it was likely we would be called into more hazardous duty sometime soon.

I had the nightmare of the battle two more times while stationed in Washington. There was little new information in this dream. The smoke, the smells, and the gore continued in almost equal amounts from the first time I dreamed it, but there was a minor change in the latest nightmare. This time there were horses. They had become agitated because of the cannon fire. I heard snorting, whinnying, and neighing behind us as we stood on the hill. I still haven't found out why that added piece of information would make any difference in my understanding of the dream.

I awoke with a start and found my bunkmates undisturbed by my outburst. Of course, their snorting, farting, and snoring kept me awake until late in the night.

I was surprised by how much my deception allowed me more freedom and responsibility than my real identity. I never realized just how merely being a woman could hamper my freedom of movement and my entrance into establishments. I had to have more pipe tobacco, so a trip to the tobacconist was routine. I was amazed at the ease with which men spoke to each other and just how tongue-tied they became when faced with a woman in a social situation.

I wrote two letters to Uncle Verdell, assuring him that I was enjoying my time away from home and my continued confidence in his keeping the telegraph office in order and profitable. I made several references to my being in the Washington and Baltimore area, giving an idea of where I was, but not enough information for him to send someone to search for me.

I asked Uncle Verdell about Edward and if he had contacted anyone about his adventures in the Army. I knew this lie would be met with ignorance. He wouldn't return home or contact anyone there for fear the information would be used for his apprehension. I felt sorry for him because he was my brother, but I couldn't extend that feeling into forgiving him for doing what he did. I was sacrificing myself, maybe my life, because of his cowardice. I was proud to serve my country, even though the circumstances were unusual. He would have to find a way to live with the problems he caused for himself and the stain he placed on his family name.

Chapter 12

Distant thunder growled. A brilliant branch of lightning etched the sky. Edward pulled back the thick canvas flap of the tent. It had been weeks since he'd slept under bedcovers and appreciation grew in his heart as the storm approached.

Yellow light glowed behind him, and a gentle flame crept up the wick of a kerosene lamp. A plate filled with biscuits, corn on the cob, beans, and ham sat untouched next to the fire.

He returned to the table. He sat and placed a pale, smudged, shaking finger near the lamp's golden light. It hovered there too long. A bubble of flesh rose along the side.

He said to himself. "How can I think about the future when the past is such a harsh mistress?"

The finger rose, and the handcrafted bowl of a metal spoon lowered over the lamp's flame.

"Am I not the man who stood on Chattanooga's highest ridge, face in the wind, inhaling the sweet smell of cannon fire?"

He took a deep breath. He had become accustomed to talking to himself. He was comforted by the sound after so much of his time now was spent around others.

"I am still that man. I have not changed, and neither has the world."

A tree branch caught in the wind and scratched against the tent. Edward jerked to his feet, pistol in his hand and ready to fire. He soon realized it was only the breeze, and he calmed, but he was apparently on edge.

He sat back down and closed his eyes. He marveled how his short time in custody with the bounty hunters had changed his mind. His one escape attempt ended when he threw a punch at the bounty hunter. He connected, and he liked the feeling. Then, of course, the hunter smashed his gun butt into Edward's jaw, but the emotion, the thrill, took hold. He relished the two weeks of training and the camaraderie of the troop. He distinguished himself in battle and rose through the ranks in a matter of months. But he was wounded many times and now had various scar tissue on his back, torso, and legs. He led a successful charge in Chattanooga, was wounded once again, and received a field commission for his efforts.

His men loved him and rushed into battle with Edward in the lead. He had to admit he liked his look. He had a long, black coat with a red satin lining that flopped in the wind and created a dramatic effect.

Tonight, he was exhausted and felt the pressure of leadership like no other. He leaned back in his chair as echoes of the day's battle reverberated in his mind.

The sound of a cannon fuse sizzling filled his ears, and then he jerked as the shell exploded. He heard rifles from a distance with their muzzles emitting a puff of white smoke long before the sound of the shot echoed around the valley—the clang of metal-on-metal, saber-on-saber. Horses neighed and snorted, shivering in fear.

Men screamed in terror and pain.

Shaking his head to clear his mind, shirtless now, he slid his suspenders from his shoulders. His face darkened as he drew liquid from the bowl into a syringe.

He regarded the syringe in the flickering light. He laid the needle on the table and tried not to look at it. He hated his craving for the drug, but it was the only solace for his almost constant pain.

Resigned, he leaned forward, picked up the syringe, and slid the needle under his skin. He squeezed the plunger.

He leaned back and stared at the approaching storm. Clouds covered the moon and stars. Rain moved across the valley below him, and a portion of his heart felt for his men exposed to the elements.

He knew many were shivering in the cold, but that was their lot tonight. He was aware that many were still shaking with nerves from the battle fought that afternoon.

"For me, the hurly-burly of approaching battle brought me great comfort. Ordering men into battle, knowing that some of them would never return home. Knowing that death was staring at me and waiting," he said as if dictating his thoughts.

He swung a limp hand toward the tent flap.

"It was an emotion I grew to know too well," he said. "And embraced."

His eyes flickered as the drug took over his mind.

"That sensation of falling off the edge of the world. There are only two things in the world that can give me that feeling. Battle and the powder."

A smile tickled the corner of his lips. The transformation was complete.

He smelled the ozone in the air and tasted the metal in his mouth. Lightning flashes filled the tent with a brilliant white light. A ghostly image lingered as he drifted off to sleep and dreamt of home. But which home? The house he co-owned with his sister in Massachusetts or the one he shared with his new wife in Tennessee?

Chapter 13

It was an open house, the day the President's office was available to anyone who had a request, a claim, or some grievance that the president could take care of.

Abraham Lincoln sat behind his big desk. He was holding his signature stovepipe hat. It was one of the hats he used at state functions, campaigns for fellow Republicans, and funerals. He always hated funerals. He had gone to too many in his life but knew they were necessary for the ones left behind. It was in his mind, a closing of the door. But his mind wasn't on funerals, campaigning, or state functions. He sat with his thumb circling the brim of his hat. It was perfect, of course; it was the president's hat, but today he was thinking about his generals. The ones he felt he could count on to take the fight to the Rebels had proved to be completely ineffective. Every battle seemed fraught with mistakes and a lack of gumption by his generals. He was trying to overcome the notion that America could become two nations.

When he finished with the public today, he would saunter over to the telegraph office in the War Department and find out what was happening on the battlefield. Had there been advancements? Would there be a need for orders for supplies or troops?

He picked up an apple, drew his pocketknife, and began to peel the fruit. A soldier appeared in the open doorway and motioned someone inside the room.

The president looked up, stood as he accepted a middle-aged woman's hand, and offered her a seat opposite him.

She had dressed in her Sunday finest. Her dress was full, and she wore a large black hat. She took off the hat, revealing a small, pudgy face and dark eyes. The president noticed a slight resemblance to his wife. He would try and remember to mention that the next time he talked with Mary.

"Thank you for seeing me. I know you're rushed," she said as she straightened her shawl.

"I'm never too busy to accept a petition from one of the voters."

Blushing, she said, "I didn't vote for you."

"I am the president of all the people."

"I have this," she opened her bag and extracted a handful of papers. "Part of my land was taken by the government to make room for an Army training camp. I didn't want to sell."

"I see. There are times, of course, where for the good of the country, we all must sacrifice."

The woman continued her appeal. "The land has been in my family for over three generations. It's where my mother and her mother were born. There was more room on the other side of the valley, but the surveyors said the lie of the land lent itself to a better placement for the exercises."

"I wish there was something more I could do about this." He folded the papers and handed them back to her. "You could bring your matter before a local court, but the demand is great. We need young men to train to serve their country. They are heroes, and we need to give them every chance we can to get back home safely to their families."

"I'm sorry, there's nothing to be done."

She took the papers from the president and stuffed them back into her bag.

"Our Constitution says that all men are created equal. We believe this with all our hearts. Don't we?" he asked.

The woman nodded.

"Then it is imperative that we recognize there is inequity in our country regarding the Negro. Do you agree?"

Again, the woman nodded reluctantly.

"So, we are united in our beliefs, even though you didn't vote for me."

The woman gave a small chuckle, a slight smile, and turned to leave.

"Not even the president can change the flow of a river or the lay of the land."

The soldier waved the woman from the room and looked down the hallway.

Another petitioner waited near a washstand.

"Next," the president said.

He nodded, returned to paring his apple, and waited as a young woman stepped across the threshold.

Chapter 14

A whipping wind. Branches of a tree corkscrewed in the storm. Blinding rain.

Lightening etched brilliantly across the black sky.

The blade of a rusty shovel thrust into the soggy earth.

Minta bent at the waist, and as she plunged the shovel into the ground, she felt a twinge of pain in her back. She took a sharp breath of the cold, damp air and winced. Wearing a cotton nightgown and boots, she wiped the water from her eyes and forehead with the back of her hand. She positioned her foot on the blade again and turned over another clump of dirt.

It was a small corral used by the men to break horses. She grew up watching them and eventually became a bronco rider herself. She thrilled as she eased up onto the backs of the wild animals, clamped her legs around their torso, and held on until they stopped bucking. She felt the rush of excitement when the horse finally gave in and bent to her will. Bronc busting made her smile.

Lightning struck a nearby tree, startling her from her digging. She frowned, stooped, and looked at the smoldering limbs. She scanned the deserted field—the acreage near the house connected to the larger plots with field upon field of cotton. The weather might cost her some yield, but she knew this year's harvest would make or break her plantation. She had prayed about the situation so many times. Now, she found herself in almost constant communication with the Lord.

"*Mother of God,*" she thought. "*Don't take me now. I got so much of your work left to do here.*"

She crossed herself, took a deep breath, and returned to the digging.

A bolt of lightning, twice as strong as the first, struck the tree again.

She dropped the shovel, closed her eyes, and placed her hands over her ears.

The cold water had covered her breasts, and her nipples had grown tight and stiff. The water revealed her dark pubic hair. She shook her head, and her mouth formed a perfect "O."

She turned, and in the smoky remnants of the burning tree, saw the ghostly apparition of a young, petite, red-haired woman, holding a parasol and a suitcase.

The girl smiled at Minta and then disappeared with the wind.

Quivering with cold and fear, she shook her head and returned to her work.

She took a packet of papers from her pocket, put it into a small flour sack, and dropped it in the hole.

She wiped her dirty hands across her face and raised her eyes to the sky. "Oh Lord, give me strength." The dirt streamed away from her cheeks and eyes.

She remembered the last time she'd fought for a man. She'd lost that time, and the husband she loved left town and was never seen again. She wouldn't let that happen this time.

She covered the hole and patted the dirt with the shovel blade. She picked up a large cow pile with the shovel and placed it over the hole. Shivering and breathing heavily, she smiled and rested her head against the shovel's handle. A twinge of pain stabbed the side of her head. She winced and closed her eyes. The pain passed, but she knew she'd eventually need her medicine.

In between lightning flashes, the three-story house loomed behind her. Two large willows swayed near the home. There was a small pond filled to overflowing to the north of the mansion. The giant barn sat to the west, and the tobacco barn just behind that. The acreage beyond the house stretched for miles. It was the largest parcel of land in the entire middle of the state of Tennessee.

She looked up and saw rain streaming from the overhangs. Whitewash streaked from the pelting water.

A narrow path led from the corral to the house. Jason had placed several planks for people to walk on in this kind of weather, so they didn't soil their shoes. Minta appreciated the fact she didn't have to slip and slide through the muck.

A "jockey" hitching post stood vigil next to the back door. She touched his head. She always considered doing that was good luck, and she'd done that since she was a small girl.

She scurried up the back steps and jerked open the door. A burst of warm air struck her in the face, and she smiled at the notion that this room held the heart of the house.

She entered the kitchen, kicking off her muddy shoes. She pulled the nightshirt over her head and dropped it onto a pile of dirty clothes in the corner next to the door. Jewels and Jason would take care of that mess tomorrow.

Naked, she padded to a counter, took a drink from a jug of whiskey, and filled a basin from a hand pump. She hummed as she worked. She took a small cloth and washed her face, arms, torso, and legs.

She cringed at the squeak, slowed her pumping, and pulled a towel from a hook. She didn't know if Edward was home, but she didn't want to wake him if he was. Instead, she tried to respect his privacy and allow him to exorcize whatever demons he was battling after his service to the Confederacy. She was proud of her husband but worried about his long-term well-being.

She looked around the kitchen and remembered how her father had supervised the building of the addition some twenty years ago. He'd turned the single-room house into a mansion with two fireplaces. Then, as cotton became king in the area, he bought up plots of land and put hundreds of acres under cultivation. The home he'd built became a showplace. He added on more and more until it sat in splendor. And now, she and her new husband were the last members of the already tiny family.

Still naked and shivering, she crept down an elaborately wallpapered hallway of closed doors. She opened a door and was about to go in when a satisfied sigh came from the door at the end of the hall.

She smiled, thinking of her husband's face as she surprised him. She opened the door and peeked in.

There was a puff of curly raven hair laid on the pillow. Then, another long sigh as a chestnut brown arm slipped from beneath the covers.

Minta's smile faded and then became a grimace. She quietly closed the door and turned. Her hand flew to cover her mouth. She rushed to her bedroom door and shut it. She contemplated her next move and how best to deal with her rival.

Chapter 15

Eloise stood at attention with her rifle held across her chest. She had practiced marching for weeks, and now it was time to put that training to use.

She followed her commander up the ridge of the training camp. A bright, white sun shone down on them over the emerald fields. Once they reached the top of the hill, they were instructed to scatter and find cover, just as they would if attacked.

They were told to keep low and try to make themselves as small a target as possible. They looked for cover and tried to imagine the enemy shooting at them. The training sergeant liked to make a joke about how bullets couldn't turn corners, so make sure you're at an angle from the gunfire.

Eloise gripped her rifle tighter and hid in a clump of trees. She found herself sweating even though the temperature was in the forties. She welcomed the cooler air. Her uniform was heavy, and at times she felt it was encasing her instead of her wearing it.

Troops advanced up the hill. The sergeant walked amongst his men and said, "Don't fire until you see the whites of their eyes."

Eloise knew this was a stolen line, but it made sense to her. Maybe it was something her great-grandfather might have heard General Washington say while leading his men against the British. If the opposition was that close, it was assured that your mini-ball would have its best chance of finding its target and inflicting damage.

It was also a distance where the other soldier could see you. She worried for a moment about being shot and killed, and maybe even worse, wounded, and her identity revealed. It was a concern that would come into her mind many times until the end of the war.

She looked down at the group as they marched in solid blocks, thirty or so men in each row, flag held high, and rifles at the ready. They were exposed, just as the Rebel troops in her nightmare had been. The men didn't run but marched to a simple chant that, at this distance, Eloise couldn't make out. Or was it a song?

"What are they saying?" Eloise asked her bunkmate and fellow soldier hiding behind a tree. His name was Samuel, and he was one of the few friends she'd made while in camp.

He was shy like her, or at least when she tried to engage him in talk, he appeared that way. Maybe he had a secret to hide also.

"I think they're singing."

"It sounds like 'Columbia, Gem of the Ocean.'"

"Why would they sing a Navy song?"

Samuel said, "Maybe it's the only one they know."

Eloise stifled a girlish giggle but found her head nodding out of control.

The troop leader yelled, "Charge!" and the men advanced on Eloise's position. They stopped singing and let out a harrowing scream. The charging "Rebels" raised their muskets and fired. Of course, they were shooting blanks, but the commander knew the simulated fire would give his men a taste of what it would be like on the battlefield. He also knew it was as close as they could come to that experience. He also hoped it would be enough to save their lives.

Eloise found the noise, high-pitched Rebel yells, rifle shots, and chaos from the charging men disconcerting. She urinated on herself. It was just a tiny amount, but it was enough to get Samuel's attention.

"What the hell? Did you piss yourself?"

"Just a bit. I couldn't help it," she said as she aimed down the barrel of her rifle. The sergeant said to pretend to shoot at the advancing men and make sure that your shot would count if it were a real battle.

"I hope it's not worse if we get into a real battle."

Eloise choked on her laughter but didn't take her eye off the advancing men.

The sergeant came up to Samuel and Eloise. He sniffed the urine on Eloise's uniform but didn't feel the need to point out the indiscretion.

"Don't forget. Hold. Hold until you see the whites of their eyes."

"Right, Sergeant," both trainees said.

Eloise let the hammer of her rifle fall on the firing pin. The empty clicking sound echoed through the small valley, joined by dozens of others.

"That's right. Make sure the other guy's sacrificing his life for his country and not you."

Chapter 16

The sun crept over the edge of the horizon and peeked through the long, green curtains covering the double windows of Edward's bedroom. He and Minta had decided months ago that her snoring and his nightmares made it nearly impossible for them to share the room.

The small, sleeping woman snuggled into the rough bed sheets and quilts. He hadn't consciously considered the affair before it started. He believed it was harmless and had come to the notion that enjoying the girl was a right for a slave owner.

Muddy boots, socks, and underwear littered the floor. A sword hung by a nail from a patterned wallpapered panel.

A shaft of golden morning light intersected the meagerly decorated room. A cock crowed.

In a dark corner of the room, a drawer in the towering wardrobe screeched, and Edward tensed as he pulled out long underwear. He put one leg into the long-johns and stumbled. The mirror on the opposing door of the wardrobe caught his reflection as it slowly opened. He'd had a long night with his "followers." He was lucky Minta hadn't waited up for him. *"What would she do if she knew?"* he thought.

Naked, he spun into the light. Long scars and healed bullet holes peppered his back. Shrapnel scars dimpled his buttocks.

His left little finger was missing from the second joint. He pulled up his long johns and turned.

A thin, Black teenager with raven-colored hair and deep brown eyes, Sophie stirred and propped herself up on one elbow. She was the result of a union of two slaves Minta had owned for many years. The parents were sold almost immediately after the birth of the small girl, and she had been raised by the house servants and knew little of her birth history. The good news was in the regularly updated pages in the middle of the family Bible. But, of course, there was a thick separation between the births and deaths of the slaves and the masters.

She had grown up a spoiled child and felt no need to cover her nakedness, there in her owner's bed. Her eyes widened in horror as she looked at him. This was only the second time she'd spent the night with him and had always left before the sun came up. She'd felt the scars, but it was shocking to see them for the first time. She nonchalantly turned and feigned sleep.

He touched his chest. A massive mini-ball exit wound covered his upper torso. He tugged at the hem of his garment and slipped his scar-covered arms into the sleeves.

He shivered. The fall temperatures had made the room cool in the morning.

The fireplace sat dark and cold. There were paintings on the walls, mostly of people Edward didn't know and would likely never meet. The wallpaper was floral, and Minta had told him it was from Paris. He was impressed and told her so. A chest and several chairs complimented the room. From behind the wardrobe door, a bright red handkerchief peeked past the mirror. Over the back of a straight chair, the threadbare uniform of a Confederate Lieutenant hung like a banner.

Chapter 17

A sign reading "ROOMS FOR RENT" swung from chains on the front porch of a rambling, antebellum mansion.

Shards of morning light split the gauzy, white curtains of a small bedroom. Virginia, a delicate, short woman with flaming red hair, milky skin, and dark, brown eyes, scurried around the room, packing a large trunk. She picked up a black-framed tintype photo of an old man. A small clock chimed. She held the picture to her chest. "I miss you so."

She whispered to herself as the clock chiming ended, "The burden of time."

She placed delicate silk undergarments in the corner of a drawer in the trunk.

There was a loud squeak.

A man on crutches with a long, gray beard stood at the open door. He rubbed the bloody bandages where his leg used to be. He was too old to fight for the Confederacy, but he felt so strongly about the war that he would don Gray and take his rifle to the battlefield. He was there for only a few minutes before a cannonball hit just feet away from him. Shrapnel caught him in the chest and face. The most significant piece took the lower part of his left leg.

Virginia looked up from her packing.

"Sorry, you're leavin' us," Mr. Hockney said.

She had grown fond of the old couple there at the boarding house. He was very much like her beloved grandfather, who had raised her after her parents died. "I'm sorry too," she said as she quickly wiped a tear from the corner of her eye. "Y'all have become so much like the family I lost."

The old man backed into the hallway, stumbling a bit and catching himself against the wall.

Virginia walked to the bed, searched for a moment, and then pulled a doll with a painted, wooden head from under the covers.

"So that's where you're hiding, Mrs. Greenwood."

She hugged the doll and then packed it next to her underwear. She touched a packet of letters tied together with a scarlet string.

She thought, "*I feel the strength of your words, my love. I read the promise of our future between the lines.*"

She walked by a full-length mirror, backed up, and stared at her reflection. She pulled her hair up from her neck and held a sheet of paper to the light. She read from the top.

She heard Edward's voice as if he were in the room with her. "I listen to the murmur of your heart because it beats with the same rhythm as my own."

She turned, grinned, spun, and picked up a box of hairpins and combs. She read from the bottom of the letter.

"The journey is long," Edward wrote, "but life without climbing the highest rampart is not worthy of the human spirit."

She picked up the packet of letters and placed them "just so" on top of a red nightgown.

"Is this your way of asking for my hand?"

She picked up a deck of cards. She had used the random chance of the draw to confirm decisions in the past. While she didn't always follow what the cards told her, it was comforting, believing that "God" was guiding her.

"Yes or no."

She shuffled the cards.

"No."

She split the cards—Jack of Diamonds.

"Yes."

She dealt the cards again. She nodded, closed her eyes, and placed them face down on top of the suitcase. She put her hand over the card.

She'd first discovered her gift when she was nine. She was able to see sparkling auras around some people, while others had different shades and colors. Her mother told her that she'd been born with a caul covering her face. Many people believed that gave the child the gift of prophecy, and Virginia had proven them right over the years. She had few friends growing up and had been particularly close to the grandfather who'd spent hour upon hour with her. When necessary, she talked with her dolls and toys and, when necessary, could guide the family in the big decisions that would affect them economically. And there was psychokinesis.

"King of Hearts."

She passed her hand over the card. It flipped without her touching it, revealing the King of Hearts.

"Yes."

She smoothed the doll's dress, picked up her parasol, and closed the trunk lid.

Chapter 18

Dear Diary,

It was a cold and dreary day with low-hanging clouds. The sun hid its face from me again, foretelling in some way the future for our small band of brothers.

The captain moved through the camp and ordered us to prepare three days' rations. With that order, we knew we would likely break camp tomorrow and begin a long march toward our next assignment. As we sat around the small fires, we struck up the refrain of "Maryland, My Maryland!".

The camp was in an apple orchard. We had gone hungry — for six days, not a morsel of bread or meat had gone in our stomachs — and our menu consisted of apples and corn we gathered from fields and orchards. We toasted, we burned, we stewed, we boiled, we roasted these two together and singly until there was not a man whose form had not caved in and who had not a severe attack of diarrhea. Our underclothes were foul and hanging in strips, and our socks were worn through.

There were some in the line that had begun to eye Junebug with hungry eyes. I tried to sleep with one eye open to make sure nothing happened to her. There was no rest at this level of awareness, but I did not want to see her harmed in support of our efforts.

Many became ill from exposure to the damp and cold; they were left on the side of the road with another soldier to watch over their recovery. The medicine wagons were full, and the whole route was marked by a sick, lame, limping group that straggled to the farmhouses that lined the way and who, in all cases, succored and cared for them.

In an hour after the passage of the Potomac, the command continued the march through the fertile fields of Maryland. The country people lined the roads, gazing in open-eyed wonder at the long lines of infantry. The glitter of the swaying points of the bayonets stretched as far as the eye could see. The people at the farmhouses did not act as friends or foes, and still, they gave so much to us, and every haversack was full that day. No houses were entered — no damage was done, and the farmers in the vicinity must have drawn a long breath of relief as they saw how secure their property was in the very midst of the Army.

Without permission and in jeopardy of being counted as a deserter, I walked Junebug up to a ramshackle farmhouse with a small family of three sitting on the porch. The father was dressed in worn slacks and a threadbare shirt. The wife sat in a low chair, darning clothes that would soon outfit a child between four and five years old. The son chased two chickens around the front yard, likely not knowing what to do with it if he caught one.

"Good day," I said.

"Mornin'," the father replied.

The woman nodded, and the child ignored me.

"I have my horse here, and it has become a burden to me. I wonder if I might leave her with you until I can make my way back here sometime in the future."

The father looked up from his whittling; the block of wood was beginning to take the shape of a small animal. He checked out Junebug.

"Why would you do that?"

"I am infantry, and caring for her is holding me back as we march."

"Why don't you just ride her?" the woman asked. She never looked up from her sewing.

"The others grow jealous of her in that aspect, and I fear she might come to harm soon."

The father nodded, spat, and said, "That don't make no sense."

I gathered my courage and told him the truth. "Sir, we have just come off a long march. Food was scarce, and there were some in the line that began to eye her with harmful intent."

"I see. I see. We ain't got much. Do she work a plow?"

I patted Junebug on the side of the neck. I realized she, too, had become somewhat malnourished, and a few of her ribs were beginning to show through her hide.

"She has not, but she is very smart, and I'm sure she would take to it if instructed."

"Instructed?" the woman asked.

"If you taught her," I said.

"Very well then," the father said as he stood. Shavings fell from his lap, and he stepped from the porch.

The first thing Eloise noticed about him as he stepped toward her was that his boots were so worn that his little toes were peeking out the sides.

"I'd like to write a small contract."

"I can't read nor write," the father said.

"That's not a problem. If there is any dispute, you can hand it to someone, and they can read it. It's for your protection as much as it is mine."

"Very well." The father patted Junebug on the neck as I had and took the reins.

"I'll set her up in the barn as you write."

He led the horse to a small barn as I searched my pockets for a scrap of paper.

I had a paragraph explaining the circumstances ready for his "X" when he returned.

"The fact that the horse belongs to a soldier should keep her from being commissioned by the Army should they come through here," I told him.

"What about if the Rebs come through?" the wife asked, again, never looking up from her work.

"Ma'am, if that should happen, losing Junebug will likely be the least of your worries."

The woman nodded, and as I turned to leave, the child said, "Why they lettin' women serve in the Army?"

I was shocked at the boy's observation, but I tried to hide the surprise on my face. I decided to ignore the boy and turned quickly. How had he seen through my disguise so easily? Do others also notice and not mention it? Are children just more honest in commenting on their observations?

I turned and didn't look back. I said, "I got to get goin' 'fore they count me as a runaway."

Chapter 19

There were times when I would receive strange and curious looks from the other soldiers. My hair grew quickly, and I took my bayonet to it with regularity. It looked ragged, but I didn't care. I knew I fit in perfectly with many foot soldiers who almost always seemed to bring up the rear. I was fine with that. I knew the roles eventually would be reversed, and the ones behind would work their way to the front.

Not because I wished it, but I was transferred to help with the wounded. I dressed the wounds of sixty-five different men — some having two or three injuries each. Yesterday I worked from daylight till dark and today I am completely exhausted, but soon I'll return to my chosen work. The days after the battle are a thousand times worse than the day of the fight — and the physical pain is not the most significant injury suffered. How awful it is — your imagination lacks until you see it after a battle. The dead appear sickening to my eyes, but I realized they are at peace and suffer no pain. But the poor wounded, mutilated soldiers that yet have life and sensation make a most horrid picture. I pray God may stop such infernal work — though perhaps he has sent it upon us for our sins. Great indeed must have been our sins if such is our punishment!

There was one, a young man who was mortally wounded and had only moments to live. I sat with him, and in his pain and struggle, he reached out and took hold of my hand. Maybe he only wanted assurance that there was someone else there with him in his moment of passing. Perhaps it was a reflex that one human does for another at the precious moment. I entwined my fingers in his, and I watched him take his last breath. I hoped there was a letter or something in his pocket that would alert the family that he'd died serving his country and that he died bravely.

Our regiment started out this morning for Harpers Ferry, which is fourteen miles away according to the maps available. I am bunked with others and will remain here until the wounded are removed, and then I will rejoin the regiment. I am growing weary of war and even more so with the business administration of the endeavor. I had been in uniform for over four months now, and I wondered how long I could keep up my ruse. Undoubtedly, the end must be in sight.

I dreamed of returning home the night before last. I loved to dream of home; it seems so much like really being there. I dreamed that I was at the telegraph office, manning the key and keeping people posted on how their loved ones were doing in the war effort. Junebug was there. It was then I realized just how much I missed her and how important she was to me. Was this not a soldier's perfect dream?

I awoke refreshed and ready for the new hell of the day. I wondered what gore and suffering would fill the hours.

Chapter 20

Undated entry

I don't know what day it is. I've lost track.

I discovered the limp form of a drummer boy laid under the dark shade of a towering oak. He looked between sixteen and seventeen years of age. He had flaxen hair and eyes of blue. As I approached him, I perceived a bloody mark on his forehead. It showed where the mini ball had produced the wound that caused his death. His lips were compressed, his eyes half-open, a bright smile played upon his visage. By his side lay his tenor drum that would never be played again. It was the saddest thing I'd ever seen.

"He looks at peace," one soldier said. He took a bite out of an apple. The sound drew everyone's attention for a moment, shaming the eater.

"He looks like he's just finished playing a march," another said.

"He's so young," the apple-eater said between bites.

"Does he have any papers? His mother is going to want to know what happened to him," I said.

One of the other soldiers searched the boy's pockets and found a slip of paper with his name, home address, and a Bible verse.

A soldier handed me the paper. I was one of the few who could read in the troop.

"His name is Benjamin P. Jones of Boston."

I could not take my gaze away from his young, smooth face. It was clear he'd never shaved, never needed to. All the potential life of this young man was snuffed out by a single act. I began to grieve for him and his loss. I lamented how his family would deal with the loss. I realized that there were thousands of little drummer boys amongst the dead on both sides. Why were their lives taken, and I remain?

Soon, we are on the move and are going to Virginia. We have served in support in the last two battles. We have got a very cruel job.

You know that we lost our good Captain, and now they think they must put me on guard on the north side of our camp. I sit right down on the ground and write just as fast as I can.

I've been close to the cannon a couple of times in the field, and several shells have exploded near me. My hearing was affected each time, and I think it was not as good as when I left Concord. My health has not been good since I was on this hill not far from Harper's Ferry, but I try and eat well, sleep, and train all the time. It seems rather difficult to be a soldier, but I have got to be one, after all. I can tell you one thing: if I live to get home, I won't leave there again.

***

Undated entry

Now I can understand why soldiers would flee battle. The sounds, the smells, the fear of death or dying is overwhelming.

There is nothing I can think of that is more frightening than the battlefield. There are moments where the chaos is so tremendous that it's hard to breathe. Yet, at other times, there is almost complete silence, with just the sound of wounded men trying to catch their breath and groaning in pain.

I have been lucky myself in that my wounds have been minor, and I have healed quickly. Others in my troop, who I make sure not to engage with too much, have died in different battles. Even though I made it a point not to make too many friends, it's impossible not to feel connected to the fallen. I have helped with their bodies that only moments prior were filled with life. The contrast is striking.

We entered a small town in Maryland. My feelings of homesickness grew as we passed the ragtag buildings that lined the main street. I walked past the telegraph office, and a feeling deep in my chest became loosened and bubbled to the surface. I felt a tear creep down the side of my face. I swallowed and swept my hand across my cheek.

A captain, long blond hair and blue eyes, a cousin of the slain musician, rode up and down the line. He asked, "Does anyone know how to send messages by telegraph?"

It was always my practice to demur when volunteers or extra work were asked for, but passing that office and what seemed a providential event coaxed me out of the line. My concern of exposing myself to scrutiny was overcome.

"I worked in an office back home." My pipe was jammed into the corner of my mouth, though I'd run out of tobacco long ago, and I shifted it from one side to the other.

"Do you know Morse code?"

"I do," I affirmed and took my pipe from my mouth.

The sun peeked from behind his shoulder and hat as I looked up at him. His eyes shone with the tears he was fighting. He reined the horse and jerked its head toward the telegraph office.

"Our company telegraph operator was struck by a mini-ball yesterday. We have urgent messages that need to be transmitted to Washington City. And I have a personal message that I must transmit."

"Is it about a relative?" I had heard many soldiers with similar requests and thought nothing of the question.

He looked down at me. It was as if he took the death personally as if he could have done something to prevent it. Instead, the guilt showed on his face, and he set his jaw.

He spoke through clenched teeth. "He was my sister's child, my nephew. He was a fine young man."

I nodded and said, "I'm sure he was."

"We spent a little time together before he enlisted. We went fishing." The captain said, a bit wistful now as he remembered the times he'd spent with Benjamin.

I pulled the slip of paper from my pocket and handed it to him. "Oh, I'm sorry."

He took the paper from me and read it.

"That's just like him to have a Bible verse with him."

"Over his heart," I said.

"Yes, Proverbs, twelve, seven, 'The wicked are overthrown and are no more, but the house of the righteous stands firm.'" The captain folded the paper and said, "Can you help me?"

I snapped to a somewhat relaxed version of attention. "It would be an honor."

He lowered his voice to a whisper. "This is a matter of utmost secrecy and discretion."

I nodded and said, "I understand."

Reiterating the need for secrecy, he said, "If any of the information falls into enemy hands…."

I took off my hat and placed it over my heart. "I can do the job," I assured him.

The captain looked down at me. "George Custer." He smiled and waited for my salute. "Are you a Wolverine?"

"No, sir, I'm from Massachusetts. I was with the 20th and got transferred. I'll return to them soon."

"A good outfit there. Come with me," he said.

"I'm Private Ed —"

"Let's hurry," he said, cutting me off.

He raced around the corner and was hitching his horse to the post as I met him at the door to the telegraph office.

"You're a Godsend," he said.

I agreed with him. "This proves to me that God continues to be on our side."

We entered, the captain first and I second, as was the manner. A boy sat at the desk and jerked awake as the key came to life and began clicking.

The boy grabbed a piece of paper and started transcribing the message. We stood, the captain with his hat in his hand and me with my pipe moving from one side of my mouth to the other.

As the message finished, the captain introduced himself and asked that the boy leave the office so that we could transmit the messages in secret.

I arranged myself behind the desk and began taking dictation from the captain.

"To President Lincoln…"

He paced in front of the desk as I kept up with his words. Finally, he paused and turned, finished with his official business.

"Now, this message is to my sister. She's in Boston," he said. Again, his voice dropped in tone, and darkness passed over his eyes.

I began keying the words.

"It grieves me to inform you that your dear child, Benjamin, was struck and killed in battle. Stop. He was doing his job, playing his drum for the troops when the incident occurred. Stop. I'm sorry. Stop, George. Full stop." He took a deep breath and sighed. "You got all of that?"

"Yes, sir," I said as I finished and signed off.

"You kept right up with me, remarkable. How would you feel if I were to ask you to stay with my outfit and take over the duties of telegrapher?" He moved his hat from one hand to the other as if embarrassed to ask.

I remembered the oath I'd taken so many months ago. My promise is to uphold the Constitution and the law. "I will serve any way asked." The captain put his hat back on and strode toward the door.

"My name is Edward Corrigan Jacobson," I said.

He turned and stood framed in the doorway as a brilliant sun set behind him. Custer dipped his chin, acknowledging, I suspected, his slight debt to me in his time of need and the professionalism I was able to provide

"I will be in touch."

And with that, I would soon be transferred again and gain a step up in rank.

Chapter 21

Rain filled the open barn door. A mist drifted into the hall. The barn had a steep, thatched roof and stalls for over 30 horses. Many of the animals were used in farming, but most were for transportation and the pleasure of plantation owners.

Minta's father had built the barn shortly after adding the new floors of the house. He scratched out the plan on a large sheet of paper and estimated how much lumber and building supplies he would need. He found a slave with construction experience who was available and purchased him for a nominal amount. Jasper had suffered a severe injury that left him with a right arm that no longer functioned. And while he couldn't swing a hammer as he used to, he could direct others in the best construction practices. When Jasper finished the project, Minta's father decided to match the slave with one of the sturdier women. Shortly after, they had a son they called Jason. Unfortunately, Jasper was sold to another slave owner soon after Jason was born. Still, his mother, Jewel, stayed and became the best cook in the county.

The barn became a vital part of the farm and Minta's favorite place. Her love of horses and her concern for them had produced closer relationships than the ones she had with most people.

Today, strung from between two poles in a horse stall, Sophie slumped, naked from the waist up and bleeding. Minta stood with arms crossed, glaring at Jason as he held a long stick in his large hands.

"This ain't right, Miss Minta. People ain't got the right to do such as this."

"She needs to learn a lesson," Minta said and pointed to the whip Jason was holding with the point of her chin. "I didn't tell you to stop, Jason."

Unseen by the two, a long, black snake encircled a pole high in the loft. He flicked out his blood-red tongue.

Jason whined. "But, Miss Minta, she ain't had no water or anything for a long time."

The snake slithered around the pole and across the loft.

Jason shook his head and said, "Ain't fair, Missie Minta, even if she's yo property."

Minta strode across the stall and snatched the whip from Jason.

Sophie slowly raised her head. "You cursed by not givin' the master a baby." An evil laugh slipped from her throat. "I'm on the way of doin' what you can't."

"You witch! You will stop preying on my husband's carnal weaknesses!" Minta cried. She turned the whip around and gripped the wooden handle. Sophie across the back of the neck with the rod. There was a sickening crack.

"That'll teach the likes of you to give me backtalk," Minta said. "Cut her down and take her back to the house. She's got chores this afternoon."

Sophie plopped into a heap on the dirt floor. Jason tried to lift her. He felt her neck for a pulse.

"She's done passed over."

Minta's eyes flew open and then narrowed. She said, "You're in big trouble now with the master, Jason."

Jason challenged her by saying, "You musta' hit her too hard."

Minta ignored him, picked up Sophie's hand, and let it fall.

"We'll say she fell out the loft or something."

"But Missie? I don't want to have to lie to the sheriff."

"You're worried you might be blamed," Minta said. She put her finger to Jason's lips. "She ain't got no family 'round here. She'll never be missed."

Satisfied with the lie, Minta smiled. If there were questions, she'd come up with another story.

Jason dragged Sophie's body from the stall then picked her up. He nodded as he turned and walked out through the barn door.

Minta smiled and hugged herself.

Something rustled through the hay overhead. She looked up as the snake snagged a ridge of skin as it slid through a knothole.

Minta's mouth fell open as the snake shed its skin. She stepped back. The snake completed its transition and slithered toward the back of the barn. She knew that it was natural and that what she'd just witnessed meant nothing in the big picture of things, but she couldn't help but feel that seeing this act was symbolic of something.

Minta turned quickly and came face-to-face with Jason as he held Sophie's body.

"I speck we need to have somebody to make some sorta talk 'fore I take her out and put her in the ground," Jason said.

"No … No, Jason. I changed my mind. Instead of sayin', she fell, we'll just say she run off."

"But —?" Jason said, "you know I have a hard time lyin' to the Massa."

"Are you gonna start talkin' back now, boy?

Jason ducked his head and turned away. Minta stomped through the barn door and into the afternoon sun.

Chapter 22

The sun rose white and scorched at the small-town center now dotted with burned-out storefronts and buildings in disrepair. The North had taken control of the area and much of the state. The administration of the occupying government was problematic with, as expected, significant continued resistance in the general population.

On the side of one building read, "Scofield Was Here" in whitewash, followed by "But He Ain't No More."

A company of citizens with staves, clubs, and other weapons huddled around a tiny bonfire. Some of them had worn Confederate soldiers' butternut and gray uniforms but had changed to civilian clothes. One man, Karol, prematurely gray beard and dusty, stood holding a sling blade. He said, "'fore we go any further, let me speak. Y'all believe it's better to die fightin' than to starve?"

He shifted the sling blade from one hand to the other.

"Dang, right!" the crowd yelled. "Hell, yes! Damn Right!"

"First, you know Edward is the leadin' enemy of the people?"

There were nods in agreement all around.

"Ain't that the truth. Preach on, brother," they cried.

Karol pointed to a corner of the courthouse and said, "The time's come to be done with him, and we'll have corn at our own price."

Someone in the back of the crowd shouted. "Sorry sumbitch! String 'em up!"

Robert, another rabble-rouser but young and clean-shaven, raised his hand.

"One word!"

Karol shouldered his tool and pushed through the crowd.

"We're just poor-country farmers. The plantation owners still rule. The shadow of our ribs in our chests is just one reminder of their abundance. They save the grain for their livestock and keep our bellies empty. Let's repay this evil with our bayonets: for God knows I speak this in hunger, not in thirst for revenge."

Another man asked, "Why single out Edward?"

"He's a dog to the people," Karol said.

Robert brought his stick to quarter-arms.

"I rode with him at Spring Hill and Franklin under Hood. So, let's not be too hasty and think about what he's already done for his homeland."

He took Karol's sling blade away from him.

"Look at the finery of his house, his filled dinner table, his well-fed horses, and cattle. I say to you, what he's done, he made sure they stayed that way."

Karol glared at Robert and said. "Though some men will say it was for his country, I say he did it for pride and to please his wife." Karol yanked his tool back from Robert. "He can't help his nature." He raised his sling blade. "There's plenty of blame to go-'round, that's for sure. We've dilly-dallied enough here. There's bloody work to do."

The fire in their hearts had been stoked. They believed they could make a difference, and this was the way to do it. The rabble took up arms again and moved toward the courthouse.

Chapter 23

A rough sheet covered a hole in the north wall of the building the size of a cannonball, but a breeze pushed the cloth away from the opening.

Roughshod feet clomped past a clerk's office, judges' chambers, and empty offices inside the courthouse.

The mob stopped in front of the door with a sign reading "County Administrator." They clamored through the open door and down another hallway. Morning sunlight streamed through the door at the end of the hall.

At the center of the room was a vast, black, dusty desk with papers, pencils, and maps. A black leather chair faced the windows.

Karol strode across the room and spun the chair.

It was empty.

"I'm here," Edward said as he emerged from the shadows holding a sheaf of dispatches and a coffee cup. He wore a dark suit and white shirt open at the collar.

There was a swagger in his walk as he moved through the group of protesters. He said, "Look at what blows in when holes in walls go without repair."

A titter of laughter moved through the crowd. It was quickly quelled as Karol said, "And what blows ill for those who allow our bellies and the bellies of our children to shrink?"

Edward took his seat. He pulled open his coat and rested his hand on the grip of a single-shot Colt pistol.

"What would you have, peace or war?" he asked.

Karol said, "War is still all around us. Just because you say we are at peace doesn't mean it's over."

Edward spun his chair and turned his back to the mob. "You change your minds with every shift in the wind. Once you call me noble, the next vile. You can't have it both ways."

Karol said, "All we ask is for corn at a fair price."

Edward turned, stood, and faced the men.

"You say there are storehouses full," he said, waving the papers in his hand. "This says that's false."

He moved to the front of the desk and said, "If that's true, I say then hang 'em! Hang 'em all! Start with me."

He pulled his collar from his neck, showing a jagged scar. "Maybe you will let me dangle longer than the last time." He pulled up his collar. "Is that your answer? If that's true, then let my neck be the first you stretch. Maybe you'll be more successful than the last ones who tried it."

Nonplussed, he looked at his papers. "You ragged rabble should have burned down the entire city when you had the chance."

Laughter all around.

Edward said, "Go, and get along with yourself, you ghosts of war that is lost too soon!"

A Union soldier, sweat pouring from his face and under his arms, entered, holding an envelope.

"Where's the administrator?"

"That's me," Edward said, "what's wrong?"

"The Rebel bastards are approaching just to the south."

The messenger pulled at the collar of his jacket as if letting off steam. The mob stirred around him. He finally surmised the nature of the meeting and the beliefs of the participants.

"Finally, a chance to vent our smoky irritation." Edward said, "They approach our homeland, and we stand here debating whether it's worth saving. Who among you is with me?"

The mob raised their staves. Two men crossed their swords as if to block Edward's and the messenger's exits.

Edward said, "Will this be the place for you to take your stand? Who but I could move these men from patriots to rebels?"

The mob moved closer. Edward raised his hands.

"How much blood is there left to be spilled? I have seen enough at Chattanooga and Nashville. Kill me now if you believe that would save your languishing rebellion, but know this, behind me is a line of men in blue anxious to rain blood on our already blood-soaked land, keen to seek revenge for some lost brother, father or friend or the Glory of the Lord."

The crowd stirred, but Karol nodded, and the men blocking Edward moved aside.

"'tis peacekeeping that we must do now," Edward said.

He moved slowly through the gathering. The rabble fell into lockstep behind him.

Chapter 24

Undated entry

I am taken with the notion that this bonding is available for men through training and battle, but not for women. It's not that women can't be friends or rely on one another. It's just that it's so rare that the opportunity avails itself. Look at men. When there are available men in a social situation, it's as though the eligible women are forced to compete, like at some kind of livestock auction for the most attractive man. Men are not that way, and I've found that in the last few months, men will never be that way.

I know I've been given an unusual perspective on the current situation because of my disguise. If I unmasked, I would likely revert to the competition, or would I be able to stand on my own two feet and throw out my chest? In battle and beyond, I've seen so much death that I think I am forever changed.

We had marched on a small road past several fields. We heard rifle fire from a battle just up ahead, but it was over by the time we got there.

I saw that every stalk of corn in the northern and greater part of the field had been cut as closely as could have been done with a knife.

The men ate the corn raw and tried to feed the stalks to the livestock. Some of the animals ate, some didn't. All the men ate.

The slain soldiers from the nearby skirmish lay now in rows precisely as they had stood in their ranks a few moments before. It was never my fortune to witness a bloodier, dreary battlefield.

We marched into the field, catching a rattling volley that swept more men into the gaping maw of death.

"Scatter and make for cover!" The sergeant shouted.

Then came the brief interval occupied in reloading the rifles. With muzzleloaders, we used iron ramrod and cartridges that were thrust into the barrel. It took strong fingers and nerves of iron to tear the conical ball from the paper and insert it after the tiny cap of gunpowder. Even with practice, and we were drilled continuously, emptying these into the muzzle, ramming home, and capping the piece took time, seemingly an eternity in the hurry of action. It was no longer alone the boom of the batteries, but a rattle of musketry, at first like pattering drops upon a roof and then as they drew closer, a roll like thunder, a crash, a roar, and a rush like a mighty ocean billow crashing on the shore, chafing the pebbles, wave on wave, with deep and massive explosions of the batteries, like the crackle of a bolt of lightning.

I lay on my back, supported on my elbows, watching the shells explode overhead and wondering how long I could hold up my finger before it would be shot off. The air seemed full of bullets, not unlike a swarm of bees. When the order was given to get up, I turned over quickly to look at the sergeant who had given the order, thinking he had suddenly lost his mind.

A frenzy, not unlike a seizure, struck each man, and, impatient with their small muzzle-loaded guns, they tore the loaded ones from the hands of the dead and fired them, sending ramrods along with the bullets for double execution.

My ramrod was wrenched from my grasp as I was about to return it to its socket after loading. I looked for it behind me, and the sergeant passed me another, pointing to my own, which lay bent and unfit for use across the face of a dead man. A bullet entered my knapsack just under my left arm while I was taking aim. Another passed through my haversack, which hung upon my left hip. Still, another cut both strings of my canteen. That once useful article joined the debris now covering the ground in front of me.

Having lost all natural feeling, I laughed at the black humor of these mishaps as though they were huge jokes and remarked to my nearest neighbor that I should soon be relieved of all my trappings.

A man but a few paces from me was struck squarely in the face by a solid shot. Fragments of the poor fellow's head came crashing into my face and filled me with disgust. I grumbled about it as though it was something that might have been avoided.

Was I losing my mind?

As the battle raged, one of the regiments was going into the fight for the second time. I watched as a soldier staggered. He had no visible wound, but he soon explained that he saw his father, of another regiment, lying dead in the group of dying and dead. A wounded man, who knew them both, pointed to the father's corpse and then upwards, saying only, 'It is all right with him,' indicating that even God thought this was a fit ending for the man.

Onward went the son, by his father's corpse, to do his duty in the line, which, with bayonets fixed, advanced upon the enemy. When the battle was over, he returned to his father's side. "Dear Father," the young man said, "why do you have to leave me now when I need you the most?"

With help from others in his troop, he buried his father. From his person, he took the only thing he had, a Bible, given to the father years before, when he was an apprentice in their blacksmith shop. He buried the book along with his father and made a crude cross at the head of the grave.

Chapter 25

As he led the posse of Rabble Rousers, the battle at Franklin stormed into Edward's memory.

The day had begun with an early reverie and breakfast. The rifles were cleaned and sabers sharpened. The camp was quiet as the men tried to put the possibility that death or injury might find them this day.

His troop had gathered near the railroad station. He had inspected the ragged soldiers in gray as they stood in a crooked line.

"We are here today to make those bastards in blue pay for the invasion of our homeland." Edward raised his saber and yelled, "Are you with me?"

Horse's hooves had pounded the dusty ground. Flashing nostrils, bulging eyes and sweat, and foam had bubbled from under a saddle. Reins had bounced rhythmically against the horse's neck.

Edward's fingers had curled in his horse's mane.

A small band of Rebs had trailed them. Edward's sword had bounced against the gray cloth of his uniform. The golden light had illuminated his face. A line of Rebel cavalrymen had followed Edward on their galloping horses across a green valley.

The sergeant had pulled his horse up short and vomited.

Edward had turned his horse and galloped back.

"Coward!" He had leaped from his horse, grabbed the man by the arm, and said, "Be a man!

The sergeant had wiped his mouth with the back of his hand and glared at Edward.

Cannons roared. Balls and shrapnel canisters had fallen like rain. Edward had remounted his horse, stood in his stirrups, and raised his sword.

"Give'em a taste of hell, boys!"

He had raised his saber in one hand and pulled his pistol with the other.

Edward had moved through a wave of Union soldiers, slashing and shooting as he galloped.

He had slid from the saddle and scanned the battlefield.

Breastworks had undulated to his left with Rebels charging over blood-covered grass. Federal troops had answered with bayonets fixed.

Edward had grinned and moved toward the embankment. He had yelled, "The day is short, and there is much work to do!"

He had severed arms, legs, and heads with his saber.

"Truly," as he had laughed maniacally, "this is what I was born to do." He had hacked another man to death.

Edward had turned and smiled at the sergeant next to him. It was the man he'd grabbed and had yelled in his face. The sergeant had looked over Edward's shoulder and pushed him to the ground. The sergeant had raised his gun and fired.

The charging Yankee ducked and slashed at Edward, leaving a deep gash on his shoulder. The sergeant stabbed the Yankee. The Yankee had pulled back and touched his blood-covered chest. Edward had stood and brushed off his uniform.

"Much obliged, Sergea—"

The dying Yankee had turned to shoot Edward. The Reb sergeant had stepped in front of Edward as the Yankee pulled the trigger.

The captain had staggered and fallen to the ground. The Yankee had dropped to his knees and pitched forward dead.

Edward had dropped to his knees and cradled the dying sergeant's head. "Your sacrifice for this noblest cause will not go unnoticed in heaven."

The sergeant had nodded, closed his eyes, and died.

***

Today, the target wasn't men in blue but those in tatters who wished to take what wasn't theirs in the mind of the governor.

Edward felt sick to his stomach at the thought of raising arms against these men, but he knew his duty, and that was to the good of all.

A colossal barn sat in the center of a clearing. Dozens of gray-coated riders carrying torches circled the structure. The night air was crisp, and wisps of fog orbited the moon.

The squad moved slowly as an overnight troop guarded the storehouse. On a hill looking down, Edward lay on his stomach and watched through a telescope. Sergeant Clyde, overweight and sweaty, scrambled to his side.

This 'mopping up' action was distasteful to Edward, but his current job required at least a modicum of effort.

Edward said, "I'll wager our support is still somewhere in Nashville."

Clyde looked over his ragged troops. Karol brought his horse to the front.

"Our ranks are thin," Edward said as he surveyed his troops. "What would you wager as to the outcome?"

"I have a gallon of my poor dead father's best home-squeezed whiskey at my house."

"Tis worthy of a bet," Edward said, nodding. "What do I have that you want?

Clyde pointed at Edward's gun, "How about that fine and shiny sidearm?"

"A worthy trade if the whiskey is as good as you say. High card?" Edward pulled a grimy deck of cards from an inner pocket.

"Since I have the disadvantage in rank, I take advantage of the first pull." Clyde pulled the deck apart. He looked first and then showed Edward the Queen of Diamonds. My God!" he said, "I'll soon have myself a fine silver pistol."

Smiling, Edward said, "Not so fast there."

Edward shuffled the cards and split the deck. He showed Clyde the King of Spades without looking at the card himself. "Spades are the swords of a soldier."

Clyde said, "Aye, sir, you know your cards both front and back."

Edward smiling, said, "I know your face, my friend."

Clyde adjusted his uniform and said, "You will have your whiskey, sir. But I'll think again before wagering with you."

Edward picked up the telescope again and focused on the Rebel soldiers. "As well you should."

"Do we try and arrest them or merely give chase?"

Edward pulled the telescope from his gaze and looked at the rag-tag militia waiting behind them. "Our mission is to arrest them if we can and to kill them if we can't."

Clyde said, "As I said, they outnumber us, two-to-one."

Edward yelled, "Saddle up!"

"Are you saying all we have to do is saunter down there and wave our sabers at them?" Clyde asked.

Edward counted his arguments off on his fingers. "One, we have the mantle of gloom. Two, we have the provision of surprise. Three, we are battle-hardened soldiers tasked to send those bastards to their maker if need be. I believe that they are as war-weary as the posse. I don't think it will be necessary to draw a bead on them."

Clyde mounted his horse and said, "Some of their numbers may also be old hands at war."

Edward sprang to his feet. He wore a long black coat. A glint of approaching moonlight caught the hilt of his saber. He grabbed the handle and jerked the blade to his shoulder. "Mount up and follow me, men," he said.

Edward stomped back to his horse and swung into his saddle. "Trumpeter, call charge."

Clyde said, "Sir, we are a good quarter-mile from them."

"Remember, we have the element of surprise." Edward turned in his saddle. "Trumpeter, your best."

The trumpeter raised his horn to his lips. He blared "Charge" into the night air.

Edward raised himself over the horse's neck. "Follow me, men! Let's make quick work of them."

The small band followed Edward down the hill.

Chapter 26

July 3, 1863
Gettysburg, PA

Eloise wandered about the small shop near the crossroads of the small town. She fingered a bolt of cotton and marveled at how soft and pliant the cloth was to her touch.

"Is there someone that could cut together a shirt for me?"

The storekeeper put a finger to his lower lip as he thought. He was about fifty, thin, with gray hair covering the back half of his head. He wore a white shirt, dark pants, and a white cotton apron.

"There's no one I can think of here in Gettysburg, but there's a seamstress on the edge of the river to the west that might be able to help you."

She nodded and said, "I need a shirt to change out of when it rains."

"Yes, the clerk said, "you don't want to catch a cold this time of the year."

Eloise said as she ran her finger over a line of canisters half-filled with candy. "I could use a new pair of sh—"

He stopped her, "Everybody who comes in here asked for shoes. There's none to be had for fifty miles."

"I understand. If my heart were open to them, I'd feel sorry for the Rebs with their bare feet marching into battle."

The clerk turned and looked up from cutting the cotton for Eloise. "They have been impossible. They take what they want and fail to pay. I would donate to you and the other Union soldiers, but I can't afford it."

Eloise reached into her pocket and pulled out a handful of coins. "I will happily pay to support your business. I have a business back home, and many times I've had to turn away people without funds."

The clerk nodded and said, "It's impossible to run a business on good intentions."

"Or under threat," Eloise said as she put her coins on the counter.

The clerk stopped cutting and folded the cloth into a small square. He had merely glanced at her since she had entered the store, but he turned his head and searched her eyes. He considered exploring his suspicions about her identity. Still, he thought for a moment about how embarrassed he would be if he were wrong.

Eloise turned her gaze away. She felt the question forming in his mind, and she wasn't in the mood to deal with it.

"That should be plenty. Do you need buttons?" he asked, his mind now occupied with business.

"Yes, of course, I almost forgot," she answered as she opened the lid on a jar of hard candy.

"Whalebone?" the clerk asked.

"Yes, that will be fine, though I fear invoking the spirit of a giant fish against me." She popped the candy into her mouth and smiled.

The clerk smiled back, counted out two coins, and pushed the others back to Eloise.

"Your fear of spirits is well-founded. There are strange goings-on around the Big and Little round tops."

"Ghosts?" she asked.

The clerk nodded and gave her a knowing look as if to confirm her fears without acknowledging the silliness of the question.

"Yes, I heard others calling it the Valley of Death." She considered telling him about her time with 'spirits of the old man and the two boys' in the farmhouse when she'd been separated from her troop. Then, she decided she needed to leave before he caused her trouble.

The clerk nodded and said, "A name we try to discourage." He smiled and whispered, "It's bad for business."

***

He found me at the river's edge. It was mere moments after I visited downtown, and I searched for the seamstress when my curse visited me. I sat at the edge of the river, washing some strips of cloth as quickly as possible. Unfortunately, I was not fast enough.

"Whatcha doing there, Jacobson?" The sergeant asked. He touched the corner of his handlebar mustache. It was a nervous habit I'd seen him do many times in the past. What was he concerned about this time?

"I got a little cut there in the briars. I'm gonna wrap it afore it gets infected."

"Good idea," he said. "I'm gonna put you on the ridge tomorrow so you can help with directing the cannon."

I noticeably winced. I couldn't help it. My hearing loss was usually cured within a couple of days of being away from the line, but I was worried that I might not be that lucky in the future. I had stuffed cotton balls in my ears, but the concussions still seemed to affect me.

I remembered how Papa had started losing his hearing and turned more of his duties over to Uncle Verdell at the telegraph office. Hearing, of course, wasn't necessary for operating the key, but Papa had a hard time admitting weakness, just like me.

"What's the problem?"

I turned away and said, "It's just the noise. It hurts my ears like somethin' fierce."

"You'd rather I place you somewhere else?"

"If you could," I said as I twisted one of the bloody rags to extract as much of the red from it as possible.

"Let me think," he touched but didn't twist his mustache again. "There's a little ditch near that wooden fence there. Let me put you at the end of that line."

"Much obliged," I said, nodding. I turned to put the rags in the water again.

The sergeant turned but said over his shoulder, "You might want to let the doctor take a look at those scratches if'n they's that bad."

"No doctor can heal this cut," I mumbled to myself, proud of the little joke I'd made on my own behalf.

Chapter 27

Everything, a horse, a vine, is created for some duty. For what task, then, were you yourself created? A man's true delight is to do the things he was made for.

— Marcus Aurelius

July 3, 1863
Gettysburg, Pennsylvania

Eloise took her position at the end of the line of soldiers on the ridge facing the meadow. She stole a glance at the faces of the men as she readied herself. She saw some with slack jaws and others with faces knotted in tension. Several looked like they were having trouble breathing, and at least one looked like he was about to vomit. She felt the same knot of fear grip her stomach that she always felt as she readied her rifle. She felt the heat under her collar, took a bandana from her haversack, and tied it around her neck. A single drop of sweat ran along the side of her underarm and quickly soaked into her uniform. She noted her breathing, rapid now, in hopes of slowing it. She counted, breathing in through her nose and out her mouth. She felt the furrows of her forehead so tight. She made a point of trying to relax in hopes her nerves wouldn't upset her aim. She shook her right hand and then her left in hopes of dispelling some of the tightness she was feeling in the tendons.

She looked over her right shoulder and stared at the loader that sat in the ditch behind the shooters. She knew it was up to him to prep the rifles for loading. She hadn't spent much time with him, and now she couldn't remember his name. She would just call him 'soldier' like she called all the other 'Blue Coats' she served with but didn't know that well.

She took her canteen and drank three swallows, reminding herself that she would need to conserve her supply because of the heat. Water was essential while waiting for battle. She had experienced the 'dry mouth' that came with nerves several times and didn't want it to happen again. She also knew, from dealing with the wounded, that their first request after falling was water. She would need to save some of hers in case it was needed.

Captain Holmes strode across the glen and inspected his men. He wore a clean, blue uniform and paused to converse with Colonel Paul Joseph Revere. Eloise stared at the young man, who was the grandchild of the famous Revolutionary War rider. She wondered if he felt an obligation to be there because of his ancestor. She also speculated whether her great-grandfather had fought alongside the young man's relative. What kind of horrible tradition was being instituted?

The colonel ended the conversation, stood up in his stirrups, and set his gaze upon the white, crossed-log fence in the center of the meadow. He made such a striking figure there on that horse. Eloise was duly impressed with the silhouette he cut, and she blushed under her big flop hat. She was fascinated with the width of his shoulders. Revere turned his horse's head and galloped away.

She turned her gaze to Holmes and remembered their meeting and how he'd rebuffed her ability to serve in any capacity except as nurse or bandage roller. She wished she could reveal herself to him now and prove to him her ability as a soldier. She remembered his tiny office, their like-mindedness in books and philosophy. She remembered the smell of the smoke from his pipe. She could feel her blood pressure rise, and her cheeks again grow rosy. She would need to find a way to keep these distractions from her focus.

She turned her face down toward her rifle as Holmes walked by her. She had made a point of avoiding him. She worried that he might recognize her, even though her appearance at the time was starkly different than she looked now.

"Jacobson, ye be ready?" the loader asked.

She looked at him. His hands trembled, too, but his gaze at her was steely and intense.

"I am ready, soldier."

The young man nodded and looked to the shooter next to her.

"Ye be ready?"

"Hush, son," the sergeant said. "We be as ready now as ever we might be."

She noticed there was no sound other than the movements of the men and the horses. She strained to hear birds or insects buzzing, but there was no natural sound.

She took another deep breath.

The sergeant screamed, "Let liberty ring!"

Chapter 28

They moved across the meadow in a thin, single line, led by a tall, bearded man. He removed his hat and waved it at the line. His hair was oiled and fell on his shoulders in curly ringlets. He shouted to the men flanking his left and right, but his words were lost in the noise.

They followed the man in the gray uniform with the shiny brass buttons. They watched him pull his saber, and even over the noise of their movements, they heard him urge them forward.

They raised their battle flag as the line advanced. They moved almost in unison behind that waving piece of cloth. They didn't question the advance but glanced at each other as if knowing that the man next to them would be the only person they could rely upon in the charge. They would mutter small prayers, knowing in their hearts that for many, that answer would be no.

They raised their guns to their shoulders and waited for the order to fire. Their line stretched as far as the eye could see. They moved as one, shuffling toward oblivion.

Their bayonets shone in the bright sunlight. Some wore floppy hats. Others were bareheaded and stumbled around because of wounds. Their uniforms resembled rags more than clothes. Many were barefoot and winced as they stubbed their toes on rocks and clods of dirt.

They marched forward. They looked up and down the line and wondered which of their brothers would endure this mad attack. They wondered if they would survive.

They heard our horseback riding commanders in the distance run up and down the ridge. "Stand ready!" they heard.

They wondered what their loved ones were doing back home. "Would they be thinking of them this day?" They gripped their rifles and thought, "*Would they survive this day?*"

They smelled urine and shit as some of the men lost control of themselves. They couldn't help themselves as they advanced. They weren't embarrassed or thought a second about what happened because they knew death was near. It brought clarity to the moment that wasn't there for them on past battlefields.

Not one turned and ran. Not one.

They knew the charge was foolish, but there must have been a reason that only their commanders knew — some life-saving strategy they weren't privy to. They would trust their leaders because they loved their leaders, especially Major General Pickett and General-in-Chief Lee. They believed that he would lead them to victory and that their sacrifice would help pave the way. They felt their hearts beat hard in their chests, and soon the stifling air around them would become filled with smoke and the retorts of their rifles.

"Fire!" General Pickett yelled.

"Fire at will!" The captains, under his command, shouted.

They watched our rifles discharge. They saw the smoke and heard the response of our guns.

They watched their brothers fall, others moved forward over them, and then those would fall. They reached for the cover they imagined they might find behind a thin rail fence. Their fantasy was that they would be able to weather the onslaught of mini-balls, and cannonballs would be stopped at the wall. In their minds, this barrier represented the possibility of survival, the possibility they would see their loved ones someday. Someday. The notion ran through their minds in unison, a single idea that unified them in life and, in many, their death. They continued to fall. They continued to move forward to their deaths.

Their blue-coated adversaries watched them fall. They knew how close they were to death and how many times in the past they had faced the same. The idea that this conflict would end soon gave them, just for a moment, hope.

For a moment, the charge worked, but without reinforcements, the soldiers in blue repelled the assault. Without the planned, flanking charge, the march would fail and fail so spectacularly that it would be remembered forever. The bravery and the dedication of the men would be recognized and spoken with reverence.

They wondered, for a split second, why they were asked to sacrifice themselves, and then they wondered no more.

They fell, many with chests expelling plumes of blood as if they were exhaling their souls.

***

"Shore up that line," the sergeant said. He waved at Eloise's company and pointed north of the boulders in the middle of the 'so-called' Valley of Death.

She followed the line of trees and approached with small, quiet steps. She knew the Rebs were close, but she still couldn't see them.

The smell of smoke from the cook fires was in the air as the dawn broke in the east. She could see shadows on the men as they quietly marched, most in bare feet. Could she be sympathetic to their plight? It was then she remembered they had vowed to shoot and kill her and her empathy melted.

"Company, move now!" the sergeant yelled.

Eloise and her troops raised their rifles and stood in a straight line. The cover from the trees was minimal, but it was better than the rocks the Rebs clung to.

"Fire!"

She pulled the trigger and watched the soldier she'd aimed at fall. It was the first time she was able to see the damage her weapon had done to another human being. Again, a pang of empathy leaped in her heart.

She looked over her shoulder and handed her rifle to the loader. He tamped down the shot and gave her the gun.

"Give'em hell," he said, just as a second volley hit the rocks and soldiers.

Chapter 29

The sign read "Hockney House. Vicksburg. Rooms to Let". A slight breeze moved the placard above the front door where Virginia stood waiting to board the carriage.

A driver yanked a thick carpetbag and tossed it on top of a small pile of luggage.

Buildings on the street near the boarding house still showed the damage from the long-ago siege.

Virginia moved through the open front door, kissed the portly Mrs. Hockney on the cheek, and hugged the rail-thin Mr. Hockney. He twisted slightly on his crutches, frowned, and looked at his boot.

"You'll be missed, Virginia." Mrs. Hockney daubed at her eyes with a handkerchief. She nodded her head in agreement.

Virginia turned and boarded the carriage. Her long, flowing dress swept the carriage's step, and for a moment, her ankle was exposed. Mr. Hockney quickly looked away. The white fabric rustled against the open door as Virginia tugged and tugged. The door finally opened.

"I'll write soon and tell you all about Tennessee," she said as she stuck her head out of the carriage window.

As he continued to avert his gaze, Mr. Hockney said, "Be careful. Your tender ways may not be well suited for such a rough and tumble place."

"Don't worry," she said as she brushed a tear from the corner of her eye. "They have everything the modern young woman could ask for."

She had considered every aspect of the situation. Was it fate that the doctor had introduced her to Edward? Was God's hand in their meeting? She would have to trust herself and have faith.

Mrs. Hockney scurried as quickly as she could up to the window of the carriage.

"Protect your heart, Virginia. If only your parents were still —" she said, choking on the last words.

Virginia looked away and brushed an errant tear from her cheek. "Many things would be different if only that were so."

Her eyebrows shot up as Mrs. Hockney asked, "How well do you really know this man?"

"I know his words, and thereby I know his heart," Virginia said as she patted her carpetbag. She tapped on the ceiling of the carriage with her parasol. "I'll write to you later and tell you of my joy."

The carriage pulled away. The horse's hooves settled into a soothing rhythm as Virginia snuggled into the seat cushions.

The old couple hugged, but Mr. Hockney continued to frown.

Chapter 30

It was a habit Minta had had since she was a small child. She would stand at the end of the staircase and wait for her father to return from whatever project or meeting he had attended. She would tap the newel top three times and say a prayer. She felt this small act was what kept him safe and returned him home each night until the time he left and never came back.

Minta stood by the stair's post, fingers clutching the rail, with her nails turning white. She tapped the wood and said a prayer. She felt a stab of pain behind her left eye but didn't think it was enough to require one of her injections. She would bite her cheek and muddle through this attack. She wanted to be fully aware when her husband came home.

She prayed, "Mother of God, preserve my home, and to your service, I pledge myself. Amen."

She straightened the front of her dress. She turned, and her dainty foot slid onto the first step. There was a large, full-length mirror across from her. The intent was to make the room appear even more substantial when people entered. Still, at this angle, it afforded her a glimpse of how people saw her. She was still striking. Tall and thin with a bright, healthy complexion. Her best features continued to be her piercing, dark eyes and her expressive brow. She seemed to have the talent for conveying a full range of emotions and expectations with her face. Many a slave had felt her fierce gaze when she was angry. There were even times when Edward would feel the heat.

She turned and moved through the rambling mansion and opened the door to the parlor. She paced in front of the roaring fire. She turned, glared at the blaze, and then jerked an envelope from her pocket.

She threw the letter into the fire and smiled. She believed fire was the perfect disinfectant and marveled at the power of the flames. It was a long-time Southern tradition. Fires were set to clear brush and trees before cultivating a field; fires were set to sterilize and cleanse equipment before use by doctors and nurses; fires were used to clean cooking utensils, and fire would also destroy most evidence of a crime.

"No," she said. "What am I thinking? I should have buried it with the others."

She wrenched a poker from the holder and snatched the envelope from the flames. She stomped on the paper and then picked up the letter. She smoothed the charred edges and then extracted the letter from the envelope.

"Impudent whore. How dare she write such to my husband?" Minta muttered to herself. It was a bruise to her ego that she had never felt before. She was always the most beautiful woman in the room and knew how to use that power over men. She liked that feeling and didn't like this new threat.

"What have you there, Minta?"

Minta turned and stared, open-mouthed at Edward. He was still dressed in the same outfit he had worn at the attack at the barn. There was a small splotch of blood on his shirt. His gaze caught hers and quickly moved to the fireplace.

"A letter for you, my love," she replied.

He took off his blood-spattered saber and jacket. He dropped the clothes on the floor near the door. He knew Jason would appear soon and take care of laundering them to-morrow. He had come to rely on the slaves, a notion he would feel was repugnant just months ago.

"Who's it to?" he asked.

"Why, it's for you. I was about to go to bed, and I had placed the letter here on the mantle when a gust of wind caught it and blew it into the fire."

Edward knew Minta might be lying, but it would be difficult to challenge her without more evidence. The house had been "added onto" so often he knew places where the fit wasn't perfect. He looked at her and tried to read the expression in her eyes. He failed.

He crossed the room with his hand extended. "Drafty old house. Let me see it."

"I saved it from going up the chimney, but the envelope is a bit scorched."

Edward took the envelope from her and yanked open the flap.

"T'was lucky to save it," she lied.

He read the letter and said, "Yes, you were." He looked up from the message and yelled, "Sophie!"

Edward continued to read.

"She's gone," Minta said.

"Sophia? That seems unlikely," he remarked.

"Feeling her need for freedom, I suppose. She decided she'd try life in the West."

Edward shuddered a bit. "Maybe Jason should try and … oh, never mind. How many are there left … fifteen?"

"More like ten." Minta shook her head.

He looked up from the letter.

"She didn't even say goodbye."

She ducked her head but glanced at him. "She told Jacob you'd understand."

Edward put his fingers to his lips. He looked up at her and searched her eyes for a flicker of truth. He was still her 'new' husband in many aspects. The whirlwind romance that put him in charge of this place hadn't allowed for any long-term reflection on the situation.

He asked. "Minta, you didn't have a hand in her leaving, did you?

Minta put her index finger on the mantle. She looked away from his gaze as she said, "No, of course not."

He returned to his reading. "Opportunity, of course. Godspeed to her."

Minta crossed herself in prayer and moved toward the door.

"With Sophia gone, the onus will now be on you to prepare the house for an exceptional visitor."

She turned. A log rolled from the back of the fireplace, catching on the andiron.

"And who might that be, Edward?" Minta asked.

"A friend I made in Mississippi, just outside of Vicksburg. A very enchanting young woman. We have a love of poetry in common."

She feigned shock in his revealing of the relationship. "Really? Why ain't I heard about her afore?"

He pulled open the collar of his shirt. He remembered the nights spent with Virginia and how quiet and tranquil the time, compared to the time he spent with Minta. "We vowed to keep the friendship quiet until things after the war became more settled.'"

Minta said, voice dripping with sarcasm. "And now they are more settled?"

"Nearly so, I've told you before this is not a 'fair' side of you. Our visitor will need special attention. Can I count on you?" Edward asked.

She thought for a moment about escalating this discussion and putting her foot down about the visit. Was this the best strategy? Keep your friends close and your enemies closer.

Minta nodded and said, "Of course."

Chapter 31

A dainty, high-heeled shoe slid onto the lowest rail at the stern of the ship. Just below, the paddle beat the water into a froth. Virginia breathed in the mist and slid her hand along the top rail. She instinctively checked her jacket pocket for the ticket that would take her from Memphis to Nashville by train. But, of course, she would leave the train before going all the way to the end. The station nearest Edward's home was at least an hour from Nashville. The apprehension in her heart was sincere, but she felt she was doing the right thing.

The war had caused the muddy Mississippi to become just another part of the conflict. The North attempted to blockade the commerce that might help the South's war machine as much as possible. Some shipping continued, but passenger travel, while challenging, was not impossible.

Virginia gazed up at the moon. She followed the riverbank for a moment and then said, "Father in heaven, hallowed be thy name." She closed her eyes. Her lips moved, finishing the prayer to herself. "Amen."

Grandfather stood next to Virginia, also looking up at the moon. He wore a long black suit and white shirt with a bolo tie. His gnarled hands grasped the railing. He was just as she remembered him. He still smelled of pipe tobacco on his clothes, and she noticed that his shoes were shined. It was the first time she'd not seen his footwear covered with dust or mud.

"The Lord asks that you seek a quiet place for prayer," the old man said.

"I couldn't find any place on deck any quieter than here."

He took a deep breath. "Are you seeking the Lord's guidance or his approval?"

"It's His guidance I always seek, Grandfather, but approval is not such a bad thing."

He tapped his finger on the rail. "Does his wife factor into your prayers?"

Virginia felt a twinge of guilt in her heart. She had been raised with a strict code based on the teachings of Jesus and the Bible. Visiting a married man in his home stretched the boundary of that protocol. Still, if she could hold on to her virtue until marriage, she didn't have a problem with playing with fire. "His letters tell me that he is no longer in love with her and that she is unable to give him the son he needs because she is dying of cancer."

"I see, I see," the old man said. "Wars make people commit foolish choices. Are you sure this man is the right one for you?"

She turned toward him, but he refused to look at her. She said, "Grandfather, you know me better than anyone. You know his letters. You know how my heart leaps in my chest when I say his name."

The old man smiled. He tugged at the lapels of his jacket. "Yes, I remember that feeling with your grandmother. Let your heart lead. It will not fail you."

She remembered the family history of the grand love affair between him and her grandmother. They were children from adjoining farms that grew up together. They were cautious and caring, loving in so many ways that they showed how healthy relationships grew.

Virginia nodded, prayed that even though her love for Edward was true, she would need wisdom and luck to circumnavigate the treacherous, churning waters of her future with him.

She opened her eyes and said, "Amen."

She smiled, scanned the empty deck, and hugged herself. The ghost of Grandfather faded in the wind.

Chapter 32

I walked into the War Department with my papers and was led into a small office. As was the practice for new hires, I was assigned to the overnight shift and believed the first night would be quiet and uneventful. I scanned the room, searching for the duty roster so that I could sign in. Unfortunately, the operator I was there to relieve couldn't be found.

I turned the corner, and President Abraham Lincoln was sitting next to the telegraph operator.

My first impression was of his long legs that were stretched out over the bottom of a chair. He was dressed in a dark suit, white shirt, and an untied bowtie. There was a small stain on the collar of his shirt, and I could see that his shoes needed shining. I noticed how his hair had a frizzy quality and was longer and thicker than I had imagined. He wore reading glasses and was pouring over a sheaf of papers. He turned to the operator and began dictating.

I put my haversack over the back of a chair and sat, waiting for him to finish. When he ended his message, he turned to me.

Looking at me over his reading glasses, "Corporal Jacobson," he said.

He offered me his hand.

I looked at the long fingers and the callus that ran along the inside of his thumb. I tried to imagine how many hands that hand had shaken in his effort to get elected, and since that time. Pressing the flesh, I think it was called.

"A pleasure to meet you, sir," I said.

"As it is you, young man," the president said.

I removed my hat and quickly rose to attention. This was the most significant moment of my life. I had admired the president for years, and now he was standing in front of me.

The president seemed embarrassed at the attention; his cheeks reddened as he waved his hand at me to reseat myself.

"Enough with the pish-posh. We're here to work." He sat down next to the operator and put his hand on his shoulder.

"Time for you to go home," he said as he glanced at a prominent rail station clock.

"Yes, sir," the soldier said. He stood, stretched, and left the room.

President Lincoln motioned me toward the stand-up desk with the telegraph keys. The room was small, with two bookcases and several straight-back chairs. Maps covered the walls and the conference table in the center of the room. A large window with white cotton curtains framed a rising sun. I glanced at the sight and, for a moment, soaked in exactly where I was.

"I have several dispatches to go before we call it a night. Let me know if I'm going too fast or if you get lost. I can stop and restate anything you need to hear. It's better to go slow and get it right than to make a mistake." He gave me a reassuring smile and brought his glasses down to his nose.

"Yes, sir," I said. His voice was more high-pitched than I'd expected, with a midwestern accent that wasn't evident in the newspaper quotes I had become used to.

He nodded and said, "I'm just an old country lawyer, but I can get ahead of myself at times."

I took off my coat and laid it on the floor next to my chair. There was an oil lamp with a chimney smudged with soot. You would think someone would take a moment to clean the darn thing, given the critical work done here, but that's the Army.

The dictation was easy to follow, not near as hard as Captain Custer or any of the other colonels or generals I'd had to translate for in the last three months.

The dispatches were specific in their instructions. The president would hover over a large pile of maps in the center of a table, marking the troop locations and what their deployment would mean to the war effort with a small pencil. I finally understood some of what was asked of us as soldiers and how our missions were pointed toward a specific goal. A part of me wished every soldier could be as well informed of the final goals of our efforts. On the ground, there was nothing but chaos and horror. Whether the attempt was successful or failed depended on so many factors I'd not understood—I still don't know in some ways.

The president read a dispatch from General Grant and smiled.

"I wish I had a bushel basket full of generals like him," he said to me over his reading glasses.

I smiled but didn't want to show any disrespect to him or the other generals I'd served under.

"I read where you were at Gettysburg," he said. He sat in a rocking chair and began peeling an apple, just as I'd seen my father and Uncle Verdell do dozens of times. Tears came unexpectedly to my eyes, and the president stopped.

I explained my reaction, and he smiled.

"One thing makes us think of another. Sometimes those things that we least expect," he said.

"Yes," I agreed. I dabbed at my cheeks and told him of my witnessing the massacre of the Rebs at Picket's charge. I told him about the soldiers' bravery as they marched to their deaths.

He paused and nodded. "They believe."

I agreed with his assessment of the men and that while their cause would rip the country apart, there was never any question of their bravery.

"Let me show you what Lee had in mind." The president pulled a map from under the stack and unfolded it.

He pointed to a ridge. "Custer blocked the reinforcements Lee was expecting that day, and he was helpless to save those men in the line of fire. I'm sorry you had to witness that."

"It was truly horrific," I said.

"I would imagine."

He refolded the map and put it in another stack.

"You really have the big picture," I said, "from here."

President Lincoln laughed. "You're right, soldier. I just wish this perch could provide a faster resolution to the war."

"Maybe we should train some parrots to fly over the battlefield and report back," I said.

The president looked up, caught my gaze, and chuckled to himself.

I joined the president in laughing. He looked at me again. I knew he was the commander and prosecutor of the war and that much of his time dealt with tragedy.

His laughter was built in volume and was filled with a tone that indicated he enjoyed laughing but hadn't had many reasons lately.

He was an easy man to like with self-deprecating humor that made him endearing. "You've been a real godsend to me, soldier," he let his gaze rest on me as he said, "and your service is much appreciated."

"It's been my honor, sir." I thought about snapping off another salute, but I didn't know how he might take it.

"Let's get back to work," he said.

I watched him as his shoulders slumped a bit as if the weight of the war was carried somewhere near the back of his neck. Finally, he turned back to the sheaf of dispatches he held in his left hand and smoothed out another map with his right.

Chapter 33

"We skirmish with the rag-tags of the Rebels while the real battles are to the North and East of us," said General John VanBurgh, a man in his late 50s, with shimmering white hair and beard. He squatted behind a desk big enough to hold a square dance. The room was warm and just a bit too humid for Edward's taste. There was an odor of cigar smoke and food left out overnight. Edward saw a small tray and a straight-back chair in the corner.

In the opposite corner, a small table with a telegraph key sat idle. A small pile of papers sat next to the key.

Edward, hat under his arm, stood at attention. A slight twitch drew John's eye to Edward's face. A single drop of sweat crept from beneath his hairline and fell down his cheek.

"At ease," John said.

Edward allowed his arms to relax.

"I'm sure you're aware of why I called you in."

Edward replied, his eyes straight ahead. "A thought did pass through my mind, sir."

"Better that than a mini-ball, if I do say so," John said as he motioned for Edward to a chair opposite him.

Edward sat and said, "Yes, sir, no question."

"Your charge on the rioters at Spring Hill. I have reports that the effort was unsuccessful because you gave them a 'warning.'"

John picked up a slip of paper and read over his half-glasses.

"How could that be true?" he asked.

"I never did any such," Edward said. "We were within striking distance. We had fewer numbers than the Rebs, so I decided it was better to move as quickly as possible, using the element of surprise to our advantage. So I called for the charge, and we lit out.

And I take exception with the word, 'unsuccessful.' We captured or killed over a dozen men."

John looked up at Edward over his reading glasses. "Your gunners were out of range, and by the time you made it down the hill, the 'party' had scattered."

"That part was out of my control." Edward glanced to his left as he lied.

John laid his glasses on a pile of papers on his desk. "Have you ever wondered why you received this commission?"

"I have wondered." Edward crossed his legs and put his hat on his knee.

"Who's the better peacekeeper than a man who's known the worst of war? You're the perfect choice to bring peace to this small corner of the world," John said as he offered his hand.

Edward studied him for a moment and then stuck out his hand. He had never respected the man, but he did know what battle was like. Moreover, he was aware that VanBurgh was a master of strategy and tactics. Those skills would be helpful in the rebuilding of the South.

"I am bound by duty and honor to follow your orders, sir."

"No doubt," John said, "no doubt."

John put his glasses back on and returned to his reading. "And your doctor is supplying you with adequate medication?"

Edward's cheek twitched, and he tugged at the brim of his hat. "Yes, appropriate to the need."

He didn't like the fact that his addiction to pain-killing medicine made him vulnerable to pressure from VanBurgh, but he had no choice but to comply at this time. Again, with the tactics.

"Good," John said, "let me know if there's anything else you or your lovely wife might need."

Edward felt the bile rise in the back of his throat. It was bad enough that the pressure VanBurgh exerted on him made him feel impotent. Adding his wife into the mix made the situation almost intolerable. He stood and walked to the office door.

John said, still not looking up from his work, "Anything at all." He knew which strings to pull and when to pull them. Everyone wanted something, and providing it to them and knowing when to provide it was the best way to keep control.

Edward walked through the open office door and closed it behind him. He had developed a method of judging men and the roles they best played in life. He concluded that VanBurgh was well suited for his place, well suited indeed.

Chapter 34

A huge, black stove squatted against the kitchen's north wall with pots at full boil and pans sizzling with slabs of bacon and steaks. The room was one of the first constructed when the house was built. A large fireplace took up half of one wall, and a small table and chair sat in front of the hearth.

Beyond that was the opened door to a dining room revealing a table spread with meats, vegetables, and confections. Lids covered many of the dishes to keep the flies from landing on the food. Spoons, knives, and ladles cluttered the counters. Steam covered the windows.

Minta moved from stove to tables to water pump. She grabbed the handle and filled a jar. She drank and rubbed her temple.

An ancient Black woman, Jewels, the size of a ten-year-old girl, hopped like a bird from one tiny step stool to the other.

Minta moved close to the stove and said, "Make sure that pie comes out afore it burns."

"Just as you say, Miss Minta."

Jewels stirred one pot, hopped from her step stool, and grabbed a towel as she took the oven handle.

"I've got to get some air," Minta said as she fanned herself with her hand. "You've got it so hot in here."

Jewels stuck her finger in a bowl of icing at another station in the cabinet and hopped to another stool. "It's hot everywhere."

Minta opened the back door and looked out on the yard. For as far as she could see, the land, the buildings, and the people working there were all property of hers. She smiled at the effort her father had made and how she had helped expand the plantation.

She watched Jason raking leaves. He looked up at the sound of the door opening, and Minta gave him a slight smile.

"I've got to get the stove hot enough to bake that cake. Ifn's you want it to rise." Jewels said.

"I do want it to rise." Minta headed for the dining room door. "I just don't want to melt in the process."

Jewels muttered to herself, "Better get used to the heat, old bitch." She put her head down, stirring the pot. "Where's you're goin' it's a whole lot hotter."

Minta turned, gathered her skirts, and rushed at Jewels.

"I heard that."

Jewels kept her head down but said, "You probably listen to a lot of things you don't want to. Don't mean they ain't true."

"Things haven't changed all that much since the war left our valley. It'd still take a jury of twelve white men to hang a white woman from a tree limb."

Jewels kept stirring her pot. "I didn't say nothin' 'bout Sophie, if'n that's what you're 'fraid of."

Minta closed her eyes, fists clenched. She picked up a butcher knife.

"Damn that, Jason," Minta said between clenched teeth.

"That's my baby boy you talkin' 'bout."

Minta glanced at the small woman and took a breath. She'd forgotten the lineage and connections. She knew confronting Jewels at this time wouldn't help her in her effort to hold on to her husband.

"I meant nothing —"

"Don't go blamin' Jason. He didn't say nothin'. Only's people who're gonna believe that story about Sophie goin' to the West to find work is the ones who want to believe."

"She said she was with Edward's child," Minta pleaded.

"Just 'cause she say somethin' don't mean it's true," Jewels said, not looking up.

Minta's eyes opened wide, and her mouth fell open. She hadn't considered Sophie was lying. She waved her hand at her chest. "So, nobody's gonna say nothing about Sophie?"

Jewels turned back to the bubbling pots. "Jason says it was an accident. I don't see no reason for anybody to have to get too excited about it. She weren't nothin' but a little cat sniffin' around causin' trouble."

Minta touched the edge of the knife. "This knife's as dull as your mind, old Jewels. Get Jason to put it on the grinding wheel when he gets in from the yard."

Jewels nodded, stirring and smiling. "Yessim."

Chapter 35

The moon shone through the tree branches around a dilapidated shack. A small vegetable garden sat to the east, and a barn in need of paint lay to the west.

Horses whimpered and stomped. An owl hooted.

The shack's door flew open, and a dirty white man in long johns rushed into the yard. He carried a rifle at quarter-arms.

From out of the night rode a tall figure. Edward emerged, wearing a long black cloak, flop hat, and a handkerchief covering the lower half of his face. His stallion pawed at the ground.

"Hold up with that rifle there, boy," Edward said.

"I got a right to protect my property," the young man said.

"Fair enough. People are talkin', Lucifer White."

He glared at the man on horseback. "Can't be anythin' of your bidness."

"Wrong, boy."

"You better turn that evil animal around and get off my property, Corrigan."

The shaking man pulled the gun up to his shoulder. Then, there was the sound of guns from every direction, 'click, click, and click.'

He held out his hand, palm up, and said, "I wouldn't do nothin' foolish there, Lucifer." Edward said.

"I cut off the head, and the snake dies. Ain't that one way to send your monkeys back to hangin' in your trees?" Lucifer threatened.

Edward said, "Put the gun down. We don't want nobody to get hurt, lessen we have to."

Lucifer cocked his firearm and aimed at Corrigan's head. A dozen masked men on horseback drifted from the shadows and into the moonlight, all armed, all aiming their guns at him.

"I don't have nothin' to lose."

Edward let a smile creep into his voice. "What about your pretty little wife and her baby? Why don't you take a look at 'em a standin' there?"

Corrigan put his hand back on the saddle's pommel and pointed with his chin at the porch. A pale woman, eyes as big as saucers, held a thin baby. They had only been married for fourteen months and were lucky enough to have the baby they both wished for quickly.

"All right, all right," Lucifer said. He lowered his weapon. "What's it you boys want?"

"We understand you're workin' your land right alongside some sharecroppin' good-for-nothin' Niggers."

A genuinely puzzled look came over Lucifer's face. It was like he couldn't imagine anyone having a problem with him making a living. "Tyrone's just tryin' to feed his family?"

Corrigan shook his head and offered his empty hands. "No, not a thing wrong with feedin' a family. We don't like you workin' alongside him. That's all."

Lucifer let his rifle slide down by his side. He heard the posse sheath their guns. "I helps him. He helps me. That's the way we got it worked out," he said. He was bewildered as to how this mattered to anyone.

"Not anymore, you don't. Leave that boy to do his work, and you do yours. Understand?" Edward said emphatically.

Lucifer's arm jerked, and the rifle moved but didn't rise to the shooting position. "Or what?"

"Or we'll have to make another visit, only this time it'll be to your buddy. And we won't stop for any chit-chat like we have here."

Lucifer's eyes widened, and he glared at the masks of the posse. "Do that, and you'll have to deal with me."

Corrigan laughed and said, "When ants take over the world!"

He turned his horse and disappeared into the night. The other vigilantes turned and galloped away.

The sound of the horse's hooves echoed through the small valley like distant thunder.

Lucifer looked back at his new wife and son. "It'll be awright. Don't worry."

But his wife couldn't put the sight and sounds out of her mind. She cuddled the sleeping baby and worried about their future.

Chapter 36

Eloise didn't mean to fall asleep at her post. In fact, it was the first time she had, which was a miracle, given the number of late nights she'd worked.

She had kept it in a small pocket in her coat, close to her heart. It was folded several times, and she would take it out and remind herself of who she was back then, why she chose to become Edward, and what she had become.

The newspaper article was poking out of her pocket when the President entered. He didn't feel it was right to disturb Corporal Jacobson. He'd worked so hard the night before, and the sun was just breaking through the window in the telegraph office of the war room.

He struggled with the notion. How could he? Sure, he was the president, but did that give him the right to move so surreptitiously and deceitfully? He felt this dishonored himself and the soldier. And then...

The president gently pulled the paper from the soldier's pocket, put on his reading glasses, and read the article. For the most part, the column was a record of a fiery young woman's speech at a hot Fourth of July celebration. *"Eloise Jacobson, was she related to Edward? That was the only logical connection,"* the president thought.

He turned the paper so he could catch the sunlight a bit better. He liked the choice of words, the rhythm, and how the speech built into a rallying cry. He was most impressed with Eloise, the writer.

He thought, *"The words are clear and concise. Nicely put together with intelligence, emotion, and fire."*

The president rubbed his chin. The beard itched at times, but he knew from his advisors that it was his trademark and that he would have to put up with it, at least, until he was out of office. Mary liked it too. She said it was like kissing a soft pillow.

"Executing a war, running a country's economy was only second to making sure your wife is happy," the president thought, chuckling to himself.

He refolded the article and put it on the table next to the telegraph key.

He removed his glasses and rubbed his eyes. He needed to get some sleep before the hell of the day began. It was an open house, and he knew it would be a long day given the grievances he was receiving in the mail.

Corporal Jacobson snorted and twisted in his seat. The president smiled and thought, *"so many wonderful young people who would carry on long after he was gone. He knew in his heart that the future of the nation was in good hands."*

He knew this conflict with the South would eventually end. The supply blockade was strangling them. It was just a matter of time. The hoped-for recognition of the South as an independent nation from England, France, or Spain would not come. He'd been assured of it and grieved that more good men would have to die before the South finally gave in.

"What a waste," he whispered to himself.

He stood, stretched, and made his way to the door. He looked over his shoulder at the snoring soldier.

He said, "You are the very best of us." It was as if he was trying to convince himself that all the effort to save the Union was worth the sacrifice.

Chapter 37

A smudged hand picked up a small sugar cube and placed it on a soft cloth attached to the lip of a glass. Another hand picked up a whiskey decanter and poured the liquid over the now steaming cube. Dripping whiskey covered the sides of the decanter and his fingers.

The dirty hand grabbed the back of his hat and a red handkerchief. He yanked the disguise forward. His black, mussed hair covered his face.

Edward parted the sweaty mass and pulled it from his forehead. He glared at the bubbling drink on the table before him, then he picked up the glass and downed it in three swallows.

He pulled the costume from his shoulders and pushed it into a chiffonier in the corner of the room.

He shuffled to the comfortable chair at the edge of the hearth and sucked his finger. He sat down hard and looked at the blaze.

Edward closed his eyes. He felt every ache and scar on his body. He'd realized long ago that there was only one adequate answer to his pain, but he wasn't quite ready for that final resolution. He felt he still had work to do.

He felt the absinthe rush from his stomach and through his system. He felt the heat in his arms and legs and, surprisingly, his nose. He had the olfactory gift, much like that of a dog.

He could smell the odors of food cooked hours ago and now in storage awaiting him downstairs. He smelled the leftover aroma of Minta's bath and her body powder from her room down the hall. He could even smell Minta's covered chamber pot in her bedroom and her slightly sharp breath as she slept three rooms away from his. There was even a metallic smell in her breath. Was it the cancer that grew in her brain? He didn't want to think about that, and with a slight nod, he fell asleep.

Chapter 38

In the front yard, a dazzling autumn sun played over the tall white columns of the house. An enormous magnolia tree rose over a brick driveway. Jason stood in the ankle-deep grass, dropped his scythe, and rushed to the front door. "Carriage comin'! Carriage comin'!"

The half-acre of the well-manicured lot featured a small pond where horses stalked each other behind a bright, white fence. The adjacent barn, also brilliantly white, sat with its large front door open behind the fence. It was clear that these buildings were well kept and maintained. Chickens and ducks pecked at the ground in front of the structure to forage, for corn spilled as the horses and cows were fed.

A black carriage circled the tree and rolled to a stop in front of the limestone steps. The horse shook his harness as the driver hopped down from the bench.

A gloved hand rested on the open window. The door opened, and Virginia emerged. She wore a full skirt, hat, and jewels. She opened her parasol and marched toward the house.

Edward appeared at the front door, arms open, smiling. His cheeks were cleanshaven, and he sported a neatly trimmed mustache and goatee. Jewels had cut his hair, and his skin had a rosy glow. His boots sparkled, and he wore new gray pants and a white, open-necked shirt.

"Welcome to paradise on Earth, Virginia, my dear girl," he said as he swept down the steps and stopped a few feet from her.

Jason stood to Edward's left. He had been cutting the small circle of grass in the front yard. He let the large scythe lean against his shoulder. With a glance, Jason perceived that Edward wanted him to put the tool away.

"This is most impressive. Much more so than described in your letters." She offered her hand. He bowed and gently kissed it. He lingered a bit too long, and she pulled her hand away. Jason watched the exchange but withheld comment.

"Yes, Briarwood surely shines bright, but my dear..." he said as he bowed but looked up at her, "...only the sun shines brighter than fair Virginia."

Minta breezed down the front steps, all smiles and delicate as an orchid. "Miss Greene," she said, "how nice of ya to come." She wore a white gown, black slippers. Around her neck, she'd tied a black ribbon, and shimmering earrings were dangling from her ear lobes.

She extended her hand. Virginia shook Minta's hand and curtseyed. "Thank you for having me."

Virginia's first impression of Minta was that she was older than Edward but was still a beauty. Her black hair still had no sign of white or gray. Her eyes were brown, with a twinkle that Virginia couldn't decide indicated anger or curiosity.

"I hope you like our little place," Minta said as she waved her hand over the vista of the grounds.

"Your husband strings words together like a poet," Virginia said as her eyes widened, "but they fail to capture the grandeur of your home."

Minta looked at the younger woman and smiled. In her mind, she calculated the relative difference between their ages. She could tell by looking at her outfit that Virginia was of low income and education. But she could see Edward's attraction to the 'girl.' Minta took in the milky, white décolletage and the ruby red hair. She finally realized this was the vision she'd seen in the tree stump that stormy night. "How did that happen? she asked herself.

Minta's chest swelled with pride. "Briarwood has been in my family for decades."

"Yes, Edward's letters are descriptive and emotional."

"Really?" Minta feigned surprise, "Pray tell, what 'is' my husband's true nature?"

Edward shuffled his feet, "Well. I'm not sure this is a good turn for the conversation..."

Minta smiled, "I'm' not sure I'm aware of this side of Edward."

"' Tis there, I can assure you, Madam," Virginia replied, rising to Minta's bait, "it's there in abundance."

The women glared at each other. The uncomfortable silence hung in the air for a moment.

Edward threw up his hands. "Enough of this pish-posh. I'm thirsty as I'm sure the both of you are on this beautiful fall day."

Jason cleared his throat. "Should I get the bags, Mistah Edward?"

Edward turned and smiled at Jason. "Yes. Bring in Miss Virginia's bags and put them in the guest room at the end of the hall."

"Next to your room?" Jason asked.

Edward said without a bit of shame or guilt in his voice. "Yes, next to my room."

He turned again and flung his arms open as if he was a ringmaster directing the audience's attention. "I believe Jewels has some lemonade freshly made for your arrival."

He offered his arm to Virginia. With a flourish, she took it.

Jason struggled with the bags, dropping the trunk. It made a faint clunking noise. Edward's head whipped around.

"Jason! Be careful. The items in Miss Virginia's luggage are just as precious as she."

"Yessah," Jason muttered.

Minta took Edward's right arm. Edward flinched and then allowed her to take his elbow.

Minta dug her claws into Edward's arm. She saw him wince from the pain, but she kept smiling at him.

The three ambled up the steps.

Chapter 39

Edward followed Virginia and Minta toward the stairs. The winding staircase had 15 steps and ran to the open balustrade that led to the upstairs bedrooms. The current center staircase covered the entrance to the kitchen and dining area. Edward glanced at the open door of the kitchen. Jewels peaked around the door jamb but quickly pulled her head back when she realized she had been seen.

"I have boring government business to attend to, ladies. When will supper be, dear?" Edward asked Minta. He glanced at Virginia. She returned his look, and a slight smile crept across her lips.

"We'll be eatin' at eight," Minta said. She turned to Virginia. "I'm sure you'd like to rest a bit after such an arduous afternoon?"

Virginia patted her temple with her handkerchief and said, "I would like to lie down for a while."

Minta said, "Let me show you to your room."

"You must be fully rested by Saturday. Don't forget the dance you promised me." Edward said. Minta looked at Edward. "*What dance?*" she thought.

Virginia blushed and nodded.

Minta extended her hand to Virginia. The young woman took it, and they walked upstairs hand-in-hand. When her fingers touched the older woman's hand, she saw a flash with a scene of a man, not Edward, dancing with her. She made a note to find out who this man was.

Edward turned, pale and shaking, and left the room.

Chapter 40

I wandered down the wagon-rutted pathway. I hoped that there might be someone passing, but the valley was empty for as far as I could see.

I stood on a mound of earth and saw the fields of corn ready for harvest. The stalks wove back and forth in the sharp fall air. I could see another path moving through the cornfield, and at the end sat an old house.

A big elm tree darkened my view, and as I walked down to it, I saw that the road went to the house and not beyond.

It stood in front of me, yellow and black. The sun was setting. Shadows filled the front and sides of the house. Most of the windows have been broken. It was a small structure with a door cut into the left side. There were loose shingles, and the grass around the house was knee-high. In the backyard, I found a well, a bucket, and rope. I dropped the bucket into the darkness, heard it glug as it filled. I pulled it up and took a long, sweet drink.

I stepped onto the porch that faced the road. I opened the battered front door. The screen was covered with flyspecks that rubbed off on my fingertips. Flies were the only moving things I could see.

The front room was empty. In the next, a roll-top desk and a bed stood at opposite sides of the room. I found some smoked meat on the counter and helped myself. The bed was rumpled as if someone had been sleeping there.

The house smelled musty and stale. The smell grew stronger as I found my way to the kitchen.

There was a basin and a table covered with a frayed tablecloth.

Posters supporting the war effort covered the kitchen wall, along with newsprint and pieces of colorful cloth. I read the stories of life, death, marriages, and all the indignities man had performed upon his fellow man.

While I was reading, I heard someone speak.

"Who's there?"

A shadow blocked the door. It was a towering figure, and it was holding a shovel.

I reached for my knife and prepared myself as best I could.

"What do you think you're doin'?"

"I was just readin'. I'm with the 20th, and I'm separated from my troop."

"Aw, soldier boy."

The man moved toward the wall. "I think I'm in here somewhere. That's me, Horace Blane Smythe."

He wore ragged railroad engineer's overalls and a hat. The boots were brown and worn through at the toe. His face was lined and weathered. His eyes looked tired, and his head bobbed slowly like the corn stalks in the field next to the road.

"Who are ye?" he asked.

"My name is Edward, Private Edward Jacobson of the Massachusetts 20th."

"You a long way from home, Edward."

I nodded. "I got separated, and now I'm lost."

"You got to be hungry. I got some beans over here," he said as he motioned toward the desk in the other room.

"I thought this place was empty. I'm sorry, I've already been in there."

"Helped yourself, I see. Well, such is war."

He moved to the hearth and began taking bits of paper from his pockets. He took a match from his pocket and struck it against the side of the fireplace.

"I'll bring some wood," I said.

"It's at the end of the back porch, on the left."

Soon, the fire was giving off a warm glow, and I saw that the room was just as shabby and worn out as my host.

"We'll have eats directly."

He placed the pot next to the fire on a rod. I took an apple box out of the corner and sat, warming my hands. The smell of the cooking food began to push out the stale air of the room. The beans smelled so good that I could almost taste them.

"I'll just need a place to stay for the night."

"When's the last time you ate?" the old man asked.

"Two days, except for me taking some of your jerky in there."

"I think they call that liberating supplies in the Army."

I smiled as he pulled the beans from the fire and handed me a metal plate and a fork.

"Where you from?" I asked.

"Oklahomee."

He told me the first of the many stories I heard that night.

"Kaufman, the man who owned the railroad, hired a bunch of toughs from the town to teach a lesson to the outlaws who was liberating some cattle. One was this real bastard, Smith, he called hisself. Smith and the toughs laid out all night with some cattle in the valley to bait us. Smith rode up from behind us, and the race was on.

Smith shot two of us hisself. Shot 'em in the back."

The old man spat and sucked at his teeth.

"Anyways, three of 'em got away. We watched 'em as Smith made one of the gang dig a hole. They put him in there and filled it up to his neck. There wasn't anything we could do to stop them. They would take shots at his head. They didn't finish him off until daybreak. Din't have rustlin' anymore after that."

"Why are you tellin' this to me?" I asked. I pulled a corn dodger from a stack on the table and sopped up the gravy from the beans.

"Somebody needs to hear it."

I was never one to enjoy grisly little stories, but if I could get a meal out of it, I would listen.

"You killed that last one, didn't you?"

He sat in silence. He seemed to be resting. He never answered the question.

"Them beans go down pretty good?"

"Yes," I said.

"I used to work for the railroad. I 'member one night I was drivin' down past Memphis. I seen this man sittin' on the tracks. I started blowin' my whistle, long and low. I throwed on the brake and put the engine in reverse. Now, it takes a long time to stop one of them half-mile-long trains. And that man was just up ahead."

A rasping cough attacked Smythe at this point. I thought it might be his last breath, but he continued.

"That man just sat there on the tracks with his head in his hands 'til the train hit him. I was doin' 'bout twenty or so at the time, and all I see was guts and blood after we stopped. That's all that was left. Found out later that he'd been beaten to death and sat up on the track to make it look as if he'd been killed by the train."

He rested again, breathed slowly, and coughed a little until he was silent again.

It's as if it was all an act he would go through for every person who came to visit. "How did you come to live here?" I asked, stuffing another bite of beans into my mouth.

"I just sorta moved in. Nobody cares that I'm here, 'cept a couple of little boys down the road. They check on me."

"What do you do for money?"

"I got a little bit put away."

The next morning, the sun rose in the front window, across the room, and into my eyes as I lay on the floor. I raised my head and shielded my eyes. I looked around and saw that the old man was gone. I walked over to the big window in the front of the room. I was standing there yawning when Horace Smythe stumbled around the corner of the porch. He had four eggs in his hands. He hunched over his cane in his overalls, holding an engineer's hat. As he came in the door, he grinned toothlessly. "Breakfast."

I washed the metal plates in a basin as he cooked the eggs on a pan in the hearth. They tasted even better than they smelled. For some reason, Smythe didn't talk too much during breakfast. I didn't want to prod him into the conversation when he didn't feel like it.

After breakfast, I started thinking about Edward, where he might be, what he might be doing. How would he be doing out West?

Two little boys sauntered into the room, the screen door slamming behind them. One looked to be about ten, and the other was only slightly older. They looked like brothers.

"Hello, boys."

The older one said, "What's going on with Mr. Smythe?"

"He's restin' in the other room."

They went into the room, and I followed.

The younger one said, "Hey, Mr. Smythe, what 'cha gonna tell us 'bout today?"

"What'd you bring me?"

The boys produced three corn dodgers, each from their pockets. They handed them to Smythe.

"How 'bout the time I was corralin' this wild bronc in Texas. I ever tell y'all that one?"

"No." They jumped up and down in excitement.

"Wa-a-ll, in Sipaw, Texas, out on the range, there was this horse called Blackie. He was mean, and he had a herd of those broncs that followed him. I'd heard 'bout Blackie, and I wanted to see that horse. I really wanted to catch 'em."

I smiled as the children laughed aloud at the expressions on the old man's face.

"I went out to this range where people said Blackie would hang around. I snuck up on that herd of horses downwind, but they still sniffed me 'bout a hundred yards off. They was off and runnin', and so was I. That horse I was ridin' was good, but he could only just barely stay up with that herd. Blackie was leadin', and he looked so purty with every move he made. Why, it looked like he weren't runnin' at all, just glidin' over the ground like a bird. For some reason, all the rest of the herd turned toward the sun as it was setting. Blackie whirled and faced me. We was in this big, old flatland, no hills. It took all I'd ever learned as a ranch hand to nab that critter. We went round and round 'fore I roped him. He pulled so hard that I was afraid the rope would break. I finally got a good 'nuff hold on him to take him back to the ranch. I broke old Blackie and rode him for six years."

"Wow," the big one said.

"Wow," the little one said.

I almost said 'wow' myself but did not.

"Tell us another one, Mister Smythe."

"Can't, boys. I'm tired, and as you know, I only tell y'all one a day."

Their faces clouded for a moment, but smiles eventually won out.

"'kay," the little one said as he stretched a leg out to the floor.

"We got to be goin' anyways," the big one said, hopping down from the side of the bed. The door slammed shut.

Horace Smythe started coughing and laid back on the bed. He closed his eyes, and his chest rose slightly. He laid there for what seemed hours, saying nothing. His stories had amazed the children and me. He had lived so much.

While I sat on the apple crate and looked out the window, I noticed Mr. Smythe's breathing had stopped. I walked across the room. I checked to make sure his eyes were closed. I didn't want the boys to find him staring at them the following day. I checked the desk and found his stash of money. I knew he wouldn't need it anymore, so I pocketed the twenty dollars and forty-seven cents. I walked out of the house and past the waving stalks of corn again, down the drive, and onto the main road.

I walked to a white house just up ahead. I moved toward the front door and knocked. The door sounded hollow as a woman with drooping hair and a frown opened it.

"A man has died in the yellow house just up the road there."

"There ain't been nobody livin' in that house for years."

"I just spent —"

"I said," she started.

"Are you the momma to two little boys? They visited with Smythe and me last night."

The woman's face grew ashen. "My boys, they got killed by some dirty Rebs. They didn't have to do it, but they just slit their throats for talkin' back."

I stumbled as I turned and walked toward the edge of the porch.

She said, "Where do you think you're goin'?"

"I don't want no trouble. I'm trying to find my unit." I tugged at the frayed collar of my uniform.

Remembering the sound of Smythe's cackling laugh and the boys jumping up and down to hear another story drove a chill down my spine as I walked to the end of the drive and back onto the road.

Chapter 41

Filmy, white curtains swayed in rhythm with a crisp, gentle breeze. There were clear indications where the rooms had been added, even though there was considerable effort to make the interior as seamless as possible. Oil paintings hung on either side of the window, and a large map of the plantation hung next to those. The plantation had been added on to and blended much as the house had over the decades. The total acreage neared one thousand, with cotton, corn, and hay indicated on the map. Behind the barn, a garden plot took up nearly an acre and provided the house and the occupants with fresh produce. The slave quarters were also indicated on the map with a similar layout and a garden spot adjacent.

A horsefly flew through the open window and traversed the rooms, exiting the front window.

Edward stared at the bug as a teaspoon clinked against the side of a glass.

Minta sat on one end of the sofa while Virginia held down the other. Jewels served them their drinks on a silver platter.

Edward sat in the wingback chair and pulled the spoon from his glass. He placed the silver utensil on a doily but failed to hide his shaking hand.

"That is hunky-dory lemonade if I do say so myself," Edward said.

"I wish you wouldn't use that coarse language you picked up in the war," Minta said.

"I like the colorful language you use in your letters, Edward. What was it you called one of your sergeants, 'Possum?' Whatever happened to him?" Virginia asked. She brushed a stray strand of blazing red hair from her cheek. Edward glanced at her as her hand moved to her face.

"I'd rather not say in mixed company," he replied.

Minta fanned herself with a handkerchief. A slight breeze stirred the curtains behind her. She touched her temple, squinted at the bright light coming through the window, and cleared her throat.

Virginia had to decide whether to let the tension in the room ease or push forward. She knew little about the dynamic of Edward and Minta's relationship except for what he'd written in his letters and the little they'd talked about in Vicksburg. She decided it was time to apply pressure. "Please, Edward, tell me," Virginia said.

Edward shifted in the chair. The cushions sank, and the straps on the bottom of the chair creaked as he squirmed.

He said, "Miss, I'd really rather not."

Minta sided with her husband and said, "When he's right, he's right."

"Oh, Edward, please." Virginia pleaded.

Edward raised his glass and took a drink. His fingers caressed the sides of the glass as he placed it on the table. The glass was smooth, and even in the afternoon warmth, it felt cool.

"It was at the battle of Franklin. He surrendered his life for mine." A tear welled in the corner of Edward's eye.

Minta noticed how Edward reacted to the memory. She decided it was time to bolster her husband's courage and tamp down his guilt. Minta said, "Shed no tears for a man who died for a just cause."

Virginia swallowed hard and hid her frown behind her glass.

"Minta, I tried to avoid —" he said.

"Do not censor yourself on account of me, Edward," Virginia said. "You've been through a terrible trauma. The only way you'll find healin' is to talk about what happened."

Edward shook his head. He reached for his collar and tugged. He stared at the empty fireplace. A part of him wished there was a fire so he could jump in. He said, "I don't feel comfortable talkin' about the war."

"And I don't feel comfortable hearin' about it," Minta said with a cat-like grin. "Let's change the subject."

A young soldier entered the foyer and rushed into the room, holding a telegram.

"Edward, what's all this?" Virginia asked.

"Sir, Madams, the general says there's terrible news."

Edward stood and took the envelope from the boy and tore it open. The soldier left. Edward read the telegram and then dropped the paper. "Terrible news." He muttered.

He turned to the women; grief etched upon his face. "General Robert E. Lee has surrendered."

Minta screamed in pain. She slid from her chair and crumpled into a heap on the floor. She looked up at Edward with fear and loathing.

"It was not in his heart to continue the fight," Edward said as he stared out of the open window.

Virginia rushed to Minta's side. She picked up Minta's handkerchief and fanned her. She took Minta's arm and tried to get her back into her chair, but Minta refused.

Edward stood and walked to the open window. He said, "I remember the last time I saw him. We sat on his front porch and reviewed men goin' home from the war."

Minta rose under her own power and weaved across the room. She had moments when she felt faint and balanced herself on pieces of furniture as she walked. It was hard for Edward to see her like this. He still remembered the way she was when they first met and how captivated he was by her. She picked up the paper. "I can read the words, but they make no sense. How could a man as good and pure as he surrender?" Minta asked.

"Everything has a beginning and an end," Virginia said.

"I know that all too well," Edward said as he staggered across the room and fell into a chair. "What is this world comin' to?"

"These are end times, I say," Minta snarled. "Did you hear? The Darkies will soon likely have the vote."

The light from the open window and the fluttering curtain cast shadows on the wall behind Edward. "That will never pass." He jerked to his feet. He leaned against the mantle and put his forehead on his wrist. A sheen of sweat formed on his upper lip.

Virginia looked up at Edward. "I ... I ... think it's a good idea. How can the healing begin without acknowledging the rights of every human being?" Edward raised his head. Jewels entered, and all eyes followed her.

"Madness," Minta said.

Chapter 42

Diary entry
November 19, 1863

I was genuinely surprised to be accompanying the president to the cemetery dedication at Gettysburg. I had worked for Mr. Lincoln for months now, as he directed the war from the tiny telegraph office in the War Department, but I knew my place in the war effort. I was a grunt, a soldier, cannon fodder in the attempt to keep the Union together.

Mr. Lamon, the president's personal bodyguard, a brooding man with dark eyes and broad shoulders, assured me I would be needed at the ceremony and showed my name on the list of people who would accompany the president's entourage to the service.

The train ride was horrendous, with several of the attendees coming down with a sickness. Even the president seemed hampered with fever and ill-temper. His usual rangy way of walking was exaggerated by his illness. It was on the train that his doctors found the skin eruptions and diagnosed smallpox.

The president assured everyone that he felt well enough to attend the ceremony, even though he was not at his best. But anyone who had a chance to see him knew that he was feeling unwell, and given the seriousness of his illness, he might not survive the trip.

This made me think of the time, late at night, as the president and I waited for news of a battle, he told me of a recurring dream he had. He was on a boat in the middle of a river. He had no oars or means of propulsion, so he felt buffeted by the wind and waves. Depending on how you viewed such things, it was easy to see the origin of the dream or nightmare, but the president seemed perplexed by what his mind was portraying. I offered a small token of empathy, as best I could, without being disrespectful. However, he still floundered to find the solution to the riddle.

We would be in Gettysburg by morning, and while I knew there would be little chance of any answers to the riddles I'd experienced in my life, I felt this dedication of the blood-hallowed ground on which I had once walked and fought would be an experience I'd someday share with my children and grandchildren.

I was bivouacked in one of the middle cars of the train while the president rode in the last car. While it was a bit cramped, it was a better place than I had experienced in several camps. Other soldiers were riding with us as a protective guard against attack. I hadn't touched a musket in months, but I felt completely at ease if called upon to protect the president.

The food was good, plentiful even, but a bit bland. I had grown tired of a soldier's diet and longed for my home where I could add seasonings and spices to any dish I might fix. More variety of meat and vegetables was also missing from the menu.

Home beckoned to me in so many ways now. I kept writing letters to maintain the ruse of my search for peace after Father's death, but I was growing weary of even that. I knew that the South was losing from working with the president and that the war would end sooner than later. Not soon enough for me, though.

The train pulled into the station, and we followed the procession through the streets of the tiny town where the war had turned in the Union's favor in many people's estimation. Soon, it would be deemed another official military cemetery, one of many now scattered across the landscape.

I looked at the gray sky and felt the light breeze on my cheeks. Winter would visit again soon and with it, even more misery. I swiped the back of my hand across my mouth. I felt the sweat and sensed a pang of panic that I, too, might have contracted smallpox. I would have to search myself for blisters when I got back on the train. God forbid that I got this horrible disease.

I could see the president's buggy up ahead of us as we marched behind it. The president wore his stovepipe hat, and I could see it bobbing up and down as the buggy wheels seemed to find every pothole and rut in the narrow road.

At one moment, I saw his head dip below the edge of the back of the buggy. My heart fell in fear that he had been taken over by the illness. Still, suddenly his hat righted itself, and I saw the president turn his head and look at the hundreds of graves that filled the cemetery.

We were marched to stand on a small ridge just to the east of the dais where a speaker's stand was centered, and some chairs sat on the back edge.

I was ordered at ease, and while the speakers were welcomed to the stage, I found a stance that would allow me to relax and listen to the speeches.

After introductions and prayers, a squat man with a high forehead and penetrating eyes stood and strode to the stand. He had a thick sheaf of papers in his left hand, and he gripped the top of the surface with his right.

He introduced himself as Edward Everett, a man I recognized as I'd once met him while governor of Massachusetts. He had come to Concord to help celebrate the opening of a ferry and glad-handed just about everyone he could stop for ten seconds.

A slight breeze picked up, and I felt the fresh air on my cheeks. I was standing behind a photographer on a riser. He hopped around the small platform like a rabbit on a hot rock, capturing image after image of the speaker, the setting, and the crowd, which was vast and, at times, restless.

Governor Everett spoke with a deep, sonorous voice that carried well into the crowd. He touched on the battle that had taken place in the valley with great detail. He praised the men who'd died there and those who would be forever changed by what they experienced.

While it was the fashion to speak in-depth, I grew restless, as did others in the crowd as the Governor ended the first hour of his speech. Little did we know he had another hour plus to deliver. I watched some of the men around me sway a bit as they stood. I feared the soldiers, and maybe even me, might not have the strength to carry us through a similar speech by the president.

Finally, the governor finished his speech and received a round of applause that seemed both a relief and a welcoming that the event might be nearing the midway point.

The president sat, head bent to one side and his hands on his thighs. He had to be jostled a bit to get his attention. He put his hands on his knees and stood, stretching a bit as he prepared to step to the podium.

He took a small slip of paper from his pocket and put his reading glasses on the end of his nose.

"Four score and seven years ago, our fathers brought forth on this continent, a new nation, conceived in liberty, and dedicated to the proposition that all men are created equal."

The president spoke deliberately and with emphasis as if each word was separate and had meaning beyond that of just recognizing the opening of a new cemetery. My heart leaped. My ears seemed to understand before my mind could interpret what the president was saying. In that split second, I touched my chest and felt the newspaper article I'd been carrying for so many years. The copy of my speech so long ago was still there. Surely it was just a coincidence that both started off recognizing the origin of the country.

"Now we are engaged in a great civil war, testing whether this nation or any nation so conceived and so dedicated can long endure."

At one time restless, the crowd grew still and focused on the tall, pale man at the podium.

"We are met on a great battlefield of that war. We have come to dedicate a portion of it as a final resting place for those who here gave their lives that our nation might live. It is altogether fitting and proper that we should do this."

I took a deep breath and listened to the voice that I had come to know quite well. I was used to hearing Mr. Lincoln ask about my well-being and news of my habits. I knew his words and tone would help those pained by their losses.

The president continued, "But, in a larger sense, we cannot dedicate—we cannot consecrate—we cannot hallow this ground. The brave men, living and dead, who struggled here, have hallowed it, far above our poor power to add or detract. The world will little note, nor long remember what we say here, but it can never forget what they did here."

At that moment, I remembered the horror of that mid-afternoon charge of the Rebs as they slowly moved across that meadow. Now, it was called Pickett's charge. But, at the time, it was madness–the way they accepted their fate for their fellow soldiers and their faces as they met their end.

"It is for us the living, rather, to be dedicated here to the unfinished work which they who fought here have thus far so nobly advanced. It is rather for us to be here dedicated to the great task remaining before us—that from these honored dead we take increased devotion to that cause for which they gave the last full measure of devotion—that we here highly resolve that these dead shall not have died in vain—that this nation, under God, shall have a new birth of freedom—and that government of the people, by the people, for the people, shall not perish from the earth."

The president took his reading glasses from his nose, put them into his pocket, and stepped back. The crowd stood, stunned, speechless, as the president turned and returned to his seat. As they had been primed by the previous speaker, the shortness of the president's speech was a shock.

As I had come to recognize it, in his voice, the emotion and depth of commitment that I knew were translated into his excellent speech. I looked at the president as he relaxed into the straight chair. Was he wavering a bit? It seemed his performance had drained the energy from his body and the color from his cheeks. Would he survive the trip back home? I let the question roam about my head for a moment and quickly tossed it aside. Destiny and the Lord had decided long ago that President Lincoln would not only survive this forsaken war but would enjoy a long and healthy life following the victory. I really believed this deep in my heart.

Later, after the ceremony, we marched back to the train station. We passed the stores, farms, and stables with solemnity and with sober, stoic faces. The people lining the road-way also were stolid. Some with scars and missing limbs stood and saluted as the president's buggy passed by.

As we marched, a captain rode up and down the line of soldiers. Eventually, I realized he was saying my name, and I raised my hand. He pulled me out of the line and pointed me toward the telegraph office.

"The president requests that you send this copy of his speech to the news desk of the Boston Evening Transcript so that it might be widely distributed."

I snapped off a salute and moved toward the small office.

Chapter 43

The newspaper headline read, "Gettysburg Cemetery Dedication." The article outlined the dignitaries expected to attend and that the president would deliver a speech. I felt a cold chill run up my back as I remembered some of the faces of the men I'd seen die in the fateful charge into the mouth of death.

For the last month at the War Department, my duties included working with the president in the telegraph room and delivering messages to members of Congress. I quickly learned my way around the capital, proud of myself for being so smart, when I walked by a horse and buggy tethered to a post in front of a restaurant one sunny afternoon. Imagine my surprise when I realized it was Junebug.

Startled and so very pleased, I walked up to her and patted her on the neck. I instinctively reached in my pocket for a sugar cube that I would usually treat her with. I didn't have any sugar, but she didn't seem to mind and appeared genuinely pleased to see me.

"I say there, soldier," the driver said. He was of medium height and weight. He had a long scar on the side of his neck and favored one leg over the other as he walked.

"I mean no harm, I promise you," I said. "This is my horse," I corrected myself, "This used to be my horse, Junebug."

The man's eyebrows shot up, and his mouth formed an "O" in genuine surprise.

"I purchased that horse from a farmer in Pennsylvania last year. She's an excellent mare."

"It's fine," I said. "I left her with this farmer who I'd hoped would keep her, but I see he decided that he couldn't."

"The story he told me was that Junebug, you say, had delivered a foal and that he was going to keep the stud and didn't need the mare."

"I see."

"He showed me papers; I remember the name, a —"

"Yes, Edward Jacobson," I said. "That's me."

The man put his finger to his lips in contemplation. "This seems wrong that I have your horse."

"You purchased her fair and square. I have no hard feelings." I turned to the horse. "Junebug, you're a momma."

Junebug whinnied and pawed the ground next to the post as if in response to the acknowledgment.

"I can't keep your horse. It would be wrong to take something from a soldier serving our country."

"You have my blessing," I said. I turned to leave.

"How would you like to buy her from me," he asked.

I stopped and searched my pockets again. I had some coins but no folding money. I had that stashed in a box in the bivouac.

I turned and walked back to the man. There was a general bustle of people around the front of the restaurant. Some would slow and watch as I talked with him. Others would reach out and touch my arm, gently letting me know I was seen. It was an acknowledgment of my service that I had felt time and time again.

"I only have coins. My money is back at home. If we could meet —"

The man rubbed his chin as if trying to determine the value of Junebug. The horse seemed interested in the goings-on and turned her head from one side to the other as we spoke. Could she possibly know what was going on?

"I want to let you know how much your service to our country means. I, too, served and have the 'souvenirs' to prove it." He touched the side of his neck. "Our victory at Bull Run," he said with a tone in his voice that let me know he was joking about the outcome of the battle.

He patted Junebug's neck and produced a sugar cube. While she took the treat from the man, her eyes never left mine.

"I don't have papers with me now, but I would be happy to sell her to you if you would come around to my home sometime this week; maybe we can come to some sort of deal."

He pulled a slip of paper from his pocket and wrote down his address.

I said, "I would be much obliged if we could come to some terms. Favorable to you, I mean."

He smiled. It was a genuine smile of warmth and camaraderie. "We soldiers must take care of one another." He patted my arm and launched himself into the buggy.

I watched as they turned and left me. Junebug turned her head once, and I could swear she looked right at me. A warm feeling of gratitude filled my chest as I turned and walked away.

Chapter 44

Stars filled a long window. The room was ornately furnished and was filled with hand-carved tables and chairs. Virginia paced in front of the large feather bed. The coverings were hand-sewn and depicted events from the history of the plantation.

Virginia picked up her luggage, tossed it on the bed, opened her trunk, and pulled out the doll. She hugged Mrs. Greenwood to her chest and walked toward the fire.

"The heat of the day gives way to a crisp and clear autumn night."

She sidled up to the fire and warmed herself. Virginia's face began to glow red.

"How might we celebrate the completion of our journey, Mrs. Greenwood?" She held the doll as if it were a baby. She touched the face of the toy and recalled the flash of intuition about Minta. She had so many questions but knew from experience that answers would come when they were ready.

"Edward is very handsome, isn't he, little baby? Yes, you are my baby until the real one comes along." She paused and experienced another flash. She said to the doll, "Oh yes, I know the scars are deep, but so is the promise of healing."

She held her up and turned the doll to face her.

"The scars do not reach as far as his heart, which is pure and driven as ginned cotton."

She sat and put her feet on a stool next to the fire. She was wearing her red nightgown and slippers. She snuggled down into the pillows and giggled. She imagined spending time with Edward and what they might do. She could see the two of them riding horses, maybe even racing. That would be exciting. She could see them at a picnic and kissing with as much fervor as possible.

"*There is nothing he could do that would cause me not to love him,*" she thought.

"Isn't that right," Mrs. Greenwood?" she asked.

She leaned back and smiled.

Chapter 45

A federal marshal leaned against the gatehouse to the compound. There were four storehouses, two stories in height, and well over four hundred yards square. The roof was clay and steeply pitched. There were doors and large windows.

Edward crept around a door and pulled a scope from his coat. He dashed toward the gatehouse.

The marshal yawned, scratched his crotch, and moved around the side of the guardhouse. He strolled around the buildings on what was now a well-worn path.

Edward slipped through the gate and into the compound. He opened the door and walked into a vast room. He opened a window, and a shaft of moonlight illuminated the mounds of golden, yellow corn.

He muttered to himself. "To the victors go the spoils of war."

He turned as the marshal's boots crunched on the river gravel just outside.

The marshal stuck his head in, looked around, and whistled. He moved his torch around, casting light on every corner of the room. It was his routine, and he was bored with the duty. He'd fought Rebs at Vicksburg and Nashville and wanted to do more. He remembered how he'd led men into battle, watched them fall and die for the cause. He was proud of his service and his continued support of reconstruction.

He moved toward a window and closed it. He turned and said, "What the hell are they gonna do with all this stuff?"

He walked across the wooden floor, opened and closed the door. The sound of his boots on the gravel outside made a fading, crunching noise.

Edward had used camouflage before in the field. He had instructed snipers on blending in with their environment, attaching pieces of limbs and leaves to their bodies to avoid detection. He was proud of some of the theories he'd developed; even though some of his commanders shunned the idea, one had seen the value and promoted Edward because of it.

When he was sure the sentry had left the area, he struggled from under a pile of corn cobs. He remembered the marshal's question, "what is the purpose of holding these supplies?" He could only think that it was punishment for the Rebellion. He vowed to stop the practice as soon as possible.

"There will be grain for my people," he vowed.

Chapter 46

Brilliant rectangles of light stretched across a pale hardwood floor. A quartet of Black musicians finished playing a languid version of "Turkey in the Straw." The rehearsal had been called for three in the afternoon, and the band was running late. They had set up quickly on the small stage in the ballroom and rapidly tuned their instruments. Edward sat in front of them in the center of the room. He knew where the acoustic sweet spot was and wanted everything to sound as close to perfect as possible.

Edward stood, put one hand on his hip, a finger to his lips, and shook his head.

"No ... no ... no. That's much too slow for dancin'." He strode across the room. He took a fiddle and drew the bow across the strings. He played the chorus with verve and vigor. "You must find the rhythm and let it flow. The music must carry the dancers as if they are feathers on the breeze."

The musicians were led by Fiddler, a man in his mid-fifties, his body bent and wiry from a career of playing and leading the band. "We'll play it any way you likes it."

Edward nodded, smiled, and said, "That's good. Let me hear it tuned up a bit."

They began again. Edward's toe started to tap, and he slowly moved with an imaginary partner. In his mind, he felt at ease. This was the one place in the house where he could let himself go and just *be*. The nagging of the pain only sated by the white powder left him as he listened. The music elevated him out of his sorrows and into the light. He said, "That's more like it."

The rhythm quickened and grew louder as Fiddler took a solo. The drummer behind him took a counter beat, and the guitarist and bassist filled in.

"Marvelous. Simply marvelous!" Edward shouted over the tune. He danced, eyes closed, and smiled.

"Stop this now!" Minta screeched.

The music died. The musicians looked at one another and then at Fiddler. He pointed his chin at the corner of the room, and they slowly moved off the stage.

"Minta?" Edward asked.

She stood, hands on her hips, glaring at the musicians and Edward. "I didn't marry a pantywaist dancer."

"Sorry," Edward said, his cheeks grew crimson, "I just got caught up in the music for a moment." He felt shame as she belittled his manhood in front of these men he respected.

"That girl's done real damage—" Minta said and tapped her foot on the hardwood in frustration. She looked down at the floor, and a flash of memory passed through her mind. She saw her father overseeing the unloading of the wagons filled with the hardwood planks. She remembered the smell and the way the slaves worked with their shirts off and how they smelled.

"Her name's Virginia, and we had many dances when I visited her in Vicksburg."

"Really," Minta said. "Your friend? Who taught you how to dance?"

Edward straightened his spine and said, "Virginia did."

He turned and waved the band back to life. "More, gentlemen! Play as if the house were on fire."

The musicians crept back to the stage and again, reflexively, tuned their instruments. They weren't interested in stepping into the middle of this tornado. They knew their place in the world and just wanted to enjoy playing the music and taking the money.

Minta's eyes narrowed. She turned and stomped from the ballroom as Edward danced again. She felt such anger that even with the memory of her father working so hard to bring culture to the plantation, she was ready to destroy it all. She envisioned the hardwood and the ballroom ablaze, and she was the one who set the fire.

Chapter 47

Eloise dreamed of home again the night before last. She loved to dream of home. It seemed so much like really being there. She dreamed she was cooking in her tiny kitchen. She looked out the back window at the cherry tree and saw that it was filled with berries. So many delicious pies were there on those limbs. Was that not the perfect soldier's dream? She would dedicate her first pie of the season to her fallen friends, fellow soldiers, and her "beau."

She awoke to a "Rebel Yell." It was terrifying and made her reach for her rifle. She had nodded off and dreamt the sound. She was on watch duty again, and she rubbed her left eye in hopes of clearing the eye mucus from her vision.

"Who goes there?" she said as she raised her rifle.

Mordecai raised his hands and stood still. "Don't shoot. I was just makin' water."

She lowered her rifle and glared at him. "I could'a shot you."

He smiled, and it was at that moment she knew she loved him. It was forbidden in the South and not encouraged in the North, but there it was. Her heart filled.

"Do you like cherry pie?" she asked.

"I do," he said, "why do you ask?"

She stopped herself from answering the question as she would a man she was interested in. She'd forgotten her disguise and where she was. The vigilance with which she'd continued her charade could all have been ended right here and right now.

"I'm just missin' home. We got a cherry tree in the back yard, and the cherries would be getting' ripe 'bout now," she said.

"I know what you mean. I miss my momma's cornbread more 'an anything else," Mordecai said.

"Do you ever dream about home?" she asked.

Mordecai propped his boot on an upturned bucket. We had been assigned to guard duty for weeks, and we were getting a bit restless. We knew we were a target because we were so close to the Virginia state line. We hoped we'd be overlooked because we were small and not well stocked, but we knew we were as vulnerable as any soldier in a blue coat.

"I dream," he started, but there was a catch in his throat, "about home all the time, just like you."

He looked at her and, at that moment, felt a real connection. He'd had acquaintances who were white before but not a real friend. He believed Edward was his friend, but there was always a slender thread of trust in his imagination that could easily be cut if the situation occurred. What would happen if they were captured and held by the Rebs? Would Edward stand up for him, or would he cut and run?

"I know I shouldn't say this, but there was a part of me that didn't want to leave. I didn't want to serve." Mordecai said as he rested his rifle on his thigh. His white shirt was rumpled from sleeping in it, and his boots needed shining. His pants were dusty, but they were still a dark blue, and his coat's buttons still shone in the moonlight.

For that moment, Eloise saw into her brother's heart. He had taken a different path than Mordecai and her, but the feelings of every soldier at some point in their lives were the same.

"I felt the same way," Eloise said.

Mordecai shifted his rifle from one thigh to the other and spat between his boots. He took on a new stature as Eloise looked at him. She had seen him under fire and bored to sleep. Now she saw him as just another soldier.

Chapter 48

One by one, I saw traces of the bullets slamming into their chests and sending them over. They fell on their backs, never to return to their feet. I sought Jesus as a salve. I felt my heart cracking open in these seconds of terror. The loud, bursting cannon shot assaulted my ears. The swords and bayonets wrestled against each other with silver shards of light and sprays of blood.

As if to convince myself, I said, "I am here for a reason."

I turned back to the battlefield. I believed I could make a difference in all this chaos.

I picked a sword out of an officer's dead hand and engaged the Reb. I ripped his skin and felt his hot blood on my face. Some of the blood went into my mouth. For a moment, I froze as if the taste would change or sicken me.

I turned my head and watched hand-to-hand combat all around me. Did they feel the same way I did? Were they insensitive? Were they callous? Was I different?

Suddenly, I saw bright lights over the battlefield. I knew, deep down, the finality of life, and it was as if I could feel the souls leaving the Earth.

I fought for my brother. I fought for my people. I fought for my beliefs. I fought for my future …

Soon enough, my eyes could not catch enough light. The darkness fell, and soldiers on both sides fell back to rest and recuperate.

As I walked back to camp, I realized I was wounded on my right side. I carefully lowered myself to the ground but was soon aided by another soldier. He grasped me by the arm, and with stumbling feet, we would try to make it to the hospital before I bled to death.

In the distance, the sun was setting. I caught a glimpse of the last of the day's sunlight. As I walked, I realized I was in the middle of a cemetery. Wherever I turned, I saw the ghosts of dead men all around me.

Was it my time? Was my service to end here? It was too silent for anyone to speak. Bullet holes and swords sprang from their bodies. Buckets of blood spilled over them.

I counted my lucky stars as they began to emerge into the night sky. I had been fortunate from the start. I had lucked into the right troop. I was able to disguise myself in just the right way and wasn't questioned.

In the end, it all came down to this. It was no surprise that people would die, but we all believed we'd be living a day where we would tell our tale. The Civil War was an act of cruelty, but this was worth the sacrifice for freedom. This experience also gave me the knowledge and a sense of who I was. I discovered myself as a strong, determined, strenuous, faithful, and lucky human being. This experience had truly taught me that life is short; death is on the horizon. For me, this may be the end of the war, but it's not the end of the road. I'm leaving New Orleans and going home. This experience has been so appreciated, and I might also take advantage of the time I have. This has been my life as a soldier, fighting in the darkest moments of the United States. Now that the night is over, the light of our unified nation will soon appear.

Chapter 49

A scarred and hollowed back. The tissue reddened and moved as he reacted to the probes.

A large metal cone descended and rested first near one clavicle and then the other. Edward breathed deeply, leading to a wracking cough. They were sitting in the doctor's small office. The tray of instruments featured everything from saws to hammers, knives, and metal probes. The doctor had gained most of his experience in the field as a Rebel medic, but an injury he suffered in the battle of Vicksburg sent him to rehabilitation at a local boarding house run by the Hockneys, a kindly old couple, and eventually home.

The doctor hopped from one side of the room to the other, waving the stump where his left leg used to be as he moved. Some patients questioned his qualifications, but Edward believed his battlefield experience gave him extra insight into his problems.

"Good doctor, believe me when I tell you I am in perfect health. You do not have to visit so often, e'en if you are under orders of the governor," Edward said. He sat on a stool and read telegrams of battle dispatches. At the same time, Dr. Hamilton, who appeared to be old enough to have treated Jesus at the cross, straightened from his crouch. He sat down on a stool behind Edward.

"I will be the sole determiner of who is sick and who is well in this household," the doctor said. He hoped his joke would lighten the moment, but Edward was distracted and missed the sarcasm. "While the general is interested in politics, I am committed by oath to find pain and heal it."

"And how am I?" Edward asked.

Hamilton pulled at his vest before he delivered his diagnosis. "There is some congestion in your lungs that is troublin'."

Edward coughed again but continued to read his dispatches. He said, not looking up, "I know, bright sunlight in the day allows me to roam the countryside, while the night air sometimes causes me to lose my breath."

The doctor stared at Edward's scars. He tried to imagine the number of times he had been wounded. How many times had he been sewn back together? Too many to think about. The doctor said, "Many people suffer breathin' problems this time of year."

Edward cleared his throat again and said, "Yes, yes, have you brought the quinine and other supplies you promised."

Dr. Hamilton reached for a large carpetbag and pulled out a white cloth sack. This supply of the painkilling powder had been diverted from the hospitals at the front line. The colonel had pulled some strings, and Edward and Minta had their relief.

The doctor said, "The healing properties of these two drugs are in dispute. There are new philosophies that say users should beware of the devotee's requirements."

Edward looked up from his papers. He said, "As killers of pain, they are effective?"

"Yes, but the need for the drug sometimes outstrips its comforting qualities," the doctor said, "Have you tried to function without their aid?"

Edward took a deep breath and stood. "Your prescription from when we met at the battle of Vicksburg continues to help. If I thought there was a problem with their use, I would stop," Edward said and snapped his fingers, "like that."

"But since there is not," the doctor said as he palpated Edward's back, "you continue to use them."

"You sorry old Reb, I continue because you have not done your job properly. Tell your employer that." Edward's voice rose in anger, but he looked over his shoulder at the kindly old gent and smiled, letting him know he was joking.

The old man looked away, nodding.

"He is your employer, too," the doctor said.

"More like my jailer," Edward muttered.

He spied Edward's syringe on the table next to the kerosene lamp.

"How are you cleaning the syringe?"

Edward returned to his papers.

"Just as you told me; with soap, alcohol, water, and fire."

Dr. Hamilton tugged at his long chin whiskers, snapped his carpetbag shut, and pulled himself up to his full height. He ran his hand over the scars on Edward's arms and back.

"Remarkable. Just remarkable how you were able to avoid the bone saw."

Edward said, scratching his underarm. "A miracle cure performed by one of your kind in a battlefield hospital."

"Piss?"

Dr. Hamilton had heard this ridiculous theory of the healing power for some time. It was an old wives' tale and had not been proven scientifically. He pulled at his chin whiskers again and chuckled to himself, "*and probably never would*," he thought.

Edward spoke with the conviction of a true believer. "Yes, urine. It was found, accidentally, I might add, to be remarkably therapeutic."

"Remarkable," the doctor remarked as he passed his hand over the scars on Edward's back.

Edward rose and put on his shirt.

Hamilton told him, "I'll continue the treatments, but I don't like the feelin' of dependence that sometimes goes along with it."

Edward said, "There are new methods of withdrawin' if someone felt out of control."

"I will take that under advisement. They involve generating electricity." The doctor advised.

"I am well familiar with the properties of electricity," Edward said wearily. He twitched as he remembered the last session and how it left a minor burn on his ankle. If the doctor knew of the device in the basement of his home, he might be more worried about his patient, Edward considered.

Hamilton hooked his thumbs into his vest pockets and said, "Very well, and how are you findin' Minta these days?"

Edward's shoulders sank. "I'm sure you've already examined her."

Hamilton knew that a half-hour exam couldn't always cover everything going on with a patient. So he made a point of asking for additional information when available. "I have, and I've given her treatment. I wanted to know how you found her," he replied

Edward sighed and said, "She has had a strident character from the day we met. A challenge, I guess you could say. She still has headaches. I guess your powders and such work on her as well as they work on me."

Hamilton frowned. "I know she is in incredible pain at times."

Edward looked up at the doctor. His eyes implored as he said, "and her behavior, it can be termed 'erratic' at best."

Hamilton patted Edward on the shoulder. It was one of the sadder situations he had in his practice. Both Edward and Minta were severely impaired, with little hope of surviving much longer. "Her time with us is limited by the tumor in her brain."

"Yes," Edward agreed. The thought of Minta dying soon both saddened and elated him.

"And what about your pen pal from Vicksburg? Are you still glad that I introduced you two?" Hamilton asked.

"Our mutual friend, Virginia, has come for a visit."

This was unexpected. Hamilton knew the state of Edward and Minta's relationship and how a visitor would strain it even more. The doctor put his finger to his lips, thinking, and considered the impact of his words, "And that has gone over well at home?"

Edward looked up from his papers and said, "It has been an interesting time."

Hamilton tossed the bag of powders on the table and turned. There were only some things a doctor could treat, but others were simply necessary to try and do no harm.

"With compliments from the general," Hamilton said as he left.

Edward picked up the bag, frowned, turned, and stared into the darkened fireplace. He looked over at the bag. It was beckoning him.

When he was in Massachusetts, the notion of being dependent on anyone or anything was foreign to him. He always felt robust and healthy. Now, there were days when he felt as weak as a kitten.

"Siren, stop tempting me. I hear your wail." He put his hands over his ears. "Goddamn you, general."

Chapter 50

General VanBurgh crouched over a flower patch, trowel in hand in the backyard of the massive mansion. He grunted as he stood and reviewed his accomplishments.

"Not a weed in sight, not a blade of grass out of place," he said as he proudly broke wind.

He was tasked with rebuilding the devastated area between the mountains of East Tennessee and the Tennessee River. He'd enlisted some men to help him—local plantation owners, Reb government officials he could trust, and even a war hero who was married to the wealthiest woman in the county. The mental pressure was tremendous, and he suffered headaches on occasion. Whiskey was helpful and sometimes put him to sleep. Still, he knew gardening was beneficial, if not a complete respite from the duties he'd been ordered to perform.

Sergeant Clyde stood downwind of the general and asked, "Are you attributin' perfection to God or takin' all the credit yourself?"

Clyde took off his hat and held it over his waist. His balding head showing white and sweating as the sun beat down.

"It's just like beef cattle. All you have to do is sit back and watch 'em get fat."

VanBurgh smiled and offered his hand to Lieutenant Clyde. "I'll take the credit for this patch. God can have the rest of the world. You bring news of the rebels led by that foulest and treasonous scoundrel, Corrigan?"

VanBurgh chuckled and said, "Yes, there is some pleasure in that. But I like the feelin' of the earth between my fingers. The things I can touch and smell and taste."

"I see, sir," Clyde said as he surveyed the patch. "You certainly have a green thumb."

"No, you don't see." The general turned, stared at Clyde, and said, "You merely tolerate the mumblin' of an old fool like me because you think it may help advance your career."

Clyde mopped his sweating brow with a small handkerchief. He said, "Sir, I assure you, I am not that—"

VanBurgh interrupted. "I know precisely your way. Just as I am aware of the 'way' of Corrigan. You are a scramblin' insect in search of a leaf to lift yourself into the air.

Corrigan is a prideful man. And you know what the Bible says of that." VanBurgh settled into his haunches and heaped dirt around a flower.

"Pride goeth before a fall," Clyde said.

"Wrong," the general said, "the Bible actually says, 'Pride goeth before destruction, and a haughty spirit before a fall."

Clyde said, "I see."

"That's just it, Clyde," VanBurgh said, looking Clyde straight in the eye, "you don't."

A Black butler entered carrying a tray with a glass of tea.

"Anticipation—now isn't that the true definition of love?" VanBurgh said as he took the glass from the servant. The butler smiled and looked up at the sun. "Elston, you are a lifesaver." He took a sip.

"What of Corrigan, sir?" Clyde asked.

VanBurgh smiled at Elston. The man nodded and left the tray on the table.

"For the moment, Corrigan serves a purpose. He gives hope to those who cling to the dream of revolution, and he keeps troublemakers in line better than the law. When he crosses the line and attacks somethin' of Union interest, I will swear out a warrant."

Clyde fingered the brim of his hat and said, "Should I continue to investigate his dealings?

"Yes, Sergeant," VanBurgh said, "Follow close, but not so close as to draw attention."

Clyde snapped off a salute, but VanBurgh ignored him and downed his tea.

Chapter 51

Edward left the doctor's office with renewed vigor. He rode to Briarwood with new hope in his heart. He quick-stepped through the house and found the door to the basement. He rushed to the device sitting in a darkened corner of the root cellar. He attached electrical connectors to giant jars filled with a milky liquid. He touched the side of the battery and felt the warmth generated by the chemical reaction.

It was an experimental device he'd found a few months ago. He read the diary entries of Minta's first husband and believed this 'cure' for his problem would be permanent and painless. He'd tried it twice before but still felt the craving. The science seemed solid. He knew from his reading that the brain operated on electricity. He had asked his doctor about the 'electric' cure but found him skeptical. How desperation causes us, such terror.

He sat in a padded, black chair and attached electrodes to his wrists and ankles. He pushed the handle of a switch closed.

POP! POW! SIZZLE!

A pulse of electricity kicked a spinning magnet into gear.

The jars of liquid that generated the electricity glowed yellow. The machine emitted a low-pitched whir, shook back and forth, and then a howl.

Edward's hands and feet jerked, and his eyes closed. The sound filled his ears, and his eyes flew open. He felt the hairs on the back of his neck rise, as well as the hair on his arms and legs.

He gritted his teeth and screamed.

According to the diary, the longer the subject could sit in the machine, the more likely it would be effective.

He let the machine run for longer than he ever had in the past. He smelled his hair burning, and the heat at his wrists and legs became unbearable.

He lost consciousness for a moment, and as he drifted, he hallucinated himself flying through soft, fluffy clouds. He shook his head and quickly returned to earth.

Edward pulled the switch, and the magnet slowed to a stop. He opened his eyes and sighed.

He took stock and recaptured his breathing. He searched his mind and his body. Finally, his scrambled mind returned to its normal state. He closed his eyes and said, "Why is it never enough?"

Chapter 52

Virginia lay on her bed. It had a canopy and a mosquito net. There was plenty to distract her with some pillows of different colors and textures. She closed her eyes and then sighed. Her fingers brushed the ruffle of a small pillow.

"Too much," she said and sat up. "There's too much anger here. Momma didn't raise me to be ill-mannered." She pushed the pillow away. "And yet ..."

The pillow moved by itself across the bed. It came to rest in Virginia's lap.

"Oh, my!" she exclaimed.

In an aqua-tinged light, bordered in Virginia's vision, the pillow slid across a rough table, finally moving to a young Minta's mouth. The young girl's long, blonde hair swept across her eyes. Virginia guessed that Minta was about ten years old.

A middle-aged man stood next to the table.

"Lie still, child, and don't let anybody hear you."

He placed the pillow between the girl's lips. She mumbled. Deep down, she knew this wasn't right.

It was difficult to make out, but she was trying to say, "Daddy."

He was thin, and his hair hung long and stringy. He had the same hollowed eyes that Edward had when he needed his medicine. Is that where the creation of the machine came from? Was this another answer? The father said, "I said, lie still as you did 'afore."

He moved on her.

A shadow passed over Minta's widening eyes. A single tear leaked from the corner of her left eye. "Daddy, it hurts," she said as the pillow fell out of her mouth. The man put the pillow back in her mouth and held her hands over her head with his left hand.

The man unbuttoned his pants and let them fall to the floor. He said, "Be quiet, child and do your duty."

The old man moved against his daughter's body in a slow and steady rhythm. "That's good," he said. "That's real good."

Virginia's vision ended, and her eyes flew open. So often in the past, she had wished her vision had been passed to someone else, and in this case, she wanted more than ever to be rid of the ability. What could be done but put into effort a reconciliation with the past so Minta might have at least a few months of peace before she passed over?

Virginia said, "Oh, my. Poor Minta." She picked up her doll, Mrs. Greenwood, and said, "Can you imagine? My poor child."

Chapter 53

Jewels sat smoking a corn-cob pipe while Virginia scurried from one table to the other. The temperature in the kitchen hovered around ninety degrees, and the humidity was nearly as high. A slight breeze moved through the open window over the sink, but it wasn't enough to make the room any more comfortable.

"You shore you wants to learn how to cook from me?" Jewels asked.

Virginia swiped sweat and flour from the end of her nose. She had been convinced by Mrs. Hockney that the way to a man's heart was through his stomach. Virginia believed that if she could cook the same foods the way Edward liked, she could better cement their long-term relationship.

"I'd like to learn to cook the foods Edward is used to eatin'," Virginia said.

"You think they'll be a time when there won't be somebody like me to do the cookin'?"

Virginia stopped stirring the batter in a large clay bowl. She had never been a slave owner, and as a teen growing up, had seen so many horrors in the fields and homes in Mississippi, she was not a supporter of the system.

"There will be a day when you or someone like you will have a fever and not feel like cooking."

Jewels kicked at the air as she set her rocking chair in motion. "You could write all this stuff down somewhere, just for safe keepin'. But, you ain't got nothin' to worry about. It's gonna be a long time 'fore my toes curl up. Lessen, I'm under some good-lookin' buck."

Virginia stifled a laugh with the back of her smeared hand.

Jewels pulled the pipe from her lips and cackled.

"Miss Jewels," Virginia said, blushing.

"I know'd it," Jewels said as she hopped down from the chair and bounced over to Virginia. She pinched the girl's cheeks and cackled again.

"I know'd it the first time I seen you. You ain't never been with a man, have ya?"

Virginia blushed again and said, "It's surely nothing to be ashamed of. I believe the Lord has a plan, and being intimate before marriage ain't in it."

"Nope, it ain't."

Virginia returned to her mixing bowl and muttered, "I'm going to wait until I'm married."

"Good for you. But a man needs more than just the hope of love," Jewels remarked as she moved the pipe from one corner of her mouth to the other.

"Are you sayin' it's necessary for my future with Mr. Edward to ... ah ... service him?"

Jewels said, "I ain't never known a person to buy shoes they ain't never tried on first."

Virginia said as she slopped the batter into the muffin pan. "Ain't too many people I know who buys used shoes."

Jewels cackled again at Virginia's joke, stuck a crooked finger into the batter, and stuck the batter in her mouth.

"For a girl who ain't broken too many eggs, you done alright."

Virginia took the pan and slid it into the oven.

"Miss Jewels, how long have you worked here?"

"You mean when was I bought?"

"Yes," Virginia said sheepishly.

"When I was a baby." She looked around the kitchen, remembering the number of renovations and additions that had happened over the years. "I seen it all."

"What can you tell me about Minta's father?"

Jewels put the stem of her pipe in the corner of her mouth and tugged at the smoldering tobacco.

"He was a mean one. Filled with hate. I believe he had his way with her if that's what you're askin'. Sick old bastard."

Virginia blushed and said, "That's not really what I had in mind," she lied. "I was wonderin' about how she grew up."

"And how she met Mr. Edward. He was fightin' with the Rebs in Chattanooga. A real hero. Miss Minta heard about him and hunted him down. She'd already run off her first husband because he didn't want to fight. 'Course, he didn't have to 'cause he had enough slaves to disqualify himself from servin'. Funny thing is, he didn't live more 'an a month later. She got herself a real hero in Mr. Edward."

Virginia had heard about Edward's actions in Chattanooga, but she had a feeling there was more to the story. Yes, she'd had a vision about Edward, but some moments were still cloudy. She would have to ask him and trust him to be truthful.

Chapter 54

In the shadows of a stall, leather straps strained against supple wrists. A horse in a stall next to them whinnied and banged her foot on the door. The rapping matched the rhythm for a moment and then stopped.

With her skirt bunched around her waist, Minta, topless, bit her lip and struggled against the binding. Finally, she said, "Be quiet, child, and do your duty."

Jason appeared over her shoulder. His overalls were around his ankles, and his naked butt shone with sweat. He was all teeth, bulging eyes, and a sweating forehead.

He lunged against her again.

"You ain't got to worry about nothin', Missie." A slapping rhythm. Jason closed his eyes.

"Don't forget, your seed, boy." She said between gritted teeth. Images flashed in her mind as he moved against her. She smelled the horses and the dung. She knew what she was doing was dirty, filthy. The urge, the ownership, it was all that filled her mind at that moment.

"Yes'um."

Minta swayed to the movement and closed her eyes. She bit her bottom lip and convulsed against the straps. A horse neighed and a breeze swept down the barn hall. A small dust cloud spun at the entrance of the building. It distracted her, and then she was back in the moment.

She tried to remember the last time her husband had made love with her. It must have been weeks, maybe a month or more. He'd been saying he was too tired or distracted by work. Now, she knew he was lying. Minta ordered, "Let yah seed spill on the ground, Jason."

"Yes'um," he said.

He grinned and continued his work. He twisted his neck around her shoulder and reached around her, cupping her breasts.

"Remove those hands," she muttered through clenched teeth.

"Yes'um," Jason said, losing interest and growing disgusted.

But his hands stayed put. Minta's nipples grew hard and poked through Jason's open fingers. She struggled against the straps, but she couldn't get loose. Sweat streaked her neck and dripped down on Jason's fingers.

"I said, 'Remove your hands, boy!" she said, with even more anger in her voice.

"Missie, I shorely will. Just a moment."

Minta said, "I said now!"

She struggled harder against the straps. Her climax this time was mixed with sweat and spit. She sputtered. "Your seed, Jason. Don't forget about your seed."

Jason said, "Just like always, Missie."

"I'll check. I swear I will, and if I don't see it, you've earned yourself a beatin'."

He trembled and then suddenly pulled away from her. He turned his back to her and climaxed. He felt humiliated, yet there was a part of him that wanted to believe that he had worth for that moment.

"Are you finished?" she asked.

Jason groaned. His breathing slowed as he buttoned his overalls.

"Yes, Missie," he mumbled.

"Let me loose and fetch a torch. I want to see what you did," Minta said as she swung her arms against the restraints.

Jason loosened her straps and sighed, "Yes, Missie."

Chapter 55

The afternoon heat had broken, the moon had risen, and a cold northern breeze swept through the open windows of the first floor of Briarwood. The dining room table was set and waiting. The candles were lit.

Edward crossed his hands in front of himself and tapped his belt buckle. It was a habit he'd developed while waiting for orders. He stood at the dining-room door and bowed at the waist. He was wearing his full-dress Confederate regalia with all his medals. He doffed his hat and smiled.

Minta straightened her bodice, curtsied, moved past Edward, and sat at one end of a long table. Virginia entered. She wore her most delicate rose-colored dress and offered her hand to him.

Edward bowed again and kissed Virginia's hand. She blushed and glided to a chair in the middle of the table.

Virginia said, "I'm forgettin' my manners. I've failed to compliment you on your lovely home."

A glittering chandelier dangled in the middle of the room. Above that was an elaborately painted ceiling that made the room appear more spacious. It was an optical illusion. A ceiling fan spun slowly, operated with ropes and pulleys by Jason as he stood in the corner of the room. He smelled the food, and he heard his stomach growl.

"We were lucky to save most of the silverware and coins when the Yankees swept through," Minta said to Virginia.

Edward seated himself and motioned toward Jewels. She began serving.

"Really? We had to bury our valuables before the raid on Vicksburg," Virginia told her.

Minta leaned toward Virginia. "We have this marvelous root cellar with a hidden entrance. It's almost impossible to find."

Jewels ladled vegetables onto Minta's plate.

When Jewels started to add a second scoop, Minta flapped her hand toward Virginia.

"I have a hard time findin' it myself at times," Minta said, attempting a joke.

"Minta, please. Let's change the subject," Edward said.

Jewels served Virginia. They both nodded after two scoops.

Virginia surveyed the room. "And this room, most interesting. I love the way the ceiling is painted so it appears to be a rotunda."

Edward said, "Something Minta's first husband toyed with, just before the war. A brilliant man. Just before he left."

Jewels served Edward and left the dining room.

"We had every reason to believe it would be all the rage, but unfortunately, so far, we are the only takers," Minta said as she took a bite of a beet.

"So, Minta, your first husband was an architect?" Virginia said as she plucked a corn muffin from a basket.

"Architect, designer, inventor—"

Minta ended Edward's sentence, "— a dreamer, all."

Jewels appeared again with the main course. She served Minta and then moved toward Virginia.

The young woman took a delicate bite of her muffin. She said, "Oh, the world is in desperate need of dreamers now."

Minta sniffed, "He'd have given away the storehouse the first time the Yankees darkened our door."

Virginia finished a bite of squash and asked, "He was no warrior?" Already knowing the answer.

Jewels hovered near Edward, her serving fork perched over the pork roast.

Edward inspected the meat and then nodded his head. Jewels put the platter on the corner of the table and took her place next to the china cabinet. She faced the wall.

"No," Minta said, "Edward is the warrior."

Edward stood up, strolled over to where Virginia sat, and picked a muffin from the basket.

"Minta, if there were more dreamers in the world, there would be little need for warriors," Edward said.

Virginia dabbed at her mouth and smiled. "You see, Mrs. Corrigan, that's the kind of observation and style that makes Edward's letters so ... oh, what's the word I'm searching for?"

"'Bully,' I believe the word you're lookin' for is 'bully,'" Minta said as her upper lip twitched just a bit.

Virginia said, "No, I was thinking of 'ideological.'"

Minta snorted and said. "There is that streak in Edward. I believe he got that from his father."

Edward tried to remember all the lies he'd told Minta about his background. He wanted to keep it vague and almost impossible to check. He knew she would be suspicious, given her wealth. Still, she was so enamored of his battlefield successes she overlooked, thankfully, any deficiencies in his story.

Virginia looked at Edward and said, "I am grateful to anyone who would produce such in a young man." Virginia nodded to Edward. He tipped his chin toward her and smiled. Minta dropped her fork. She said, "Jewels, I'll need another fork!"

Jewels ducked her head and moved toward the china cabinet.

"Forks right over there on the bureau, Missie Corrigan," Jewels said. She knew she could get a beating for being sassy to Miss Minta. However, she believed it was safe to "smart off" a bit, given the guest at the table.

Minta fumed for a moment, stood, and pushed her chair back from the table.

A round mirror over the bureau showed Edward and Virginia ogling each other. Minta saw the reflection and the flirtation behind her back. She grabbed her fork and stomped back to her seat.

She considered her next move in this small war. She looked up at the ceiling and imagined her first husband looking down at her. What would he say? Would he laugh at her?

"Oh, for the days when men were men," Minta opined, "the time before the war of Northern aggression."

Chapter 56

Edward stood next to the downstairs rail. Virginia stood on the second from the bottom step. They were eye-to-eye, and the proximity was palpable. His hand rested gently on hers. They tried to hide their interest in each other. They knew the trouble it would bring if they grew closer together as Minta became sicker. Keeping their distance would be wise.

"So, we ride tomorrow morning?" he asked.

"How could I say no to such an enticing offer?" Virginia replied, blushing.

"Looks like the devil's work," Minta thought when she saw them. She swept into the foyer and said, "Wasn't the dinner just the best?"

Edward jerked his hand from the post. Virginia left her hand on the newel.

They both nodded in agreement about Minta's review.

"I was just about to invite Virginia to sit a spell on the front porch. Won't you join us?"

"No, thank you," Minta said and then cleared her throat. "I was thinkin' Virginia and I might take a shoppin' trip to downtown Nashville tomorrow. I'd like her to see the sights."

"Oh, my, that would be wonderful—" Virginia said but was interrupted.

Minta affixed a snake-like grin to her lips and said, "— then it's settled. You'll need to get to bed early. It's a long trip, but a rewardin' one."

Virginia dipped her head and turned. "Until tomorrow then, Miss Minta."

The girl turned and took two steps up the staircase. She looked over her shoulder as Edward smiled up at her.

Minta swept by Edward. He snatched her hand and pointed her toward the library. He guided her inside with just a bit too much force. She sidestepped him, slammed the double doors, and pushed him toward an elegant divan. He weaved past it and continued, not allowing himself to be trapped in a small space.

The candles had been lit for the night's reading and talk. He pulled open his elaborate collar and huffed, "What is wrong with you?"

Minta balanced herself and tugged at her bodice.

"I'm sure I don't know what you're talkin' about, my dear."

She crossed the room. Her mood turned on a dime, and her eyes flashed with a reflection of the candlelight. She had an agenda, and she knew how to pursue it. "I will not have this in my house," she said.

Edward said, laughing, "*Your* house! That's rich. I believe the house became mine when I married you."

Edward stumbled a bit over his shiny boots as he approached the tray of spirits. He poured himself a bourbon and downed it in one swallow. He quickly poured and drank another. "This is like water to me now."

She sidled up to him and whispered in his ear. "This woman —"

Edward pushed her away and said, "I am friends with 'this' woman, Minta. Do you understand? I have feelings of sincere friendship for her."

He poured another drink.

"Feelings!" Minta exclaimed. "Feelings?"

"Like I've never had afore," Edward said. "She is an equal of mine in both emotion and intellect."

Edward moved to the fireplace, took a poker from the stand, and prodded the flickering fire. The embers leaped to life and produced a low flame. He weaved a bit as he pushed the kettle next to the fire and replaced the poker.

Minta said, "Oh ... well. That changes everythin', doesn't it?"

Edward said, "And I will not have this sniping and evil back-talking."

Minta stifled a smile with the back of her hand. "I am not evil, my dear."

"You are, at times, most malevolent," he said, slurring his words, "— as bad as that growth in your head."

She slapped him. As she reared back to give him another, he caught her hand.

"How dare you speak that way of me!"

"Daring is one thing I do very well," Edward told her.

"So, when is the great warrior goin' to take action instead of hidin' behind his words?"

Edward broke the glass in his hand. "Is this the violence you would have me do?" he asked.

Minta grabbed him by the hair and kissed him. It was an animal kiss, with a lingering, biting passion from first only one side. Still, given the liquor and his lightheadedness, now both sides were equal. Edward broke away from her and turned his face.

"Leave me. Leave me alone," he gasped.

Minta wiped her mouth with the back of her hand. She answered, "As you wish."

She moved toward the door, locked it, and turned. She slipped off her dress and stood glaring at him in the flickering firelight. Edward turned from staring into the fire.

Minta strode across the room, her bodice falling to her waist. "This is the kind of fire she can never give you."

She grabbed Edward by the back of the neck, startling him, and bit him hard. It would leave a mark. He screamed, weaved, and fell onto the sofa. "Woman!"

She stepped out of her pantaloons and jerked his belt from his trousers.

"Here's something she would never do because she is all starlight and roses." She slapped the belt against her thigh. She closed her eyes and enjoyed the pain. She straddled him, rubbed the back of her hand against the front of his breeches, reached between his legs, and found him already hard. "She doesn't 'really' love you the way you like to be loved."

She grabbed his waistband and jerked his pants to the tops of his boots. She lifted her skirt, licked her hand, and rubbed it against her crotch.

In a moment, she was atop him, moving with the rhythm of the grandfather clock that sat across the room from them. The cushions on the divan swished, and the straps that held the pillows in place strained. The room temperature rose, and Edward felt a drop of sweat begin in his hairline and fall down his cheek as Minta continued to move against him. There were no words between them. After their initial short period of 'court and spark,' they became entwined like this almost every night, then every other night, then once a week, then once a month, and so on until they decided separate bedrooms would be best for them.

Minta remembered their first months of marriage and believed this lovemaking session would end the threat from the small girl just rooms away.

Edward moaned and struggled against her, but she held his shoulders. "You're not going anywhere," she said.

Their breath became synchronized, and Edward tried to get up again, but this time with less effort. "*Maybe it was the alcohol,*" he thought. Maybe a small part of him still had love in his heart for her.

Edward said, without thinking, "What is the point of this when we cannot have children?"

Minta was hurt by his words for a second, and she winced for a moment before her face split into a wide grin. "Maybe that is the very reason."

She shuddered against him as he closed his eyes and buried his face in her naked breasts.

"There, there," Minta said. "Let your tears of 'feelings' fall here."

Edward glanced up. A flash of anger crossed his face as he climaxed.

Minta looked down at him as she clamped her thighs around him with a devilish gleam in her eye.

Chapter 57

As I was placed on the operating table in the hospital, the doctor began cutting my clothes away from my side. It was caked with blood, and even with a stick to bite on, I found myself moaning in pain.

He cut away a portion of the side of my pants and pulled back the flap. I jerked up, trying to cross my legs before he could see, but it was too late.

He looked up at me, eyes wide and forehead wrinkled.

"Corporal, I mean, young lady," he whispered. "What do you think you're doing here?"

His words were not loud enough for others around us to hear, but he was clear.

"Why didn't he expose me?" I asked myself. "How many others had he seen in a similar deception?" I considered asking him and thought better of it.

"You are not alone in this," he said, anticipating the questions in my mind.

"How many others?" I asked.

"Five, maybe six that I have seen." He said as he sewed up the bayonet cut in my side and wrapped my wound. "There was one woman who was clearly pregnant and not detected until she gave birth. She wanted to be next to her husband." He turned to me and whispered, "I guess it was somethin' we should have expected."

"'Expected,' you say."

"Yes," the doctor said, "but very dangerous."

"Yes, I —"

The doctor interrupted, "your explanation is not necessary. You are a patriot who wanted to serve. I can understand that."

"Yes, that was my original motivation," she said.

"And now?" The doctor asked.

"Now, I'm not sure. There was a rush of excitement that I felt when under fire. I didn't expect that."

The doctor pursed his lips, "I've heard quite a bit about that effect also."

"I would appreciate if you —"

I leaned back and looked at the discolored ceiling of the tent. I had thought I was alone in my ruse. It was good to know there were others, maybe dozens, that had followed the same path. I could understand the husbands and wives. I could even understand the women who were patriots. But I was surprised at how they were successful. Of course, I had to work at my disguise. I wondered how they had pulled it off.

"Your secret is safe with me," the doctor said.

I chuckled to myself and thought, *"Until I give birth."*

Chapter 58

The doctor who'd helped me recover from my wound asked me to be transferred from the front to help him. As a result, I aided in dressing the wounds of seventy different men today, some with two or more injuries each.

Yesterday I was at work from daylight till dark. Today I am completely exhausted, but soon I will catch my breath and go at it again. I remember confronting Oliver Holmes about aiding the war effort by rolling bandages and smiling. I used gauze to help close a wound. Where was the woman who sat at home and helped play the only role "society" allows?

For me, the days after the battle are a thousand times worse than the day of the fight—and the physical pain is not the most significant suffering. And until you see the destruction after a battle, well, it's impossible to describe. The dead appear sickening to the living, but they suffer no pain. But the poor wounded, mutilated soldiers that yet have life and sensation make a most horrid picture. I pray God may soon end such infernal work, though perhaps he has sent it to us for our sins. Great indeed must have been our transgressions if such is our punishment.

We are near Harpers Ferry. I am ordered along with others in my troop to remain here until the wounded are removed and join the regiment. With the doctors and nurses, I expect there will be another great fight here.

That night, the doctor and I had been away from the hospital to see some wounded men and returned late. I fastened my horse to a peach tree, where I fed him some oats and hay from a barn. I slept and dreamed of my loved ones so far away.

I have made the acquaintance of two rebel officers—prisoners in our hands. One is a physician. Both are very intelligent, Southern gentlemen. One is wounded in the torso and the other in the leg. They are great favorites with our officers though they have not divulged any troop or cannon movements. One of them was brought off the field during the fiercest battle by our 5th Army of New Hampshire officers. They both have said they are Masons, as is one of our doctors. They shared the secret handshake, but I was not able to see it. Father was the same way when he met another Mason. Not for women, he would say.

One of the two, the younger one, gave me a bit of gold lace. This was cut from another rebel officer's coat while still on the battlefield. While it was difficult for my Yankee ears to understand him, I found him a most engaging conversationalist. And we shared a love of orchards—mine cherries, his pecans. I felt he was privy to my secret and might have been courting me in his clumsy and didactic way. How many others have seen through my disguise? Is the need for cannon fodder greater than who is standing on the line? I know some officers care deeply for their soldiers and go out of their way to make sure they survive. But, if they knew I was a woman, would they dismiss me or keep me from the greater harm? I guess I'll never know.

The war would end. Life and love would pick up. Why not explore those possibilities when hostilities ended? I know my experience hasn't helped my appearance. As they say, "you're not getting any younger," so when the war is over, I would need to double my efforts to end my spinsterhood and find a husband.

While the lieutenant continued to recover, he complained about his yearning for tobacco. I found a corn cob and fashioned him a pipe that looked and worked as well as my own. He was a lieutenant, and while his wounds seemed to be healing, he succumbed to a fever in the night. I've seen that happen so many times, but the suddenness of death never fails to shock me.

Chapter 59

April 15th, 1865

It was a door I'd entered and left so many times in the past, and yet on this day, I was unable to get anyone's attention. The streetlamp flickered on the corner, and I could see my reflection in the window. Who was this person? While the actual time was short, my face was yellowed and lined like an old woman. I'd seen too much in my day, too much death, too much sorrow, too much …

I rapped on the window again.

What could have happened that the telegraph office was closed?

Today was supposed to be my last day helping President Lincoln. But, unfortunately, my exposure to battle and cannon fire had damaged my hearing so much that I had become useless to the president. I could hold my ear trumpet to my ear, but I would still miss a word now and again. Those missing words could make a big difference. Besides, my service and the service of all soldiers would end soon. Lee's surrender less than a week ago would quickly bring the conflict to an end.

While I was happy to know that I would soon be going back home, I was melancholy about the people I'd grown to love in my time away.

A crier passed me on horseback. "The president has been shot!" he yelled.

I felt the cold, night air against the back of my throat, and I gasped. How could it be? The war was over, and victory was ours. What kind of cruel God could let something like this happen?

I ran toward the crier. "What happened? Where is the president?"

The man in black turned his horse and looked down at me. There were tears in his eyes, and he swallowed hard before he spoke.

"The president was attending a play, and someone shot him in the back of the head. He is at the Peterson house on Tenth Street."

I turned to get my bearings and walked toward the hotel.

There was a crowd of men in front of the Peterson house. Many were well dressed and wore top hats as if they had attended a social event of some kind.

I moved through the crowd as best I could. My uniform helped with some of them, as they deferred and let me pass, but others couldn't seem to care less about my service to the Union. How quickly they forget.

I walked through the entry hall and looked up the stairs. I saw Mr. Lamon sitting on the stairs with his head in his hands. He was crying, and I watched his big shoulders move up and down.

"Oh, that it was me instead of him," he murmured.

I put my hand on his shoulder and said, "I'm sure there was nothing you could have done."

He glared up at me. His cheeks were flushed, and the veins in his neck were distended.

"I should have been there," he said. He closed his eyes and moved aside as I stepped past him. "I love him."

"We all do," I mumbled.

A soldier I knew from delivering messages from the telegraph office to the president allowed me to pass into the sitting room. I glanced at the open bedroom door as I walked toward the fireplace.

The president lay at an angle with his head at the north corner of the bed. Two doctors stood next to the bed. One was finishing bandaging the president's wound. The other prepared a solution in a small glass.

Mrs. Lincoln sat in a red chair next to the fireplace. She wore a dark blue dress with white frills at the wrists and collar. I noticed that there was blood on her wrists, and there was a smear on her skirt.

"Mrs. Lincoln," I said.

She lifted her eyes and looked at me. A flicker of recognition registered on her face for a moment, and then the sadness passed over her features again.

"Corporal Jacobson, I've seen you several times at the White House."

"Yes, Ma'am," I said. I squatted next to her chair and stroked her arm.

"I saw the man who shot him."

"Did you recognize him?" I asked.

She shook her head.

"I've seen hundreds of men struck by bullets, Mrs. Lincoln. I've seen men survive what doctors would say were impossible wounds. Please, don't lose hope."

Mary said, "How can I go on? When Todd passed, at least I had him—"

"I'll say a prayer," I said.

She nodded and twisted a handkerchief in her fingers.

"We have given so much, and now we are asked to give even more," she whispered.

"We have all given," I said.

I walked into the bedroom. One of the doctors stood near the bed while the other talked with a well-dressed man who held the brim of his hat and scraped his thumbnail against the satin fabric.

"Doctor, is he going to pull through?" I asked.

The doctor turned and shook his head, no.

"Is there nothing that can be done?" I asked Mrs. Lincoln.

"Pray." She looked up at me from the crumpled handkerchief she held in her hands. "Pray for him," she said.

"That I can do," I replied.

I looked back for a moment as I left the room. Mrs. Lincoln continued to sit in perfect stillness. Her gaze fell somewhere between the middle of the rug and the door. I tried to think of something else to say but couldn't think of a thing.

She suddenly began wailing, her face flushed, her handkerchief came up to her mouth as if it might muffle the sound. I felt so sorry for her. She had lost so much and now so much more.

As I reached the street, I noticed that the crowd had grown even larger. Still, the usually accompanying noise of such a gathering was missing. The men whispered and held their hands over their mouths.

It finally dawned on me the gift the president had given me. So many times, I'd marched, filled a line of soldiers, and pointed my rifle as directed by my betters. Still, it was rare I knew anything about the shape of the battle and why we set up here instead of over there. How could that make any difference for one person? When President Lincoln showed the maps and the troop movements, I could see the method to the madness. Where we went and when we attacked made all the difference. When in the vortex of battle, it was impossible to have that perspective. Thank you, Mr. President.

I had experienced so much of the war, the bad and the good. I would be forever changed in so many ways. So many men I'd stood next to that had decided the Union was necessary for the country's future. They were led by one of the most exceptional people I'd known, who now lay dying.

The streets bustled, which was strange for this time of night. People were visibly upset, sitting on benches, weeping and such. The former soldiers I ran into seemed glassy-eyed and dazed by the horror. This news was just one more thing to add to their grief.

I entered the bivouac and sat on my bed. I said a silent prayer for the president, for America, and tried to sleep, but that night, it would not come.

Chapter 60

Against a cold, black, moonless sky, a dozen white-hooded riders clamored around the lower limbs of a large elm tree. On the bed of a wagon sat a trembling Black man. Edward, in his Corrigan disguise, nudged his horse forward. The horse snorted as if affirming the meeting.

"We don't cotton to uppity niggers in this part of the country," Edward said.

"My name is Pauly Jones. I've got a mother who loves me and a family who's depending on me," the man told Edward. He was small in stature, thin, and his hands were tied behind his back. He wore gray pants, suspenders, and a white shirt. His face was contorted with tension, his eyes large, and his lips pulled tight over his teeth.

Laughs came all around from the other masked men.

Edward said, "We know the latest tactics of the likes of you, Nigger. I couldn't give two shits about you and your family. You done wrong and—"

Pauly interrupted, "—what did I do wrong?"

Edward looked over his group and pointed at one of the men. "This man here said he heard you talk about niggers votin' and how that was a good thing."

"I didn't say nothin' ... no, wait. I said it might be a good thin' now's the war's almost over and all. I said that to Lucifer." Pauly stopped and looked at the hooded man. "That you, Lucifer?"

Edward took a deep breath and turned his back to Pauly.

"I can't believe—" Pauly said.

"—you admit you said it?" Edward asked.

Pauly stiffened and stood but almost lost his balance. His shoulders shook, and a single tear fell down the side of his cheek. "Damn straight, I did, and I believes it too."

"That's enough for me," Edward said. "Stretch his neck for him."

A rope appeared and drifted over the limb directly over Pauly's head.

"This ain't right, Lucifer. I talked to you like we was friends."

The man riding the swaybacked mule sat silently. His white hood looked new as if it was the first time he'd worn it.

Edward, losing his patience, said, "I can't believe this shit. Yank HIM!"

The wagon jerked from under Pauly's feet. He gasped and swung his feet, thinking he might have a chance to live if he could only pull his legs up to his head.

A masked man sidled next to Lucifer and patted him on the shoulder. The holes in the hood were black, but he knew Pauly, his friend, would know he was there for him. He knew this in his heart because he was a Christian and believed God could console anyone in any situation.

Pauly swung from the tree limb as the group thundered away on horseback.

One hundred yards away, Sergeant Clyde parted the undergrowth from behind a low bush to get a better view with his spyglass.

Chapter 61

Nashville, after the war, was slowly returning to a bustling city of commerce. Horse-drawn wagons filled the streets, and the docks on the Cumberland provided a steady stream of new products and suppliers.

The shoppers flowed through the downtown streets and around Minta and Virginia as they strolled along a cobblestone sidewalk. They wore full, billowing skirts, bodices, and handmade shoes. They both carried parasols.

"Please tell me all about Edward when you first met him," Virginia said as she covered her face with a handkerchief to shield her from the dust kicked up by the riders on horse-back and buggies.

Minta said, "He was the man more likely to lead than to follow."

Virginia coughed and said, "I guess that's what made him into such a successful military leader."

Minta guided Virginia around a horse pile. A buggy flashed by them, again, kicking up more dust.

"Are you quite sure you're all right? That's a pretty bad cough." Minta had let a tone of concern creep into her voice.

Virginia said, "I am sometimes overtaken by coughing spells. It's all right. It's just the dust."

They strolled by "Stella's" dress shop, stopped, and peered through the window. There was a headless mannequin in the window sporting the latest fashion designs from France.

Minta said, "That blue one." She looked Virginia up and down.

"That one would look best on you, what with your figure and colorin'," Virginia said.

"I've never found myself to be very attractive in blue."

"You are attractive in anything you wear," Virginia said.

Minta smiled. She knew this to be true. She'd had many suitors growing up, and her first marriage was more arranged than romantic. *"Maybe that was why it didn't succeed,"* she thought. She turned to Virginia and said, "Should we go inside?"

"No, not this one, thank you," Virginia replied, "I fear the cost is out of my budget."

They continued past a restaurant, a bank, and a dry goods shop. Many had posters and declarations of support for the recovery. Still, not one window featured support for the North or South for fear of turning off shoppers.

"Is that the Tennessee Theater?" Virginia asked.

Minta smiled and pointed her parasol. "I remember attendin' a benefit performance by Mr. John Wilkes Booth durin' the occupation. What a marvelous actor. The newspaper said, "'his genius was equal to anythin' the tragic muse has produced.'"

Virginia said, again coughing into her handkerchief, "I remember reading about that in the newspaper."

"It was a little more than a year later he did this world its biggest favor," Minta said as she put her handkerchief to her nose. More dust from passing horses was beginning to affect her, too.

Virginia's lips fell open in surprise. Minta swung her parasol over her shoulder.

"Surely, you do not condone the murder of any human being?" Virginia asked.

"Maybe I saw too much durin' the war. But if the cause be true, hang the individual," Minta said as she pointed to another storefront. "Look, they're havin' a sale at Baldwin's. They have the best bolts of fabric in the whole mid-state."

She took Virginia's hand and led her into the store.

***

Minta looked at the top of the staircase. "You look marvelous, my dear."

Virginia stood on the top step. She wore the blue dress from Stella's dress shop with white gloves and a large blue hat.

"I fear it is not me as much as it is the dress," Virginia demurred.

Minta agreed and said, "There is always a bit of trepidation when tryin' some new style."

Virginia nodded and then took a faltering step and grabbed the rail.

"Come along. Edward will be home soon."

"Edward is already home," he said as he appeared at the door.

"Edward!" Virginia bounded down the stairs and curtseyed. He bowed.

Edward said, "You have found your feet."

"You inspire me to try many new things."

She coughed and placed her handkerchief over her mouth.

"That cough again. Maybe my doctor—," Minta said.

"I assure you it's nothing. My doctor in Vicksburg guaranteed my health before I came."

Edward offered his arm. "Shall we have a look at what Jewels has been up to today?"

She smiled and took his arm.

"Tell me about your day in the big city," Edward said.

The couple strolled into the dining room, leaving Minta standing at the stair rail.

Chapter 62

Virginia sat at a writing table. She pulled the nib of her pen from her lips and looked at the flickering lamp. She set pen to paper and began with a flourish.

She wrote, "Mrs. Hockney, you would not believe the beautiful mansion and gardens of Briarwood."

She glanced at the new dress that Minta had bought for her. It was green with white piping. She knew the ensemble would complement her red hair and pale complexion. She wondered about Minta's motive for the purchase. Still, she dismissed it as the older woman just trying to be friendly and courteous. Was there an ulterior motive?

A ladybug emerged from the side of the desk and marched across the top. The bug circled the inkwell. Virginia smiled at the bug as she dipped her pen in ink.

"There you are, my pretty one. And where do you think you're going on such a blustery night?"

The ladybug continued its stroll. Virginia kept writing. "And the food. Prepared by this tiny woman, the meal we had tonight would satisfy the most discerning palate." She considered how much detail she should include in this report. Should she write about the apparent tension between the man and woman of the house?

***

In his bedroom down the hall, Edward leaned back; a needle stuck in his vein. The militia had required additional guidance tonight, and the needed extra energy was exhausting, both mentally and physically.

He decided it was time for him to cut back on his nighttime activities. He was getting older, and it was time to turn the reins over to someone else. Maybe someone younger who still had a fire in his belly. Retirement from the movement seemed more appealing as every day passed. Lucifer, the young sharecropper, seemed to take to the philosophy nicely. He might be a good headmaster and recruiter of younger members.

Edward loosened the leather strap around his arm. A tiny bubble of blood oozed from the puncture. His eyelids fluttered and foam accumulated at the corner of his mouth.

***

She decided to give even more detail in her letter to Mrs. Hockney, knowing at a certain level that Mr. Hockney would likely be reading this too. They seemed joined at the hip in many ways. Was that a healthy way for a relationship? She believed she and Edward would someday share their lives, and she wondered how that would look. Virginia wrote, "I was right about Edward. He's everything a woman could hope for in a man."

***

Edward coughed into a handkerchief. A small ball of blood was nestled in the cloth. He eyed the piece of phlegm like something from the other side of the moon.

He wondered if he looked as bad on the outside as he was likely corrupted on the inside. He stood, wobbled to his feet, adjusted his pants, and weaved across the room.

***

Virginia wrote. "He's as charming and opinionated as his wife but with a kind streak."

***

Edward snuck down the hallway and stood by Virginia's door, hand poised over the knob. It was a place he'd imagined himself many times before she'd even decided to come visit.

He pulled his hand away, put it back on the knob, and then pulled it away again.

He turned, his face fallen, moved down the hallway, and opened another door.

Edward entered, eyes downcast. "Jason said you wanted to see me."

Minta sat at a dressing table. She was naked. An intricate pattern of scars crisscrossed her back. They were not as profound or severe as Edward's, but the source was different, creating a different design. They had been created by a whip and not from battle.

"Woman, cover yourself," Edward said as he averted his eyes.

Minta stood and moved toward him. She was with her husband, and she felt no shame in showing him her body. She straightened her spine as if challenging him. She thrust her breasts out like a proud peacock and flaunted her toned stomach and thighs.

She would not be told what to do, especially in her own room, in a house her father had built.

"Why should I?" she said, looking at him. "We are man and wife. We have no secrets in this house, now do we?"

He picked up a robe and held it in front of her. She snatched it away from him and tossed it on the floor.

She knew it was time to confront him. "That girl would never be able to satisfy the warrior heart in you."

He picked up the robe.

With exhaustion in his voice, he said, "I am no longer a warrior."

She threw the robe on the floor again and grabbed his hand. She placed it on her swelling breast.

A nagging pain started at her temple. She knew the coming agony would be exquisite, but she was on a mission and wouldn't be deterred.

"Here, take this, that you might suckle again, like the baby you have become."

He jerked away, turning his face. "How could you?"

Minta's cheeks grew red as she said, "How could I not if you would act doe-eyed in the presence of such a silly little girl?"

Edward turned, eyes blazing. "You talk of the woman I will someday soon marry."

Minta slapped him, picked up her robe, and pulled it close to her body. The affront stung, and she hoped that the slap produced just as much pain as his words.

***

Virginia wrote. "He's tall and strong and sensitive. I am worried about how the war affected him, though. I wish there were a way for him to talk more about his feelings." She noticed that the inkwell was running low. She thought about adding more but didn't know where to get it. She'd ask Minta tomorrow. She was surprised at how accommodating the woman had been.

***

Edward's eyes watered from the pain of the slap, but he wouldn't acknowledge it to Minta. He raised his hand to strike her. He stopped, breathing hard.

"Is this what you want?" he asked.

Minta's eyes narrowed.

***

Virginia wrote, "I feel there is a secret that I've yet to fathom. My normally clear vision is cloudy, maybe by emotion. I hope to figure it out soon so as not to jeopardize our future."

***

Edward pulled his hair from his face and wiped a tear from the corner of his eye. He felt sweat roll down his side, and there was a pang of pain in his left arm. He'd suffered a severe cut there last year, and it was still healing. The doctor had said the nerve damage might increase as he recovered.

"You and Virginia together? As long as I live, that will never be!" Minta bellowed.

"You have never been more wrong," Edward whispered, "and right in your life."

***

In Virginia's room, she placed her hand in the ladybug's path. The bug climbed on her finger and sauntered across the back of her hand.

She said to the tiny bug. "If only I could be like you. Just imagine what I would learn if I could be as small as you and could fly?"

Chapter 63

Jason finished saddling Edward's horse. He was always good with animals, chickens, cows, and pigs, but this horse always unnerved him—he was too big and powerful. Jason felt the animal could crush him if he took a notion to do so.

Edward polished the top of his boots on the back of his pants legs. He had seen his underlings similarly shine their shoes, but he had never tried it.

He looked up. He had postponed his afternoon with Virginia because of work, but now he was excited about their spending time together.

Standing in the barn's door frame, he saw a shiny pair of small riding boots.

Virginia's big-brimmed hat tipped up. She was wearing black riding pants and a white, cotton bodice. The outfit was too hot for the weather, but she would put the discomfort out of her mind. Her growing up in Mississippi had allowed time for training in riding sidesaddle while living in the deep South had also acclimated her to hot and humid weather.

"Are you sure Minta won't mind seeing the doctor today instead of tomorrow?" she asked Edward.

He wore a brilliant white shirt that flowed into a pair of gray woolen pants. He had learned to ride almost before he could walk and felt more at home in the saddle than the cramped office his current station in life required.

"She was disappointed when I told her," he said, "but she agreed she needed attention."

"The headaches?" She asked.

Edward nodded. A pang of guilt sped across his face as he affixed a blanket to the side of his saddle. His argument with Minta last night had likely triggered the pain. Edward felt guilty, an emotion he seldom experienced. It was almost imperceptible to Virginia, surprisingly, since she was usually overly attuned to nearly every aspect of her surroundings.

She strode across the barn hallway and to the other saddled horse. "I'm used to a spirited ride."

Edward rubbed his chin. "Ridin' pants on a girl?"

"It's all the rage up North. I find them very freeing," she said, grinning.

"I'm not sure I approve," Edward said, shaking his head.

Virginia's eyes flashed darkly as she said, "Is it important for me to seek your approval?"

Edward slid his boot into the stirrup and mounted the horse. Jason handed him a picnic basket. "Not at all."

She swung into the saddle and nudged the horse in the flank. "I'll follow you."

The sun shone in Edward and Virginia's eyes as they galloped across the hills and meadows.

The setting seemed familiar to him. But even though he'd lived in the area for so long, he was still lost at times. The landmarks were clear to natives, but he sometimes was confused.

They rode toward a large, spreading oak tree in the middle of a meadow. He suddenly realized where he was and felt the same kind of panic in his gut he had before topping a ridge at a battlefield. "Not that tree," Edward yelled over the thundering of the horse's hooves.

She dug her heels into the horse's side. She was determined. It was as if she knew deep in her heart that this was a sacred place.

"It's fine. I'll race you there!" she yelled.

Edward nudged his horse in the side.

They pulled the horses up short and tied them to a low limb. Edward scanned the area sheepishly.

Virginia dropped from her horse. She danced around the lower limbs of the tree. She was like a sprite caught in a breeze, and he could not take his eyes off her. He'd indeed never seen anything as beautiful and vivacious in his life.

Edward looked down from his saddle. "Not here."

Virginia smiled at him, beckoning.

"Look at the view from here. It's the most beautiful place in the whole valley."

He put the location and what had happened the night before out of his mind as best, he could. Then, finally, Edward took a deep breath and dismounted. "I guess it'll do."

He untied the picnic basket from the saddle. The blanket was spread at the opposite side of the limb.

"What do the locals call this place?" she asked.

He looked around the meadow. "I don't think anyone has a name for it."

"Then it's up to me to name it," she said, again bubbling.

He marveled at her youthful exuberance. It was her most attractive trait. He loved her smile and how it made him feel. She could find a positive light in any situation, something he had a hard time with, given the brutality of war he'd seen.

She jumped and hung from one of the lower limbs. To her right, a single thread of rope dangled, glistening in the morning dew. It was a strand that had caught on the tree bark after Corrigan's men hung Pauly from the noose. She didn't notice, but Edward did.

"From this time forward, I dub this place—. What should I call it?" Virginia asked with a playful tone in her voice.

"Come down from there this instant," he insisted. "I'll not have you break a bone foolin' around where you shouldn't."

He dropped the basket and pulled her from the limb and to his side.

"You're hurting me, sir," she said.

He remembered the incident with Minta the night before. The violence between them created a palatable frenzy of excitement and sexual tension. Still, he knew it was unhealthy for them and their relationship. His life with Virginia would be the beginning of a new chapter—one where there was peace and not war.

He loosened his grip and bent down to pick up the basket. He turned his back to her and walked into the shade.

She asked, "How about Virginia's Ridge?" She skipped to him. "It would be egotistical to name it after me, wouldn't it?"

"Would it be all right for me to call it such?" he asked, with a gleam in his eye.

She moved toward the shadow and near to his side.

"How could I stop you?" she asked. "What has that wizard of the kitchen, Jewels, packed for us?"

She spread a tablecloth and pulled out towels.

"The delay of twenty-four hours has whetted my appetite even more," he replied, glancing at her. "Looks like fried chicken, my favorite."

"Still warm. How does she do it?" Virginia said as she picked up a piece and tore into it.

"Your appetite seems to be whetted by the ride," he remarked.

She grinned and said, "My appetite is one thing I can always count on."

He handed her a biscuit. His finger brushed hers.

"You've written to your friends about us?" he asked.

"I told them everythin' about your wonderful plantation."

Edward winced. He remembered the Hockneys and how they had an opinion on just about everything, and they didn't hold back. "Everything ... Even my wife?"

"I like her. She's honest and frank."

She passed him a sack of boiled potatoes. It was heavy, and she struggled a bit with the weight.

"Really?" he asked, a bemused expression on his face. "Thank you kindly."

He took the bag with ease, chuckled slightly at her weakness in handling the weight, and spooned out the potatoes.

"Minta's something," he remarked. Of course, it was an understatement, but her dominant personality first attracted him to her—that and her feverous support of the cause.

"It would be difficult not to have been affected by the occupation, and of course, her sickness."

The hanging tree loomed over them. A shadow fell over half of Virginia's face. Edward found it strangely attractive, and he stared for a moment longer than he'd meant.

Edward cleared his throat. "Yes, she still wishes she could extract a pound of flesh from the Yankees."

"Has she told you all that happened?"

Edward took a deep breath. "She has kept that to herself, but I know it took some time for her to recover from her wounds."

"Wounds?"

"Yes, she resisted the Blue Coats, and they made her pay for it. I know she was whipped and suffered other atrocities."

Virginia took a bite of a biscuit. She chewed, swallowed, and said, "Just as you have kept to yourself how you were affected by the war."

"The scars and loss of blood and limb. Yes, it all weighs on me."

"I mean—" she began but was interrupted.

Edward let out a tired sigh. "How did I survive while others around me died?"

"You have no reason for feelin' guilty because you survived and others did not," she said as she took a big bite of biscuit.

"I never feared dying. I somehow knew I would live through any battle if I stared into death's eyes and made him look away," Edward admitted.

"And you never felt fear?" she asked.

He took a moment to consider his answer. He wanted to impress her with a profound and poetic response, but he chose the truth instead. "I always knew if I could sacrifice my life for the ones I loved, I'd have a throne in heaven. That thought gave me great comfort."

"And the politics of the war?" she asked.

"This was a minor consideration. I believe in state's rights, but the excitement of battle and my brothers in arms was why I was successful."

She glanced at him and smiled. "*Just as I'd surmised*," she thought.

He wiped a drop of sweat from his face and glanced over at the tree. Again, guilt played at the edges of his conscience. He had led many a posse that sought justice outside the law, but in this instance, there was a nagging pang of distaste in the act.

"There are so many secrets in your family. Why did Minta's husband leave? What is that contraption in the cellar?" she asked.

"*There are even more secrets than you can imagine*," he thought. How would she react to his having a secret identity and a different life as a Yankee?

He pursed his lips and took a bite of chicken. "How did you know about that? Have you been exploring?"

"I believe I know just about everythin'," she replied, realizing that she may have overstepped. "I'm sorry. I've upset you."

He glanced at the ground. She pointed to her eye.

"Second sight, that's my secret," she said, chuckling.

He looked up at her with a quizzical gaze. "What is the extent of this talent?"

"Most times, it shows me things both past and future."

"What of the future?" he asked.

"Of us?"

"Yes," he said.

She took another bite of biscuit. "It's cloudy, hard to read. I've lost my objectivity. But I do know we will be connected for the rest of our lives."

She rubbed his arm. He jerked back, looked at her, and then down at his food.

"If only that could be true," he said.

"It's important that someday you and your wife be able to tell me all your secrets."

She unbuttoned the top two buttons of her shirt and said, "'Tis warm for this time of the year. Look at how the leaves are already changing color."

"Soon, their grip will loosen," he remarked.

She said, "But just as surely spring will follow. That is the nature of life."

"To that, we can feel assured."

He took another bite of chicken. "It is unwise to fight the nature of things."

She nodded and said, "Unless the nature of things is unnatural."

Edward turned and looked out on the meadow. He chewed and swallowed, but the food resisted going down.

A squirrel moved from one side of the tree to the other. "Look how our little friend makes ready for winter," she said as she pointed to the squirrel.

"I wish I could convince the governor it's time to make ready for winter," Edward said remorsefully.

"In your letters, you mentioned his pigheadedness," she said as she took a bite of chicken.

"Wrongheadedness. My commission was forced upon me, but I felt I could be more effective working within the system to restore our land than from the outside. The bad news is, I believe he would like to extract his pound of flesh from the South."

She moved across the cloth and pulled at the edge of his collar. It had become bent under during their ride.

"How do the scars of the warrior heal without medical attention?"

He pulled away from her and took a bite of potato.

"The damage that was done has pulled together quite well."

"That wasn't the case the first time ..."

He retorted, "That was a mistake."

She turned quickly.

"Let me state that again. We should not have gone down that road so soon in our friendship. I wasn't ready for you to see me the way I am, shirtless."

He felt the shame burning in the back of his throat, and he coughed.

"Your letters led me to believe our friendship had deepened beyond shyness at that point," she said as she tipped his chin up. She looked him in the eyes and continued, "Are you concerned that I would love you only for the body I have seen and not your mind?" She smiled and ripped off a piece of chicken from the wishbone. "No. that would never be."

He reached for her and pulled her into his arms. "No, of course not."

She kissed him and then laid her hand on his chest. They kissed more passionately, and he moved his hand inside her blouse. The buttons popped open, exposing her under-bodice.

She moaned.

He moved his hand over her nipple with his fingers. He groaned and untied the bow.

"Edward," she gasped, her breath rapid and ragged.

He freed her breasts and kissed her neck, moving down her chest.

"Enough! My virtue remains intact, sir, and so it shall until my wedding night."

She moved away from his embrace, tied her bodice, and buttoned her blouse.

"And so it should," Edward said, resigned. He pulled away from her.

The sun set as Virginia and Edward raced to the barn door. All the way home, he'd thought about the tenderness of her love and her principles. How she had rebuffed him based on her beliefs. He marveled at how much stronger she was than him, which would make a difference in their chance of having a prosperous future together. They pulled up short and laughed as they both dismounted. "Let's change as quickly as possible," Edward said.

"Yes, the dance," she agreed, eyes flashing and her smile wide.

Minta stood at the barn door. She pulled her shawl to her shoulders and touched the side of her head, wincing in pain. She took a deep breath and relaxed her jaw.

Edward looked at her and then at Virginia. Minta glared at Virginia.

"Those breeches." She tut-tutted and said, "Let's hope your attire tomorrow at church is more appropriate."

Virginia blushed and told her, "I assure you it will be."

Chapter 64

Men in their most elegant suits in the upstairs ballroom and women in long gowns swirled over the hardwood floor. The quartet played with volume and enthusiasm through "Turkey in the Straw" and then segued into "Battle Cry for Freedom." They played with tempo and professionalism. They remembered the direction given earlier from Edward and now exemplified the master of the house's imagination.

Karol stood next to Edward at the edge of the dance floor. They enjoyed the music and clapped along with the beat.

"Let tomorrow be our day of destiny," Karol said.

Edward gave him a glance and a slight nod. The cover of the music allowed him a moment of acknowledgment of the mission they had planned.

Virginia glided up to Edward and took his arm.

"May I?" she asked.

Edward smiled and took her hand. Virginia twirled from Edward's embrace, smiled at him, and danced back into his arms.

"You've lost not a step since the last time we danced," she said.

The room was filled with finely dressed couples and opposing groups of singles. It was advertised as a major celebration, and the food and drink were top-notch. Jewels had done an excellent job overseeing the production. Minta supervised the decorations and the presentation. She had made sure there were two punch bowls, one with spirits and one for the teetotalers.

The floor was filled with spinning dancers as the music drove the crowd into a merry frenzy.

Virginia said, "I appreciate all your lessons more than ever since I now have you in my arms."

He spun her around and then pulled her close. He teased, "I believe you've been practicing."

"Not that much. There was a girl at Hockney's house who helped me a bit," she confessed.

"She did a marvelous job. I'd like to send her a thank you note for helping you."

Minta stood next to the punch bowl. She downed one cup of the liquid after another, spiked with a liberal amount of Kentucky whiskey, and soon felt the effects. She was not a big drinker, and this exception to her rules made her lightheaded and giddy within minutes. Men on either side tried to engage her in conversation, but she stared at Edward and Virginia.

"That young woman left Mississippi a while ago," Virginia said.

"Did she open a dance studio somewhere?" Edward asked.

"I'm not sure where she went. Mother Hockney said she left to seek her fortune." Virginia spun around.

"I see. Given the conditions in this country, that is something many people are trying now. Even some slaves, ah, former slaves," Edward said. He remembered Sophie and how she'd left without saying goodbye. He was still surprised by that.

Edward and Virginia danced near Minta. Virginia smiled. Minta frowned. Edward quickly turned Virginia toward the middle of the floor.

"Why doesn't Minta dance with you?" Virginia asked.

"I don't know. Since her father left, her heart has shied from all forms of entertainment," he answered, looking over at Minta at the refreshments table. He saw her sway a bit and realized she was drinking the spiked punch.

The music ended, and Edward and Virginia made their way arm-in-arm through the crowd to the punch bowl.

Minta slid next to Edward. "You dance wonner-fully," she said.

Edward turned from her and took a cup of punch from a servant. Minta reached for it, but he gave it to Virginia.

Virginia said, "Thank you kindly, sir."

Edward said, "To your health."

They clinked glasses and drank. Minta grabbed a drink from the servant. She swayed a little as she moved to the center of the room. She tapped the edge of the glass with her fingernail. The crowd quieted.

Minta yelled over the din of voices, "Ladies and Gentlemen!"

She strode toward the stage. She looked from left to right, keeping eye contact with some of the participants she had known for decades and had depended upon for years. Yet, given the circumstances that must have launched much gossip, she would put on a brave face and appear as gracious as possible.

"Ladies and Gentlemen! As many of you know, my husband is bein' visited by a charming young woman from Vicksburg. We are honored to have her with us at this time and hope to convince her to stay much longer," Minta announced as she raised a glass.

"To Miss Virginia Boswell."

The crowd raised glasses and cheered.

Virginia smiled, turned to Edward, and clinked glasses. She drank. He took a deep breath and drank.

Chapter 65

There was a chill in the air and not a star in the sky. The moon hung like a large, white teardrop. In the east corner of the plantation, a shallow creek gurgled beside a Dutch barn in disrepair. An enormous black horse splashed through a shallow portion of the water.

Dozens of men congregated around three large tables filled with maps, icons, and weapons inside the barn. Some of the men wore tattered Confederate uniforms. Some wore bedraggled suits with large cotton patches. Karol played mumblety-peg with a knife. The young men around the table laughed as the older man entertained them.

There was a glimpse of Lieutenant Clyde near the back in the dark shadows, but Karol couldn't be sure it wasn't just an animal tied in a stall. Clyde had obtained stealthy skills over many successful engagements.

Clumps of snuff dippers stood near the barn door. Their spitting and laughing made the meeting casual and comfortable. Their raucous discussions ended as a tall man in silhouette stepped through the opening.

The man's boots gleamed, his pants held a severe crease, and his brilliant white shirt fell open at the neck. He removed his hat, then put both fists on his hips. At his waist was a long saber sheathed in black leather and gold.

His long black coat had a bright red lining that flashed around his legs.

All conversations stopped.

He glared at the men and let his gaze sweep from left to right. He'd known many of these men as soldiers for months, and he trusted them. They'd served, and he respected them. Corrigan yelled, "This is the sorriest excuse of Gray backs I have ever seen."

Edward broke into a dazzling grin. The group erupted in laughter. There was much jostling and knee-slapping as the crowd relaxed, and Edward moved into the light coming from a window in the roof that allowed a shaft of moonlight into the hallway.

Karol said, "Those who are fit to be tied can't find the time to concern themselves with the latest fashion."

"True, true. You, sir, are the greatest example." Edward said. More laughter.

Karol said, "Have you finally gathered enough horse sense to lead our joyful band full-time?"

Edward's face became stony as he said, "When I could not be with you in the flesh, I was always with you in spirit."

Karol asked, "When was the last time your 'spirit' rode through a volley of mini balls?"

Edward turned and faced Karol.

Feelings of disgust and pride fought in Edward's mind. He'd hoped to lead through example and steadfastness. He expected to lead with intelligence and integrity. He knew if his movement, his rebellion, were to be successful and bring order and justice to the valley, he would have to make another sacrifice. "So, this is what it comes to?"

"Aye, sir, show us your hornet stings!" Karol shouted.

Edward shook his head. "I will not."

Another man said, "Your courage and commitment have never been in doubt, kind sir."

Karol said, "Your commitment durin' these last days of the war, sir, yes, but what of your dedication to our just cause now that the hostilities are ending? Word has it your devotion to your wife, and your doctor is the greater attachment."

Edward visibly colored at this. He turned his back on the rabble-rouser. This was not as he'd planned. He had a speech in his mind. He hoped it would be enough to inspire the group to continue their work. He remembered how effective his sister's speech had been those many months ago—how he had been inspired to join the Army and how he'd changed his mind. He remembered how in the South he'd evolved and how he had become addicted to battle. He was not the writer and speaker his sister was and likely ever would be. He was a man of action, and this group was demanding something else. He realized in this instance; words would not be enough.

He let his coat fall to the dirt floor. A man wearing a tattered Rebel uniform rushed to pick up the jacket. He dusted it off and stood stiff, arms extended.

Edward slowly unbuttoned his shirt. He opened the front and slipped the sleeves off his arms.

The scars on his chest and back turned red with shame.

Edward closed his eyes and then searched the eyes of the men as they stared.

Some were open-mouthed, while others fought the urge to look away.

Edward laid the shirt on the ragged man's arm and turned, arms stretched.

There were audible gasps. Several stared while others turned their eyes to the ground. Of course, many had seen the missing portion of his finger and some of the scars on his arms and neck, but only a few people had seen him half-naked.

"Have you seen enough?" Edward asked.

There were nods all around from the men.

Edward snatched the shirt from the ragged man and put it back on as he strode to the map table. Many of the men gathered around, and several stood on tip-toe to see the presentation.

A Middle and West Tennessee map was on a table with several large charcoal "X's" marked. Edward moved to the table as he put his shirt and coat back on.

Edward missed one of his buttons. His shirt collar sat against his cheek. He flicked it back with his finger, but it persisted.

Edward remarked, "I see where we will visit several Yankee storehouses."

Karol said, "It's there where the food is."

Laughs all around again.

Edward nodded and agreed, "Quite so, quite so. I have seen it."

"We expect them to be as snug as a bug in a rug in their beds as we do the Lord's work," Karol said.

Edward retorted, "Or the Devil's."

Again, a tittering of laughter as the crowd grew restless. The speech had worked, but there was more to be done.

Karol said, "Either way, our bellies and the bellies of our young'uns will be filled."

Edward snatched the maps in his fist. "Enough talk. I grow tired of these hit-and-run skirmishes," Edward cried as he pulled his sword. "'tis time for war!"

Rebel yells, cheers, and the rattle of sabers filled the air.

*****

From memory, Edward led the vigilantes along the route mapped out in the barn. He felt the excitement and anticipation he'd always felt before going into battle. It was a heady mix. Even though there was a chill in the air, he felt sweat on his arms and chest. His attraction to battle was whetted, and he rode with enthusiasm.

The men charged through one tiny town after another with their white robes flowing and their guns and sabers raised.

It made for a frightening sight, and while some cowered in their houses and looked out of windows, others left their homes and businesses and lined the streets and cheered the men onward.

Some still felt anger against the northern aggressors and wanted to fight back in any way they could. Others wanted the world to go back like it was before the war. They looked to Edward to lead them back in time, and he was happy to oblige.

Edward didn't share any of these thoughts at this moment. He considered the maps in his memory and how best to engage with his opposition. He was a master strategist and knew how to win.

***

Edward visualized the lie of the land, the placement of the small creek by the warehouse, and the road that ran by it. He directed half the men to the north side of the warehouse while he took a small band of men past a sleeping federal sentry on the south side. Edward bonked the guard on the head with the handle of his saber, ran another through with his blade at the door, and led the others into a storehouse filled with bags of grain.

Two wagons were driven into the barn, and the men loaded bag after bag of grain into them. Edward smiled and got a knowing nod from Karol as they escaped with their booty.

***

Later that night at the Dutch barn, the vigilantes distributed their plunder. A list of sympathizers was produced, and they were each given a bag of grain for their service. Some of the men had brought their children and were so happy they would lift the youngsters in the air.

Edward watched as the booty was divided. Once they'd successfully obtained the needed food, he knew there would be a call for even more raids.

He was pleased with his notion. In a way, the excitement of the mission, for a moment, quelled his need for the white powder. But soon after he returned home, the craving would return. He cursed himself in his weakness and wished somewhere there was a cure.

***

In another raid, the federal soldiers had been briefed on the last attack and now patrolled in front of a munitions storehouse with new awareness. They stood stiffly and walked with deliberate strides, thinking the extra effort would ward off a surprise attack.

Edward wore his best suit and tie, appearing as the successful administrator, sauntered up to the guard and tried to pass.

His huge black horse was braced into a buggy harness, and he pulled him up sharply as they closed on the guardhouse.

"Who goes there?" the sentry asked.

"I am here to inspect the holds here, young man," Edward said.

The horse shivered and shook his head. The noise distracted the guard.

"That's quite some horse you have there," the young man remarked as he moved to stroke the horse's neck.

Just then, Edward's men swarmed from behind and under the carriage, forcing the soldiers to give up without firing a shot.

Edward drove a wagon filled with guns through the door and past the guardhouse in less than ten minutes.

The young guard sat in the barn, tied, and gagged, left to send a message at the cruelest and obvious level.

***

Later, again at the Dutch barn, vigilantes distributed the guns and ammo. Edward knew that nothing succeeded like success. Recruiting would be much easier now that they were better armed and ready to fight.

He picked up a rifle and sighted down the barrel. It was a fine piece, probably leftover from deactivated troops and rebuilt weapons damaged in battle—it was only one of the thousands that were warehoused all over the area and would be needed to make the uprising a success.

As he spied down the sights, he noticed a faint glitter from a small mound near a tree to the north of the barn. He didn't make much of it but made a mental note to explore the area later to guarantee the site was secure.

He knew how spies worked and how valuable intelligence was to a war effort.

In the distance, Lieutenant Clyde lay on a small mound, looking into the torch-lit hallway.

Clyde felt disheartened to see his friend wielding the stolen firearm and sharing his pleasure with the dozen or so men that surrounded him. How had he failed so badly to read the character and disposition of this man?

He put the spyglass to his eye once again, brushed a mosquito from the side of his face, and resumed his viewing. It was that insect that momentarily had caused Clyde to move the glass and create a reflection of the torchlight and unknowingly reveal his position.

Chapter 66

The sun rose over his shoulder as Edward galloped past the magnolia tree in the front yard of Briarwood and dismounted. Jason took his horse as Edward rushed inside. It had been a successful night of pillaging supplies and arms from the enemy.

As he entered the parlor, he saw Virginia sitting at one end of the table, reading a book. Dirty and exhausted and in need of his 'medicine,' Edward hauled himself to his chair.

She said, "I don't know the business of this state, but there must be someone who can lift part of the burden from your shoulders."

"Yes, ye are right," he said as he poured himself a drink from a decanter on the table. "You don't know the business of this state."

The insult stung, and she knew if she were a man, it would have provoked a fistfight at least, and maybe even a duel.

Virginia closed her book and stood. It was a conversation she'd been dreading, but maybe now was the time. She felt she needed to confront Edward's attitude and help him find some positive things in his life.

Edward pleaded, "I'm sorry, I didn't mean for it to come out that way. I'm just so tired."

Virginia said, exuding as much control and calm as she could. "I'll bring you some breakfast."

She exited as Edward picked through the morning dispatches. A fire raged in the hearth, but there was still a chill in the parlor's air. He looked up at the portrait next to the china cabinet. The painting showed Minta sitting on a straight chair, looking like a queen. It was the look she gave the slaves at times when she wanted to intimidate them. She was a beautiful woman, but there were times her 'problems' outweighed her presence.

"Jewels outdid herself tonight. Too bad you were out so late," Virginia said, "We would have liked your company."

Edward replied, "I wish I could have been here, too."

He started to eat. As Virginia reseated herself, Edward sniffed himself.

"I reek. I'll have Jason draw me a bath."

Virginia said, in genuine appreciation, "He and Jewels are so helpful. They are the best people. How long did Minta have them before the war?"

Edward had to think for a moment. "Years. Jason was born in the quarters."

Virginia returned to reading her book. She said, "We stopped owning slaves two generations ago in our family. There wasn't even that much debate. We took the financial loss. It just wasn't 'Christian.'"

Edward stopped eating. "Your family was so much more 'enlightened' than Minta's."

Virginia blushed and set her jaw. "I didn't mean it that way. We decided we would live our lives a different way, that's all. Maybe I'd better go out on the porch and drink my coffee there." She rose and was about to pick up her cup.

"I'm sorry, I'm just so tired. I'm sure I'll feel better after my bath. Please stay."

She said, "Maybe we should talk about all the things we have to be thankful for. Have you considered how lucky you are to be alive and thriving?"

"I'm not sure I'd call it thrivin'."

She nodded. She decided maybe the time wasn't right, but she knew deep down that his outlook was. He offered his hand. She hesitated and then dragged her chair to his end of the table to be near him. She held his hand while he fed himself.

Chapter 67

Minta knelt by her bed, hands folded, head bowed. She muttered to herself and then got to her feet. She wore a long cotton nightshirt with satin slippers. She said, "Amen and Amen."

The pain she felt today was so sharp and exquisite that if she was stronger, she might even find some pleasure in it. The notion that pain might equal enjoyment sparked a memory of her making love with her first husband. He had struck her, and after the shock of him doing it, she found it thrilling. She had never approached Edward with the idea of trying something similar. The frequency of their lovemaking had stalled, but maybe now was the time to revisit the idea.

She filled a syringe, pulled a strap at her elbow, found a vein, and gave herself the injection. She closed her eyes and licked her lips. She got into bed and turned toward a window filled with sunlight. The room spun reassuringly.

"Merciful Mother, how can I save my husband from makin' such a fool of himself?"

She turned over and hugged her pillow. "A wife always knows what's best for her husband. This woman is not the best replacement for me. I feel it in my bones."

***

Down the hallway in Edward's bedroom, Jason filled the bathtub with a bucket of steaming water. Edward poked at the fire. He stepped to the tub and swished the water with his fingers.

Jason said, "Make sure you don't catch no cold, Missta Edward."

"Thank you, Jason. What would we do in this house without you?"

"I don't rightly know. Good day." Jason turned and left.

Edward dropped his robe and stepped into the water. He soaped his arms, face, and legs. He closed his eyes and lowered himself into the water. He rubbed the soap over his hair and rinsed it. He slid to the bottom of the tub and closed his eyes. He wished he could hold his breath like this for hours, but he soon needed air and sat up.

He emerged from the water rubbing his eyes.

He heard her move across the hardwood floor and tried not to look in her direction. He said, "Virginia. Please, no."

He tried to cover his scars with a washcloth.

She stood, holding a book of poetry. She kept her hand on the doorknob, unsure if what she was doing was a good idea.

She smelled the soap and a hint of jasmine as the hot water splashed near the edge of the brass tub. She turned and smiled, convinced the setting was her best invitation.

"Your door was unlocked. I hope it's all right," she said.

Genuinely shocked by her being in his room, Edward said, "No, it's not all right. You should be in your own room."

Virginia pulled up a chair next to the tub. "I just found this marvelous poem I wanted to share with you," she told him.

"Poetry? You should not be here. We've talked about this."

He lowered himself into the water to cover his scars.

"I used to wash my father's back, and he really enjoyed it. May I?"

She put her book on the floor and moved the chair closer to the back of the claw-foot tub. Her notion of trying to talk Edward into expressing his feelings had failed. She decided it was time to be bold and catch him at a vulnerable time.

"Virginia, how many times must I say no? Leave me," he said with as much emphasis as he could muster.

She pulled the chair up to the rim.

"Give me your cloth and lean forward," she instructed.

"You ... you ... cannot forget what you see of me."

She nodded, readying herself for what, up to this moment, she could only imagine. "You fail to realize, my love for you cannot be caught in this all-too-weak flesh. I love what is in your mind and your heart."

Edward shook his head in disappointment and dread and said, "I am afraid you will find the container too much."

"Nonsense. Lean up," she ordered.

She snatched the cloth from him. He took a deep breath and rose from the bubbles. She picked up the bar of soap from a holder attached to the tub and soaped the cloth.

She stared. It was much worse than she'd imagined. The small exit wound on the back of his shoulder created a star-shaped scar. There were many long cuts, apparently made by sabers and knives, and there was another wound she couldn't place the origin of on his neck. Had he been hung? She took a deep breath, closed her eyes, and scrubbed.

"No one has shown me such kindness since my days in battle."

She washed him and said, "Tell me more."

The track on Edward's right arm emerged from the bubbles. She stared at the scar and continued to wash him. She had not seen that kind of wound before and wondered how it was caused. He noticed and pushed his arm under the water.

"So many deaths. The breastworks, aye, that was easily the worst. I've seen the ditches fill with blood, both Reb and Union. I was the one who had to send the men over to their deaths," he told her, his voice breaking at times and trailing off at the end.

Virginia's eyes widened and reflected the bright sun filling the windows. She was amazed at his honesty and openness.

"They would rush over, take a shot, and fall back wounded or dead. Eventually, the mounds were covered with the dead and dying," he said as he brushed a tear from his cheek. "It was horrible."

She asked, "Are you sadder for the dead or because you were able to survive?"

"I'd truly never thought of it that way, Virginia. Although I must say, I sometimes find myself feeling guiltier for living than dying."

Virginia nodded and rinsed his back.

"So, now what do we do?" she asked.

"You leave while I get ready for work."

She kissed him. He reached for her, but she stood and walked across the room.

"Good day, sweet Virginia."

"Good day, fair Edward," she said without looking back.

Later in her room, Virginia knelt at her bedside. Her hands were clasped in front of her. "Forever and ever, Amen."

She looked up. Sitting on the edge of the bed was the ghost of her grandfather.

"I must admit to being startled by the sight of his scars," she confessed.

"How deep are they?" the old man asked.

Virginia settled herself into the covers. "I know what you're asking, Grandfather. They are only skin deep. They do not reach into his soul."

The old man asked, "Are you sure?"

It was something she'd considered. Was Edward too damaged to love her or anyone? He would likely need to hate his enemy to kill him. Would that hatred ever be replaced with love? She nodded. "Yes, I'm sure, with all my heart."

There was a knock on the door.

"Yes, who is it?"

The irony wasn't lost on Minta as she stood in the hallway. Yes, it was polite to knock and ask permission to enter, but it was her house, which had been her home for decades. So why would she need to ask? "It's me, Virginia. May I come in?"

Virginia replied, "Certainly, Minta."

Minta entered and crossed the room. She sat where the now-fading visage of Grandfather had sat.

"I feel I owe you an apology," she began.

Minta was dressed in her long skirt and bodice. The top was green, setting off her beautiful eyes. The bottom was black and almost seemed to move on its own.

Virginia asked, "What for?"

"I feel I haven't given you the proper respect," Minta replied as she extended her hand. Virginia took it and squeezed.

"I really don't feel it's necessary," Virginia said.

Virginia pulled the pillow across the bed without touching it. Minta caught the movement out of the corner of her eye and reflexively scooted away.

"So, how have you enjoyed your visit?"

Virginia smiled and said, "It's been most pleasurable. I especially enjoyed our shopping trip together."

She pushed the pillow near Minta, again without touching it.

"Good, well, I'm glad the air's been cleared."

Virginia offered the pillow to Minta.

"This is a lovely pillow. The embroidery is so elaborate. How long has it been in the family?"

Minta hesitated and then took the pillow from Virginia's hand.

Minta experienced a flashback of Horace's face as it loomed over her. She felt the pain and his suffocating weight on her.

Virginia tugged at the pillow and glanced at Minta.

"It's actually very new. I believe I bought it last year from a peddler," Minta replied and threw it back on the bed.

Virginia interrupted herself. "I feel ... oh, never mind—"

Minta glared at her. She didn't like the meddling nature of this girl, who knew too much and was clearly angling for her husband. Minta knew she was dying, but she wasn't dead yet.

"Good day," said Minta as she walked across the room and closed the door behind her.

Virginia stared at the door and then closed her eyes. She said, "You poor, poor child."

***

Dried off and wearing his robe, Edward sat at his desk. He prepared a syringe. As the needle hovered over his arm, he took a moment and rubbed his bottom lip. Then, he squirted the morphine onto the dark, green curtains framing the window to his left.

There was a screeching noise. He looked up as a mouse ran across the floor. He picked up the poker and rushed toward it. He missed and returned the poker to the fireplace.

He looked out the window.

"This burden, this burden," he muttered to himself. The pain crept into his mind and spun like a tornado. He clenched his teeth and winced. How much could he take? He'd been wounded, bled so much for the cause. Now, he was suffering for love. He'd force himself past it.

Chapter 68

Later that night, down the hallway, Edward stood, hand on the door as if feeling the love emanating from the room. He twisted the knob. Four candles still burned in the bedroom, but the light near the bed was dim. He could make out the figure there, but the image was indistinct.

He crept across the room, took off his robe, and slid into Virginia's bed. She wore her red nightgown and was lying with her back to him. She had refreshed her perfume, and the scent made Edward even more ardent. He touched her shoulder.

"Edward, we've talked about this," she scolded him.

He felt his cheeks reddening, and he quickly turned. "I've disappointed you. I'll leave."

She took his hand as it rested on her shoulder. A small voice inside of her whispered that this was the moment she'd been waiting for and that to tarry any longer would be wrong.

"I've changed my mind. Life is too short, and I can't wait any longer," she said as she turned to him and kissed him.

"Do not fear if there is blood," she said as she smoothed the front of the red gown.

Edward asked, "You knew this would happen?"

She kissed him. "I saw that we would be together like this, but I didn't know when." She took his trembling hand in hers.

"Now, my love, make this night everything I hoped for and dreamed about."

Edward felt torn. He wanted her, but believed just being close to her would sate him tonight. So why had she changed her mind? She'd seen his scars, and she had accepted him as he was. The notion of unconditional love—was it possible?

"Are you sure?" he asked.

She placed her hand over his mouth.

"Speak your love to me with action instead of words," she murmured. "Remind me of our time in Vicksburg and your promise of love. Remind me of some of your letters, and I'll recite some of mine."

His mind was blank, and he looked at her dumbly. Finally, he said, "I'm too tired. Can't think."

"Do you remember the letter I wrote you about the chicken I'd taught how to fall asleep on command? Surely, you remember?"

That was something he should have recalled. He remembered when he'd found Minta saving one of Virginia's letters from the blazing hearth. How many more had met a fiery fate?

He was distracted now, and anger had begun to boil in his chest. He would confront Minta again about her meddling in his private life.

Virginia touched his cheek, and she kissed him. His mind returned to the moment, and he debated what to do next. He didn't want to ruin their future by making love with her now. "I've changed my mind," he said, "We should wait until we're married."

She put her finger to his lips and said, "Let it happen now."

She kissed him as she guided his hand to her chest. He pulled at a blue ribbon and freed her breasts. They were tear-shaped and topped with erect, pink nipples. He caught one in his mouth. A moan resonated from deep inside her.

She ran her hands over his scars and drew him to her. They kissed, long and deeply— the shock of their bodies so close that it excited them both.

He mounted her and slowly guided himself into her. She bit her bottom lip and closed her eyes. She found the pain, both exquisite and nagging. Is that all there is?

There was a quick intake of breath, followed by rhythmic breathing from both parties. He finished and moved to her left. She glanced at him and giggled.

"Oh, Edward," she whispered. "I guess I can be called a maiden no longer."

"No, that phase of your life is over," he said. He moved to leave, and she touched his shoulder.

"Will you say anything about this to Minta?" she asked. He'd considered that before as he stood holding the doorknob. Life is too short, and no one knows what tomorrow might bring.

"No," he said, "I'll not speak of it."

Virginia let a sly grin creep across her face. She reached for her doll, Mrs. Greenway, and hugged her tight.

Chapter 69

A brilliant sun shone down on beautiful gardens, filled with a corps of sweating, Black gardeners. Clyde and VanBurgh sat on a raised patio, enjoying cigars and cognac.

Clyde said, "The infiltration was very simple. I took on the same appearance as the attendees and found the door flung wide open." He was growing to resent these meetings and wished he could receive his orders on paper. He tried to hide his distaste for the governor, but it was not easy.

The governor pulled a sour face but tried his best to hide it. He didn't like underlings who worked to puff up themselves and their accomplishments.

VanBurgh said, "They weren't suspicious?"

Clyde shook his head and said, "They welcomed anyone with enough hatred of the North."

This was his first assignment at espionage, and he was uncomfortable spying on his friend and brother-in-arms. Clyde felt a drop of sweat fall from his hairline and down his cheek. The temperature was moderate, so he shouldn't have reacted in the way he was. It was as if his body was trying to tell him something. He considered swiping it away but decided against it.

VanBurgh said as he waved his cigar at a small shrub, "And you're sure it was Edward that addressed the crowd?"

VanBurgh knew the answer to this question, but he wanted to test the man's loyalty sitting before him. It was a simple exercise he'd used in the past to make sure he was able to trust his underlings. It was underhanded, in a way, but VanBurgh felt it was necessary.

Clyde paled as he said, "Trust me, it could have been no other." He remembered how Corrigan had exposed himself to the crowd and how some had reacted. He, too, was shocked at the sight, not to the point of vomiting as some had, but it was striking. How had the man survived? It was a miracle.

"Continue your mission then." VanBurgh said, "But lay low. Put nothing in writing. We don't need a record of your work at this time."

Clyde found this part of his assignment unusual. He knew a paper record of all military activities was needed for review. *"Why was this task different?"* he thought but merely said, "I will do my duty."

Clyde stood and saluted. VanBurgh returned the salute.

Chapter 70

Flames from a blazing fire illuminated the two figures as they sat at a round table in the sitting room. Edward leaned back and studied the cards in his hand. Virginia pulled a card from the stack in the middle of the table.

"Dealer takes one."

Discards rested alongside a chewed cigar in a crystal ashtray. Edward picked up the cigar and took a long draw. Virginia coughed.

"Sorry, my dear," he said, "does the smoke bother you?"

"No," she replied, swallowing hard, "it's comforting. It smells of the same cigars my grandfather smoked."

He leaned back and blew a thin column of smoke into the air. "I am amazed at a young woman's interest in cards."

Virginia laid down her hand. "I win!"

Edward moved forward and laughed. "You are truly remarkable."

"I like to deal," she said, fingering her cards. "There's a sense of geometry that I find fascinatin'."

She gathered the cards as Edward looked at a small piece of paper. The telegram listed the number of attacks the rebels had accomplished and which he had secretly led. She shuffled.

"How about poker?" He looked up from his dispatch and asked.

She nodded and dealt five cards each. It was Edward's favorite deck of cards. He'd had it with him for months and carried it into battle many times. They were worn, and he could identify some of the cards from the creases and the scuffed backs of the cardboard. He thought he could cheat if he wanted to.

"So you count the cards?" he asked. He had heard of people with the ability to do this but had never experienced it himself.

She smiled over her hand. She pulled two cards from the center of her hand and moved them to the end. Edward looked at his hand and moved a couple of cards from left to right.

"No, it's more a gut feeling. I can 'feel' the cards that have been dealt and guess at the ones still in the deck."

Edward smiled at the cards in his hand. "So, you know the cards I hold?"

"I know most of the cards you hold," she replied.

Was it time to tell him fully of her gifts? Minta had not cottoned to her probing of the past, and she didn't want to push Edward away at a time like this. She had seen him in the telegraph office and at his home. He'd never let on his talent for Morse code and where he was from.

"Which are?" Edward asked.

"What is the sport in that?" she asked, giggling at her joke. Edward smiled, too. "True," he agreed.

He pulled a small wooden box of kitchen matches and counted out thirty sticks for each of them. He took two matches from a stack and tossed three in the center of the table. "I bet three."

She studied her cards, pursed her lips. She took three from her pile and added two more. She said, "I see you."

Edward put his cards face down and toyed with his matches. He knew how much you could tell about a person by playing cards with them. He'd 'read' many a soldier by the way they played their hands.

He tried to read Virginia's character by the way she played her cards. He could tell a lot by how players held their hands and the flickers of recognition around their eyes and mouth. He was rarely wrong.

She had a good poker face, but he was becoming distracted by her beauty.

"I fear the house might grow cold if I'm not careful," Edward said.

Virginia laughed and pulled her cloak tighter around her shoulders. Even though the room was temperate, the idea of it being too cool made her react. It was a suggestion he'd made to see how susceptible she was to what he'd said.

"Are you chilled?" he asked. He would make the fire in the hearth even more intense if she needed it. He tried to be sensitive to her needs, wherever that might lead.

"No, sir. I'm fine, but I promise you I will leave enough 'fire' to get you through the next winter." She was amused by her pun, and she stifled her laughter. She realized that in the past, she had played for more significant stakes, but she'd never felt a hand of poker meant more to her.

Edward smiled. He remembered the lovemaking from just moments ago and realized he'd have years to enjoy his time with Virginia.

"I see your bet and raise you four," he said. He moved the sticks into the pile.

She smiled at him over the cards fanned out in her hand. "You forget, sir, I know most of your cards."

He said, smiling. "But not enough, I believe." He was intrigued by this new aspect of her and wanted to test the extent of her abilities. They both laughed.

She said, "I call." She laid her cards on the table. "Three of a kind. I believe that beats your pair."

She reached for the matches. He grabbed her hand, leaving it on her wrist just a bit too long. She blushed and snatched her hand back. He laid his hand down, showing his pair of aces.

"How did you know?" he asked. He hadn't believed her claim of her extraordinary power until now, and he was trying to figure out just what to do with that information.

"I told you. I have a feeling for the cards. I sometimes even use them to help me make decisions."

"How so?" he asked.

She shuffled and held the cards to her breasts.

"I draw." She nodded.

She cut and held the half-deck up to his face. "It's a nine of diamonds."

She laid the deck on the table.

"Then I ask a question. 'Will Edward and I be together forever?'"

She drew the card and held it up to him.

"If the card is higher, the answer is yes."

Edward stared at the ace of spades. He stood and picked up a glass from the mantle. She, of course, already knew this but wanted to place the idea in his mind that they would find happiness together.

"Cards and life are never that fair," he said as he turned his face from her. His tears glistened in the fire. She stood next to him.

"You turn from me as a child," she said.

She took his chin and turned his face toward her. Tears filled her eyes as she looked up at him.

"I am crying with joy and anticipation. Why do you weep?" he asked.

She took a deep breath and swallowed hard. "There is something I must tell you about Minta. It's something I saw that happened in this room many years ago."

An astonished look moved over Edward's face. "How could you know? What on earth could that be?"

Virginia said, with a hurt tone in her voice. "It might explain the 'trouble' she has with her mind."

"The doctor has explained that," Edward said. He knew in a way it was cruel for him to be with Virginia now, but Minta was so disagreeable at this time. He felt sorry for her and her disease, but life is short, and true love is rare.

He said, "She has cancer in her brain. It has produced 'problems' for her. She has little time left on this earth."

Virginia took a deep breath. She knew her observation might cause Edward to be more sympathetic to Minta and drive a wedge between them, at least for a while. "There was an incident when she was a child," Virginia said. She leaned forward and touched his hand. "Her father took advantage of her in the most horrible—"

Suddenly, Sergeant Clyde burst into the room with a dispatch. He was in his blue uniform, and Edward noticed his brass buttons were shining.

"Sorry to interrupt, sir, Jason let me in," Clyde said, "but there's been more trouble."

Edward's face turned ashen. He looked at Virginia and pulled his hand away. He turned and said, "Yes, my friend."

Clyde had a small slip of paper. He handed it to Edward and stood at attention.

"I have a full troop assembled out front, awaiting your orders."

Edward wiped the tears away from his eyes and read the paper. He looked at Virginia, took a deep breath, and spun on his heel.

"It seems we have no choice but to take those Reb traitors apart limb-by-limb," Edward said.

Clyde turned to leave.

Edward wondered if there was a way he could wriggle out of this confrontation. He would likely have to face off with the very men he'd recently led on raids on Northern storehouses. His mind was torn. And the idea that Virginia had just proposed involving Minta shook him to his core.

"I'll get my coat." Edward took Virginia's hand. "A kiss for luck?"

She smiled and kissed him. Clyde tried to look away, but he couldn't help himself. He was a man who had been to war and had seen so much. It was hard to surprise him, but he was shocked.

"I will pray for your safe return," she said.

Outside, dozens of riders were gathered in front of the magnolia tree. Clyde mounted up as Edward strode out of the front door. He stopped at the top step.

"We ride because the cause is just. In the United States, the law is king, and we are merely its servants."

The troops responded. "Hooray! Yeaaaaa-haw!"

Jason held Edward's horse. Edward bounded down the steps and jumped into the saddle.

"Those who die tonight do so for the ideals we hold deep in our hearts," Edward said.

The troop responded. "Kill'em all. Yaaaaaaaah!"

The troop turned and thundered away. In an upstairs window, Minta stood half-hidden by the deep green curtain.

Chapter 71

Stars filled the sky, bright, shining, and twinkling. The fall air was crisp, and a mist hung near the ground. Several Rebels patrolled outside the barn. They had become separated from their unit and were foraging for themselves until they could reconnect.

Edward and his troops stopped at the top of a ridge. A torch flashed from across the canyon as a signal.

Edward's giant black horse weaved his way from the back of the troop.

Lieutenant Clyde sidled his horse next to Edward. He asked, "Did you think you could fight this battle without me?"

"No, Clyde, I knew there was no path to victory without my good friend riding by my side." Edward patted his horse's neck. The animal had accompanied him into many a battle and had grown at ease with the sounds and smells of combat.

Clyde asked, "Would this be the time to offer a wager?"

Edward pulled his deck of cards from an inside coat pocket. "To victory or survival?"

Clyde said, "Victory, of course."

Edward cut the deck and showed Clyde a three of hearts.

"Surely you would like to pull again," Edward said.

"That will not be necessary."

Clyde pulled a card. He slowly turned over the four of diamonds.

"I'm sorry, but there it is," Clyde said. "Almost too close to call."

"And yet, you are a clear winner. You seem reluctant." Edward responded.

"The cards do not lie," Clyde said. He knew cards didn't prevaricate, but there was a feeling deep in his gut that told him Edward had lied to him for months and that their friendship would soon be tested.

Edward crossed himself and entwined the reins in his fingers. "That's the signal." He stood in his stirrups. "How many do we have on the other side?"

Clyde said, "A hundred men."

Edward lowered his scope. "Then there it is," he said, "I do this in the name of my beloved country." He raised his saber and said, "Trumpeter, sound the order. CHARGE!"

The troops descended from both sides of the hill.

Dozens of hidden Rebel soldiers dashed from the barn door and caught their horses. They armed themselves, fanned out, and rushed toward the descending troops.

Clyde slapped the reins against his horse's neck, urging him on. He soon matched Edward and his horse stride for stride.

"CHARGE! With all the might of Heaven on our side! Let God's will be DONE!" Edward screamed as he slammed into one of the Rebel guards' horses.

Edward scanned the field as he topped a small ridge. The location reminded him of a breastwork and the horrors of war.

A Reb soldier caught a mini ball and fell into the creek.

Two Union soldiers ganged up on a Reb and slashed him to pieces.

A volley of rifle shots took three Union soldiers off their horses.

A Union soldier lay in a shallow pool, blood soaking his uniform.

Bluecoats and Rebs fought saber-to-saber and hand-to-hand.

A flag carrier stood with the Stars and Stripes unfurled during the fighting, bugle to his lips—until a mini-ball shattered his head.

Edward jumped from his horse. A Reb soldier swung a pick at Edward. He slipped under the attack, then turned and faced off with the soldier. It was Lucifer.

"Away with you, boy," he said, "do no harm to others or feel the edge of my Dog Hill saber."

Lieutenant Clyde battled two Rebs but turned to see Edward freeing Lucifer. Clyde shot one Reb and slashed the other man.

Edward and Clyde turned and continued fighting—Clyde killing and Edward freeing Rebel soldiers.

Suddenly, Edward's horse leaped from an embankment. He slammed into Clyde and pushed him into the mud.

Clyde's horse ran away. Edward's horse ran too.

Edward said, "I believe you know too much now, my friend."

"I know your allegiance is not to the Union but the Rebs!" Clyde cried.

Edward pulled his saber and pointed it at Clyde. "This is how the world ends."

Clyde also pulled his saber. He said, "Why do you pull your saber and point it at me, your friend?"

"My 'friend' who spies for VanBurgh and reports to that son-of-a-dog Grant."

The men crossed swords. Mud, water, and sweat dripped from their sabers and their arms. Their faces contorted with pain and stress. Edward pushed his hair from his face as Clyde moved forward, right foot leading his attack. Edward retreated but continued to beat Clyde's best moves.

Thrust ... parry ... thrust ... parry.

The metal moved through the air with blinding speed and startling sound.

CLANG!

"I was merely following orders," said Clyde.

CLANG!

"As am I," Edward said, "I follow orders of the heart."

A vicious slash from Edward almost disarmed Clyde.

"With God is my witness, my heart orders revenge on those who betray the cause of the Union," Clyde retorted. "Especially the dog that is Corrigan!"

Edward's eyes flashed as he realized his identity had been revealed. On the battlefield, he'd often thought of himself as a separate person, fighting with a fury that belied his true nature. But now, maybe, this was his real character. He cried, "If that be the case, then fight on!"

They crossed swords and met face-to-face. They disengaged and thrust. Clyde slashed while Edward parried. A small cut appeared on Edward's cheek. It was a minor wound, but in many ways, it cut him closer than any other he'd ever suffered in battle.

"Did you really think you could pull off this madness, Edward?" Clyde asked. He backed over a stump and nearly lost his balance. Edward saw the opening but failed to take advantage. What was keeping him from following through?

They moved up the hill with moonlight glancing off their swords.

"Did you really think, Clyde, I wouldn't know the history of every man in my troop? This is where you made your first and fatal mistake."

Clyde and Edward crossed swords.

Sweat and blood drip from their faces.

SQREEEEEEEEEEEK!

As their swords slowly scraped against each other.

Close enough to share the same air, Edward sneered. They separated and parried. Clyde slashed Edward on the arm. It was a deep gash, but Edward didn't feel it. The cut bled, which made Edward even angrier. How dare this insect wound him in this way? He switched his saber from his right hand to his left.

"I am no longer Edward Jacobson." He jumped to the top of a rock.

"I AM CORRIGAN!"

He leaped on Clyde and pushed him into the mud.

Eye-to-eye, Edward placed his saber against the side of Clyde's neck.

"Let loose the demons of war! Death to all who oppose us!"

Edward raised himself up and slashed Clyde's jugular vein. The blood, under tremendous pressure, spurted high into the air, baptizing Edward. He stood, looked down at his dying friend, and said, "Death to all."

He ran to his horse, mounted up, and raised his bloody saber.

"I AM CORRIGAN!!!"

Chapter 72

Bright sunshine poured through gauzy white sheers surrounded by dark red velvet curtains. The office was dark wood and had an aroma of cigar smoke and candles.

Behind a large desk stood two flags, the state flag of Tennessee and the Stars and Bars. Governor VanBurgh sat at the desk, surrounded by reporters.

"It is with great trepidation and sorrow that I must call out the state militia to root out a subversive element in our society." VanBurgh read from a piece of paper.

"How will you do this?" a reporter asked.

"There is a patriot to the United States who —"

***

A single rider galloped across a vast western prairie. Edward gripped the reins tighter and kicked his horse in the side. He made a plan with only one thing standing in his way. He considered a route to the freedom that he'd initially sought in the West—he would take back roads, cross the Mississippi and maybe even go as far as the Pacific.

***

VanBurgh continued speaking to the reporters, "with great personal risk named dozens of the leaders and followers of this most violent and disruptive body."

VanBurgh lit a cigar and said, "Warrants have been sworn out for one hundred twenty Rebels, including their leader, a man who goes by the name of Corrigan. Most of you know him as Edward Jacobson."

There was a visible shock in some of the faces of the reporters. Many of them had interviewed Corrigan, and even one or two considered him a friend or at least an acquaintance.

"Do you mean the governor's administrator?" a reporter finally asked.

VanBurgh knew this would be the touchiest part of the announcement. He would have to admit that posting Edward to the administrator job could be an embarrassment. "An undercover operation to root out traitors has uncovered this conspiracy. Jacobson was its leader." The reporters looked at one another in shock. They'd covered Jacobson and his rebuilding projects for months. They knew his history, his marriage, and his wealth. It was difficult to swallow, but this information would make for many a follow-up story.

"W-w-who will lead this r-r-roundup?" one reporter stammered.

VanBurgh took a draw on his cigar.

"The arrests will be coordinated by this office and the commander of the state militia. Anything else?"

A reporter asked, "One more question, sir. When they're captured, will the trials of these men be held in Nashville?"

VanBurgh looked up and glared at the reporter. "I have been given the authority from President Johnson to assemble a federal court to try these men. This is serious business, gentlemen. I only hope the level of violence can be kept to a minimum. Let me just say it is a sad day when men choose to cling to the past rather than embrace a bright, new future in a United States of America."

The reporters rushed from the room as the governor turned and drew more smoke from his cigar. A breeze swept through the open windows and set the sheers into a gentle wave.

Chapter 73

"*The machine, the machine, the machine,*" Edward thought. He stared at the thing as it squatted near a small window in the basement. It was painted black, the seat had a leather-covered chair, and the straps that held the arms and legs were also leather. The round magnet that sat behind the seat looked like a small moon that emitted waves of energy.

He pulled the restraints tight and eyed the switch. He felt weak, putting so much hope into this ridiculous device, but he had no choice. This time it had to work.

There was a whirring that increased in volume. He smelled ozone, just as if lightning had struck nearby, and he felt his nerves jangle as the power from the batteries grew. There were sparks from the magnet, and he clenched his teeth and closed his eyes.

He screamed and looked at the switch. He touched it, his hand shaking, and disengaged the device.

The magnet over Edward's head slowed to a stop. He opened his eyes. His jaw was locked in a grimace of pain. This pain was replaced with a feeling of frustration.

He pulled the disconnect switch on the machine. The whirring noise died.

He knew his addiction would be a hindrance in his escape. He couldn't be worried about his mind being clouded by the powder when he was on the run. He thought, "*This is insanity.*"

A blister the size of an egg rose on his wrist.

"Such bullshit. Your invention fails me again. The ache for the powder remains," he said to himself.

He ripped the strap from his wrist and yanked at the ankle belts.

A mouse moved from the shadows and looked up at Edward.

He looked down at the tiny animal. The mouse sniffed the air and was confused by the stench of burning flesh and the ozone produced by the machine.

He said to the mouse, "Just as you cannot become a cat, this proves I can never be something I am not."

Meanwhile, Virginia looked at herself in the mirror two floors above as she finished buttoning her dress. Her usually reliable second sight was clouded today. While that was sometimes comforting to her, the uncertainty today, she felt, was a hindrance.

She wasn't paying attention to the sound of the pounding boots in the hallway outside her bedroom.

Corrigan burst through the bedroom door with his eyes like hot coals. His hands were twisted into fists.

She was looking at herself in the dresser mirror. She saw him in the reflection and was startled. She had never seen him like this. It was almost like he was another person, someone she wouldn't have recognized if she had walked past him on the street. His disheveled appearance and his dark eyes seemed to bore a hole through her back. A bubble of fear crept up the back of her throat.

She would try and defuse the situation and downplay Edward's threatening demeanor. She said, "I was just about to come down and ask you if you would like to take me on a picnic down by the river this after—"

She turned, the back of her hand going to her mouth.

"Oh, my."

Her mind's eye cleared, and she saw the scene of the battle and his fight with Clyde. She saw the anger in his face and the hurt in his eyes. She saw him changed and how he had become the monster that now appeared before her.

Corrigan stormed across the floor and grabbed her by the shoulders. He threw her halfway across the room with disregard for her health or well-being. Her head and torso landed on the bed, but her hips and legs bent toward the floor. He rushed to her and tossed her legs on the bed. He unbuttoned his pants without looking at her.

Her plan to help him with all the love in her heart died as she realized the terror of what he was about to do. "No, Edward, please," she pleaded.

He jerked her skirt over her head, covering her face. He pulled her bloomers to her ankles and jammed himself inside her.

He knew deep down that this was wrong. He had resorted to this only in wartime when necessary to make subjects compliant or release pertinent information.

Virginia cried, "No, Edward, Edward, please don't do this. You must stop now!"

Corrigan's face twisted into a horrible mask.

"This isn't you. My love, Edward, please stop," she pleaded, biting her lip in hopes of easing the pain. It didn't work.

"It's time to end this charade," Corrigan growled in a voice she'd never heard. "This is the man you love."

After all, he had done, all the killings, and now Clyde's death, he knew he did not deserve love.

He raped her for a torturous minute and then climaxed. He jerked away from her, bolted upright from the bed, and left the room in shame.

"Not Edward," she murmured, "Not you. Not you." She reached across the bed and clutched her doll.

Chapter 74

They stood together at the rail fence. They watched the night sky darken and fill with stars.

"What was it like back home for you?" Eloise asked. She was ending her time with the Army in a "mopping up" operation in Tennessee. They were close to Fort Rosecrans, and they were preparing to go out on patrol soon. She propped her rifle against the fence and pulled out a packet of tobacco. She pinched off a small portion and inserted it in her cheek.

"I was a drummer for this travelin' band," Mordecai said.

Her experience with music was limited to listening to Edward play piano and the dances she'd attended, which seemed so long ago now. She had no knowledge of how musicians worked and why the sound they made was so pleasant. "And you played for weddings and such?"

"Along with other events, dances, concerts, too. We rode far and yon, all the way to Canada a couple of times. We were supposed to take a tour of Europe afore the war broke out."

She looked at him standing there, tall and thin. His dark eyes flashed as he looked at the brilliant, full moon.

She let herself have a moment of imagination. What would her life with him be like? She loved the idea of traveling and seeing the world beyond America's shores. He had similar interests and seemed open to travel. She wondered just how impossible that dream might be.

"I've always dreamed of seeing Europe," he said.

Her heart leaped, but she kept her voice steady and said, "All the usual tourist sites, I guess."

He turned to look at her. She spat and wiped the bottom of her lip. He smiled, he'd had an aunt that dipped, and she was always his favorite.

"I always wanted to go to Italy," she said. "I wanted to see the ruins and walk the streets where my favorite philosophers had walked."

He had never read philosophy and was impressed that Edward was so learned. He wondered if they would have been friends if there'd been no war. But, he decided, not a chance. He said, "I see. So, I'm not as well-read. What is your fascination with them?"

She turned and looked at him. "Marcus Aurelius is my favorite. I could study him all day."

"What was he about?" he asked

"He was a soldier, just like us. He advised people to seek out experiences and make choices that would enlighten them." She felt this was her opportunity to shine a bit and show off some of her talents. "*Would it impress him?*" she thought.

He asked, "And you've tried to live your life that way?"

"Yes, oh, how about this, 'it is not death that a man should fear, but he should fear never beginning to live.'"

He had never heard anything like this insight into how to live one's life, except for the teachings from the Bible and the advice his mother had given him growing up. "That's good," Mordecai said, "I like that. I was frustrated when they told me all I would get to do was play music. I wanted to fight. Look what that got me."

"I was at Gettysburg. It was a horrible slaughter. I've never seen anything like it," she confessed. She looked at him and knew how he would have been changed, just as she had by the experience—and not in a good way. "I'm glad you missed it."

Mordecai said, "Maybe you're right. Maybe I should be glad I've seen as little blood as I have."

She put her hand on the rail and leaned over to spit. He put his hand near her to steady himself. They were close to touching, but there was a small gap between them.

"I got to go make water."

She nodded. Mordecai walked to a small clump of bushes. She heard him urinating and the rustle of his clothes as he buttoned his pants. "I guess I should have taken my rifle with me."

She spat again and leaned over the rail.

"Yep, you're a terrible soldier."

She realized that it might have been a hurtful thing to say to a soldier. She had heard him play and was amazed at this talent. They were just days away from returning home and beginning their lives anew.

They both laughed, leaning against the rail fence again, and their fingers touched ever so briefly. A shudder of recognition of the feelings they shared burst through Eloise's body. She turned her head but couldn't keep the smile from her lips.

"Sorry about that," Mordecai said.

"Sorry about what?" she asked, unknowingly teasing him. It was a joke only she could enjoy.

He was a musician, an artist. He'd known plenty of men who were attracted to other men, but he never believed he was one of them. But he felt a real connection with Edward. He would have to think on this one. Was it friendship? Was it more? "Sun will be up in a couple of hours," Mordecai said as he looked to the East. "If you want to get some sleep over yonder, I'll take watch."

"Maybe I should," Eloise agreed. "No tellin' what tomorrow might bring."

She felt her heart leap as she watched his profile move in the moonlight. Her first beau. How could she tell him, and how could she go on living this lie?

She put her rifle against a boulder near the fence and settled against it as best she could. She smiled to herself again. Her artistic yearning seemed to match Mordecai's. She loved music, poetry, and philosophy. A moment of truth would have to come someday. There would soon be a time when after the war, she would begin to live.

Chapter 75

In his barn just ten miles away, Edward saddled his horse. The huge black animal shuddered and swayed under the weight of the saddle. Jason entered, carrying a small sack.

"I got everythin' you asked for, hardtack, jerky, cornbread dodgers, and meal. And they's a sack of coffee and tobacco."

"And the gold?" Edward asked. Only three people knew about the stash of hidden money in the basement. Minta had let it slip during one of their lovemaking sessions. While it was an odd admission at the time, Edward had remembered. Jason had been told after he was cleaning and found the stash. Minta had trusted him with the information. Edward had not.

"And the gold?" Edward asked again, this time with a bit more force. Jason nodded.

Edward turned.

Jason's usual grin turned into a frown. Finally, his gaze dropped to the floor.

"Did you remember my medicine?" Edward asked.

"Nawsir, I'm sorry, I left that up in your bedroom. Miss Minta said you weren't goin' to need it."

Edward smacked him with the back of his hand. Jason's lip bled.

Jason muttered, "That's the last time." He knew the end of the war would mean an end to slavery, and his freedom was near.

"What did you say?" Edward asked.

Jason felt his heart leap. It was a moment that he'd waited for all his life. It was his time. But he said, "I didn't say nothin'."

Edward cinched the saddle.

Minta screamed, "So, the coward would rather live lookin' over his shoulder than stand and fight?"

He looked at her outlined in the light shining through the barn door. She was dressed in cotton slacks and a white, embroidered shirt. She had a small, black ribbon tied around her neck. Her cheeks were bright red, and her eyes fixed on him with the intensity of a flame.

She stood next to the stall where she'd had revenge sex with Jason with not a whit of recognition, guilt, or memory.

"Minta," Edward said, "you're the last person in the world to criticize me for choosing to live over choosing to die."

Edward grabbed the sack from Jason and threw it across the saddle.

"What is courage? I fear the definition has changed in our bright, new world." Minta said as she glided across the hallway and sidled up to Edward.

"Stay and fight," she said. "The meanin' of your life grows ever greater in death. If you live, you will lead the South in victory. If you die, you'll be a martyr to the cause."

He looked around the plantation and said, "You really believe I would rather die than live in this moss-covered hell?"

She touched his cheek. Her love for him had never been greater. She thought she could stop him from running away and that he would stay with her forever. She believed in the revolution, and she believed in him.

"I trust you'd rather choose to be a 'legend' instead of a footnote told over cigars by Blue-backed bastards that rape the land and enslave the people."

Edward shoved her aside. He mounted his horse.

"How far do you think you will get without your medicine?" she asked.

He kicked the horse in the side and left the barn.

Chapter 76

Sorrells and his posse mounted up. He knew this was only the next in several assignments he was ordered to carry out, just as all soldiers had to follow. Sorrells was a good soldier and thirsted for advancement. This mission could make that happen.

The group was not as motivated, and they demonstrated their apathy by sitting on their horses, waiting for orders.

The posse followed Sorrells away from the governor's residence at full gallop.

***

Edward tied the horse to the post at the north end of the circular drive. He burst through the front door and stomped toward the staircase. He grabbed the rail and forced himself up the stairs.

A gust of wind blew blades of dried grass over the threshold. Minta entered, out of breath about three steps behind Edward. "Your weakness mocks you!"

She followed him upstairs.

***

Sorrells and his band rushed toward a fork in the road. They darted past a sign reading, "Shelbyville, three miles." Sorrells had studied a map and had estimated just how long it would take to reach their destination.

A thunderstorm rumbled behind them as they rode.

Sorrells realized the coming storm would hamper the search. Still, he knew his duty, and he was prepared to do whatever was necessary to complete their orders.

***

The shadow of a cloud passed across Edward's window. Thunder crashed in the distance. The green velvet curtains hung next to a table filled with Edward's syringe, powders, a bowl and pitcher, and a leather strap. A small oil lamp burned. The light was trapped in a smudged chimney.

Lightning cracked, illuminating the room in a pale white hue.

Edward gathered the bags of powder into a cotton sack. He put the syringe into a small, black box and snapped the lid shut.

Minta was within arms-length of him when she said, "The proudest day of my life was when I heard of your bravery at the battle of Chattanooga. I could almost see you as you stood there, surveyin' the battlefield, dispatchin' your men, and plannin' the battle."

She pointed to the portrait of Edward hanging over his fireplace.

Lightning filled the window again with near-blinding light.

She said, "I could see you standin' there, the wind in your hair, wearin' your black coat, screamin' at the top of your lungs to 'Charge!'. At that moment, I could not have loved you more. That's why I commissioned that painting."

Edward paused in his packing and looked at the picture. "It was my finest moment," he mumbled.

She drew closer.

"Until now."

He knelt before her. She stroked his hair. He put his arms around her thighs and drew her close.

"The embers of revolution need only the slightest stirrin' from a stiff breeze. The Yankees know this. That's why they fear you so much," she told him.

"You're wrong. There'll be no revolution, only more death. And I'm afraid—" Edward said, shivering.

"Any warrior who says they are not afraid of death is lyin'," she replied, pulling his face close to her. She looked down at him and continued, "But what divides the truly great from the mediocre is the willingness to sacrifice all for a just cause."

Rain pounded the window. A jagged fork of lightning lit the room in an eerie white glow. To Edward, Minta's face looked like a skull bare of skin and flesh. He shook his head and closed his eyes.

In the doorway, a plank creaked as Virginia entered.

Minta said, "Any pain, any act, is justified if the cause is true."

Another creak. Edward looked at Virginia. Her eyes were downcast, hands folded.

She looked up at him and smiled. He stood.

His face was a mask of shame and guilt. Here was the woman he'd declared his future too but had ruined it by attacking her. He took a deep, ragged breath.

She stretched out her hand to Edward.

"Get out, whore!" Minta screamed. "Your corruption of this great man has ended!"

Virginia turned to Minta. She looked at the woman with pity and understanding and said, "Your hatred holds you because you preserve the past. It's not your fault. Your father had no right to do what he did to you. You must let that go. You must forgive him." Virginia said.

The incidents of abuse flashed in Minta's mind. How many times had it happened? She had lost count. She remembered how his visits ended soon after her thirteenth birthday. What happened to make him turn his attention away? She had no idea.

Minta's rage melted. "M-m-m-m-y father. My father was an inventor, a gentleman farmer, and a decent—I," she choked on the last words.

"You're mad," Virginia said as she crept forward, "I've seen what went on in this room and also in the cellar."

Minta gasped. "How could you? You weren't even born then."

"I have the 'second sight.'" Virginia turned to Edward. "And I've seen that our fates are tied deep into the future."

Virginia offered her hand to Edward. But, she said, "There's nothing she's done or can do that can keep us apart."

He looked at her and then his wife. He moved to his wife. He clearly felt each step he took and the breath in his lungs. He refused to look at Virginia and kept his gaze on Minta. Finally, he opened his arms, and Minta smiled. She knew she had won and that even with all her visions and youth, Virginia was no match for her.

Edward hugged Minta to his chest. Over his shoulder, Minta looked at the girl and smiled in victory at Virginia. She had won.

"All of God's children are worthy of love, Minta, even you," Virginia said as she wiped a tear from the corner of her eye and added, "And I love you."

A long, terrible moment as Edward squeezed tears from his tightly shut eyes.

Suddenly, his eyes flew open, and he set his jaw.

"This is the end. The time for revolution is now!" Edward cried.

He swept the lamp off the table and into the green curtains. The fabric ignited and trailed up the rotting wallpaper.

"GET OUT, VIRGINIA! SAVE YOURSELF!" he yelled.

A clap of thunder shook the glass in the large windows, and a flash of lightning filled the room.

Edward pushed Minta away from himself as the room ignited. The curtain wrapped around his wife.

"Edward!" Minta yelled, "NO! MOTHER OF GOD, NO!"

The wind pounded the window as a tree limb snapped and broke the glass. The gust of air fed the fire, and the room exploded into a pillar of flames.

Virginia moved toward Edward, and he shoved her away. She fell and then got up and turned.

"Run for your life!" Edward screamed.

He had seen so much death, so much suffering. He could save her, but not himself. He had sacrificed so much for the war, but now it was time for him to sacrifice himself to make things right. He was ready to die.

In Minta's clouded vision, time slowed. The pain was excruciating, but she had lived with pain for years and, at moments like this, considered it a friend. She opened her mouth to scream, but no sound would come. Instead, her lungs filled with smoke, and she saw her hands and arms disappear. The parameters of her mind narrowed. She felt regret, sorrow, but deep down, pride in what she had accomplished. Her beloved South would rise again under the leadership of her husband and crush their oppressors. She knew, in her heart, that what she would leave behind was more important than her life.

In her last moment, she looked at the two of them from inside the tower of flames. Her heart filled with pride as she took her last breath.

Chapter 77

Dozens of federal troopers fraternized while Militia Commander Andy Sorrells stroked his goateed chin. His dark eyes flashed as he reviewed his orders. He was a big man with thick shoulders and a protruding gut. He had stood in the back of the room as the governor met with the reporters. He had already received his orders but wanted to witness the shaping of the story in which he would play a significant part.

He left the building, crossed the courtyard in front of the mansion, and stood on the rough-hewn staircase. The governor and the military magistrate had complete control of the area. He knew that following orders might stop a bloodbath of Rebel sympathizers. Intelligence told them there could be thousands ready to continue the war or resist the Johnson government.

Sorrels knew the uprising's leader must be apprehended. His small group would arrest Corrigan and charge him with sedition. He had not seen the report on the rebellion, but he was a good soldier that carried out orders. It was the same for all of them, except for the generals.

"Portions of this mission are secret and will remain so in the common interest of the United States. I'll call out ten names, and you'll join me in the first troop. The rest of you will receive your orders from Lieutenant Commander Grams."

Sorrels had received several battlefield promotions for bravery and successful leadership efforts. The commendations in his file had fattened it to almost a quarter inch. He had fought at Vicksburg, Atlanta, and in Nashville. He'd distinguished himself as a capable soldier and knew in his heart he would serve for the rest of his life. So he put on half-glasses to read.

"Theodore Williams, Robert L. Giordano, James C. Smith, Edward P. Jacobson, Mordecai A ..."

***

Sorrells' troop moved down wagon-rutted roads with as much speed as the horses could muster. They circled the county courthouse in Murfreesboro, and the sound of their hoofbeats reverberated through the town. They had received their orders, and they were determined to do their duty. They knew saving lives sometimes cost sacrifice, and they had been ready to pay that price, no matter what, to keep the peace.

As they moved southeast, distant lightning flashed behind them. It was as if the weather was chasing them.

Thunder rumbled.

The troop faced forward, but soon blinding rain enveloped them as the wind blew the water sideways.

Sorrells stood in his stirrups and pointed forward to the men who followed. "Advance!" he yelled, "Ride as if your life depended on it!"

***

Virginia brushed rain from her eyes. She ran past the corral and saw a tree that seemed to have been split by a bolt of lightning. She glanced at the stump and stopped for a second. She tilted her head and looked at the splintered remnant.

A vision came to her of Minta in the corral with a shovel. She saw the older woman bury a packet of letters, and suddenly, she knew everything.

She turned, rushed to the barn, grabbed a horse, put a rein on it, and leaped upon him. She didn't have time for a saddle and was thankful she was wearing her riding pants. The life she had hoped for, the dream, the vision, was over, and she cried. She couldn't help herself.

She was a dutiful woman and had done as Edward said. She hadn't looked back, but she believed he was behind her.

She looked at the front door as she reined in the horse and jogged to the front of the house, but Edward wasn't there.

Suddenly, a column of fire erupted from Edward's bedroom window. "*Who could live through that,*" she thought.

She watched as the decomposing siding burst into flame, catching the roof ablaze. The rotted wood ignited and quickly spread to the front, sides, and back. Her hands were knotted in front of her, and her face was twisted with tension. She had to run.

She didn't look back as she galloped away.

***

Water puddled in the wagon grooves in the dirt road. Trees bent to the will of the wind as the storm reached its full strength.

Jason and Jewels didn't look back as they drove a flatbed wagon loaded with bags and wooden boxes with provisions they had taken from Briarwood. Those provisions included a small cut of the gold Edward had hoped to use to start his new life and the revolution.

They had seen the fire as it exploded from Edward's bedroom window. They believed it was their opportunity to escape to the North. They thought the wagon load would give them value in a new community.

Up ahead, they saw Sorrells' soldiers dash toward them. The troops veered toward Jason and Jewels for a moment. Jason gripped the reins, believing their attempt at freedom would be met with arrest. It was a fear that had stalked them both their entire adult lives. The notion that traveling without the proper documentation would mean confrontation and possible violence, even with the end of the war and the hostilities in sight.

Sorrells' troops breezed past them, and for the first time in their lives, Jason and Jewels took a long, deep breath of freedom.

***

Virginia gripped the reins and closed her eyes. The rain beat her face and shoulders. She believed Edward was trapped in the fire and that it had taken his life. She would grieve her loss in due time, but she knew escape was the best she could do for now. Finally, she came upon a signpost, read it, and headed west. She had enough money for the paddle wheeler and home. It was her only thought.

A pang of grief and guilt stirred in her heart, but she would have to put those emotions on the back burner until she felt safe.

***

Sorrells' soldiers pulled their horses up short in the front yard of Briarwood.

They were locked and loaded, ready for a confrontation that could end in blood. Instead, they breathed as heavily as their exhausted horses.

In the reflection of their eyes, they saw the house crumple into a pillar of flame. The men and Eloise stared, slack-jawed. She had seen a lot in her time during the war. She had seen row upon row of houses burn to the ground after a battle, but this fire burned as bright as the sun.

Sorrells hopped off his horse and dispatched his men to search the entire plantation. "Don't miss an inch," Sorrells said, "search everywhere." He felt the pressure of finding Corrigan and what it meant if they couldn't arrest him. He knew it would likely be hours before this fire was quenched enough to search for evidence. And how would they prove it was the scoundrel Corrigan?

The posse found the barns, slave quarters, and other outbuildings were saved from the fire. Then, as the rain pounded the fire into submission, the troop ended their search.

"All right, men," Sorrells said, "let's head back."

They mounted their horses and returned to Nashville.

***

Virginia knew all her hopes and dreams had ended. Her future with Edward was over. In many ways, she felt her life had ended in the fire. But, without love, what is life?

She had believed when reading his letters that she had the intellect and emotions to heal his wounds. She thought she knew him and all that he was. Now, she realized she knew nothing and that there wasn't anything she could have said or done that would have made a difference.

The war had taken his body and his mind. She had failed.

She looked over her shoulder at the smoke in the distance and then turned.

She screamed. "OH, GOD! NO!"

Chapter 78

I had been transferred to Tennessee in the fall of 1864 after my talent at the telegraph office was no longer needed. It was just a few months before Christmas time, and my longing for home and family made me most melancholy.

I was assigned to an overnight patrol of the perimeter of our campsite. I welcomed the opportunity to be unobserved and scrutinized for a time. However, the facade of being a male I was forced to erect every day was exhausting. While I still believed in the cause of the Union, there were times when I began to question the method to find a solution to the conflict.

I looked up at the moon and took a deep breath. The Tennessee sky at this time of the year was both inviting and harsh. Rain, followed by bright sunshine and, almost inevitably, heavy rain and storms.

The moon wore a yellow hue and displayed an astonishing clarity. There were times when the wonder of the natural world was overwhelming in its beauty. Then, I heard a crack and turned. It was likely just an animal in search of food. It didn't occur to me that another soldier would find his way this close to our camp.

We were briefed on the mission. Even though the war was over, there was a report of an uprising in middle Tennessee led by a former Confederate colonel by the name of Corrigan that would need to be quelled.

The outlaw had gathered over one thousand followers, and our numbers were matched. We were all sick of bloodshed and would be happy to see this "mopping up" operation ended as quickly as possible.

Chapter 79

We had been given the overnight shift in front of the guardhouse at the fence around the fortress. We had heard that the fort might come under attack and everyone was on edge. Unfortunately, our effort to serve the warrant at Colonel Corrigan's home had failed, so our support of the posse ended, and we were reassigned. After the fire had gone out, we searched the ruins and found several bodies, concluding that Corrigan had died in the blaze.

***

Mordecai stood at one corner of the small guard house, and I was stationed at the single, large black door.

There was a time when I didn't believe someone could sleep standing up, but as the troops were sent home, fewer of us had longer and more detailed assignments to cover the shortages.

I tugged at my coat in hopes of retaining more warmth. I didn't know it could get this cold in Tennessee at this time of year, so I hadn't dressed appropriately. Maybe the weather would be enough to keep me awake.

The good news for me was that I had finally received my separation date. I looked forward to the time I would leave the Army, but I knew I would miss the friends I'd made during the war.

I also knew Mordecai, and I would have to talk about my feelings for him. That would include coming clean to him about my taking on Edward's identity and what that would mean for our future if we were to have one.

I looked up at the moon as a cloud gently passed before it. I realized the Taurus new moon was called the Marcus Aurelius moon. I remembered how the spirit of the moon personified an authority that is exercised intelligently and rightly. It represents a spirit encouraging tolerance and acceptance of ideas and customs, which may be strange at first glance. It described the ability of humans to express empathy and generousness. I remember how Mr. Lincoln had talked about reconciliation after the war and that the South would need to be a full partner in the healing and rebuilding of the nation.

I was roused from my thoughts by the sound of a racking cough somewhere out there in the dark. "Who goes there," I asked. "What is the password?"

"Johnny Reb," he said with a gruff and low-pitched voice.

"Are you gonna shoot me?" I asked and raised my rifle and pointed in the direction of the man.

I felt my breathing slow and my eyesight gain more focus. The moon continued to provide considerable illumination. In the distance, far from my rifle's range, I saw a gray flop hat move near a boulder.

"Johnny, I got a bead on you, so you ought to come from behind there," I said. The man moved; rifle raised. He, too, realized that he was out of my range.

The soldier shouldered his weapon and moved toward me. "Don't shoot. I am greatly famished. Let us eat, and we'll pray together."

When he said that, time stood still for a moment. "*How could it be?*" I thought, "*So many months, years, had passed, and he was still alive?*"

"We'll pray together," I whispered, "Edward." I remembered how we'd knelt next to our dying father's bed and held hands as we prayed.

"Edward," I said, and then louder, "Edward?"

The figure moved closer, and even in the moonlight, I could tell it was him.

He was thinner, and his hair and beard were long and black. He was wearing a gray hat, which he took off to better help me identify him. He still walked the same and moved his arms in an almost musical rhythm. He had always found a way to keep himself neat and presentable in the past, but now he looked like a monster.

"What in heaven's name?" I said.

I had seen so much that stretched believability. There was a part of me that thought I'd someday see Edward, maybe only when we were both in heaven, but here he was clothed in the uniform of the enemy. An enemy that had been vanquished, but remnants still wanted to fight. He moved toward me, and I wished he was surrendering.

He moved to within twenty feet or so and put his rifle next to a stump. "All my men have scattered, and I have no idea where I am. I saw you at my farm as the house burned. I have to say I was surprised."

He remembered how he'd concealed himself in the loft of the barn and had hidden in a stack of hay as the soldiers searched. He had seen Eloise as she followed the others. He was so surprised he almost let out a yelp of recognition and joy. As they left, he mounted his horse and followed the posse to the fort. He didn't really have a plan, but he had so many questions for his sister.

"I never thought I'd see you again, Sister. And what the devil are you doin' here in that getup?" he asked.

He was wearing the uniform I'd seen so many times in my sights. The gray cotton and the brass buttons shone in the moonlight.

I said, "I'm serving my country against the rebellion from the Southerners."

"But that's impossible. You're a woman," he said. His face was lined in soot, and he moved his hair away from his eyes and mouth.

"When you left, someone—" I choked on the words. I'd seen so much and done so much in his name. I felt shame and guilt. "Someone had to save our family's name," I said as I raised my rifle.

He grinned, "Ehhh, you're a good soldier, bought the whole hook, line, and sinker."

It was amusing for him to find a willing debater. I had clearly expressed that it was now his time to take the other side that July Fourth.

"It appears you did, too." I relaxed a bit and pointed my rifle at the ground. Then, I said, "You changed your mind about fighting."

"I merely realized that it's time the South was allowed to make its own way in the world." He moved forward, inching his way toward the guardhouse.

"So, you won't fight for the Union, but you will take up arms with the Rebels? What about slavery? What about the Union?" I asked.

"The institution of slavery was crumbling under its own weight. I have seen it. Slavery would have ended all by itself without the interference of that devil Lincoln."

I choked back a sob, "You cannot speak ill of him. He was a great man. I knew him." I raised the rifle again, pointed it at him, and said, "I've fought in your place. I've fought to save you and our family from disgrace."

Edward advanced with his hands out, palms up. He knew this was a universal sign of surrender. He said, "I never asked that of you, Eloise. You should have stayed out of it. I have lived with what I've done."

I raised my rifle. "As do I."

"Will you shoot me now?" He chuckled and raised his hands. "Will you take me, prisoner? How will you explain that you are a woman and I am your brother, a dirty Reb?"

I lowered my rifle again. "You should just escape while you can. Take care of yourself, and we'll have more of this discussion when you are safely home. This war is almost over and done. Let's not make it even more of a tragedy."

Edward said, "Might I have at least one last brotherly hug before I return to my side of the argument?"

How could he know how much I needed to feel him in my arms? Was he able to read my mind and see all the days and nights I'd wondered what happened to him and how much I missed him?

He moved forward again. He had picked up his rifle with bayonet fixed and carried it at quarter arms. As he came closer, I realized that while the inside of my sibling might have changed, the outside was still very much my brother.

"Come no closer," I said.

I was about to raise my rifle again when I saw out of the corner of my eye my friend and my love, Mordecai, move with alacrity into the standoff.

"Mordecai, no!" I yelled.

But it was too late, he'd already engaged with Edward, and they fought with knives and unsheathed bayonets. Edward's bandaged arm, the cut he'd suffered in his fight with Clyde, hampered his movements and strength. He winced, feeling the pain he'd grown accustomed to from so many other battles. But today, the cut he'd suffered while fighting Clyde hampered his movement, flexibility, and strength.

The grunting and clanging of steel upon steel filled the small impression in the earth. The hollow had been created months before after the fort had been shelled by Rebel artillery. The ground had melted, and the grass now grew where there was nothing but mud just weeks earlier.

I took out my bayonet and advanced into the fray, but it was too late. Mordecai had found my brother's stomach with his blade, and by the time I was able to disentangle them, Edward was stabbed a second time. I stifled a scream, not wanting to bring more soldiers into the fight.

Mordecai arose from the ground and stared at Edward's face. He looked at me for a moment and shook his head.

"What kind of sorcery is this?" he asked.

"'tisn't sorcery, just nature. We are not twins, but we both take features from our mother."

I sat on the ground and cradled Edward's head in my hands. He smiled up at me and gasped. His eyes fell to my feet. "Are those my boots?" he asked.

In a moment, his eyes took on the glassy stare that I had seen too many times on the battlefield and in field hospitals.

Light snow began falling, and I closed his eyes and stood.

"He was my brother, and I am his sister."

I looked at Mordecai's face as I let him know the secret. I felt a moment of relief and then terror.

"We were but a year apart, he the elder," I said. I looked at him and asked. "You must not share this with anyone, Mordecai. I'm trusting you."

Still dumbfounded, Mordecai nodded his assurance that he would hold his tongue. He knew of many instances when brother had fought against brother on opposite sides of the battlefield. In his mind, a twisted logic formed, mirroring this situation.

I looked up at the falling snow and offered up a prayer of forgiveness and sorrow for what had happened. A wave of shock and anger filled my heart, and a tear slid down the side of my cheek.

"We should report this," Mordecai said.

"Let's find a fire first. I am mightily chilled," I suggested.

I knew, deep down, the chill was more than just the temperature. The shock of seeing Edward again and in a Reb uniform was almost too much for my heart. I had to sit on a small chair near the fortress tower to catch my breath. Mordecai was kind and understanding. He, too, had suffered a shock. He'd taken a life up close for the first time, and I noticed how his hands shook.

We turned and moved back toward the tents and fires of our camp. Mordecai kept his promise and never mentioned the conflict.

The campfires flickered in the light, falling snow. They became shimmering candles of light that led us away to our comrades. I looked at the young faces as Mordecai walked with me. So many of them would likely lose their lives tomorrow in a battle in a war that was over and that, for the most part, meant nothing to anyone.

I knew Edward's body would be discovered at first light. Later in a newspaper report, I found out that he had been identified as the leader of the unsuccessful Rebel uprising that had threatened peace and reconstruction.

I had been stabbed during battle, but the emotional pain I felt at the news of my brother's betrayal and death was the most painful wound.

I tried to understand how he had been recruited into being a Reb after reacting to my speech on July Fourth, a day that now seemed a lifetime ago.

Deep down in my heart, I knew that this would likely be a mystery that would never be solved.

Chapter 80

Virginia was lucky the Hockneys had saved her room in the boarding house. They had read the glowing letters of her time in Tennessee, but they felt there was an undertone of problems that could be disastrous. They were right, of course.

She'd left Edward's burning mansion with nothing more than what was in her pockets, the clothes on her back, and the horse she rode on. She arrived in Vicksburg dead tired and starving.

She needed a family, and the kindly old couple were as close as she could come to that now. So she worked in the kitchen for her room and board. She remembered some of the recipes Jewels had taught her, and the dishes became popular with the tenants. The months passed quickly, and soon it was time.

Of course, it was the middle of the night, but Mr. Hockney had successfully roused the doctor from his home and escorted him back to the house.

"Mrs. Hockney," the doctor said, "I'll need hot water and a clean cloth."

The house grew quiet as the other guests tried to respect the activities happening in an upstairs room. A gentle breeze blew through opposing windows as Virginia lay in the four-poster bed. Finally, at dawn, her labor neared the end.

Virginia cried in pain, tears filling her eyes. While the temperature in the room was cool, she was sweating, and her hair was matted to her head. Her furrowed brow twisted even more as the waves of pain moved through her body.

"NOOOOOO!"

The doctor ordered, "You're going to have to give me one more push, dear."

Virginia calmed a bit, nodded, focused, bit her lip, and pushed.

The doctor looked up from between her sheet-covered legs—a tiny peep and then a full-blown baby's cry.

"It's a boy," the doctor announced.

"Of course it is," Virginia said, "Oh my, Doctor."

The doctor put the baby on the new mother's chest.

She looked at him, wiggling and moving against her breast. He would search for her nipple soon, but for now, he was satisfied with hearing her heartbeat and feeling the warmth of her skin. She said, "He's beautiful."

"He's an excellent young man," the doctor said. "I'm tired. This is my fourth baby in as many nights."

Virginia cuddled the babe in her arms and said, "A baby born of love."

"One more little push," the doctor said. He smiled, gathered the placenta in his palm, stood, and put the tissue in a large bowl.

The doctor said, sadly, "I've delivered too many children to the world that will never get to meet their fathers."

Virginia said, eyes sparkling with tears and sweat, "His father's loving spirit lives in me, Doctor, and in this tiny heart."

The baby cried, and Virginia scooted up in bed to allow him to feed. She stuck her nipple in the baby's mouth.

The doctor took a thick book from a shelf in the bed stand. "The name of the father... for the family Bible."

He flipped to the middle. He dipped a nib into an inkwell and positioned the point at the last line on the page.

"My husband's name was Edward. I'm naming the baby after him," she lied. She needed to grow accustomed to the lie for the baby and his future.

The doctor wrote and then said, "So it is, so it ever will be." Then he packed up his syringes and utensils and snapped his black bag shut.

Virginia nursed baby Edward as the doctor left. She thought Edward would have been so proud of his beautiful boy and how he would have loved him. Would this have been the catalyst that would have saved him from his destruction? Of course, she would never know, but she believed, and that was enough.

She sang a song she would sing to the boy dozens of times in his life.

"I've placed my cradle on yon holly top,

And aye as the wind blew, my cradle did rock;

O hush a ba, baby, O ba lilly loo,

And hee and ba, birdie, my bonnie wee dow."

Virginia looked up and smiled at her grandfather's spectral image at the end of her bed.

"I've placed my cradle on yon holly top,

And aye as the wind blew, my cradle did rock..."

Chapter 81

How could this be any more annoying? I see how long the grass has grown. It tickles my ankles as I walk toward the grave. Heroes like my ancestors should be shown more respect. As I approach the gravestones, it dawns on me why the grass is so long, and it makes me so sad that I must stifle a tear. I thought about the men, all the boys who would lie in distant graves, tended by strangers who feel no more for their sacrifice than the loss of a cat.

How will I find them in this mess? And then, the oak tree in the middle of the cemetery, as it always has been. Why didn't I remember that? What is going on in my head?

The headstone reads my father's name. The one next to him is my mother. The slenderest of memories of her still rest at the edge of my mind.

She stands over my bed, bends down, and kisses my cheek. A dim light from the hallway bathes her in a yellow glow. She smiles down at me and says, "I love you. Tomorrow is another day."

A week later, she was dead from the fever.

"I've taken that phrase to heart all my life," she thought, *"Tomorrow means another chance to try and succeed. Tomorrow means another opportunity to fail and find out why."*

After all, I have seen and done; the phrase holds more meaning for me now than ever. As we celebrate the victory of the Union and the rejoining of the broken country, I see just how important tomorrow is.

Maybe this is the message I should deliver at this year's Fourth of July celebration. I still grieve for the death of my president, or could I say, my friend, Mr. Lincoln.

As I was writing the speech, I remembered how I had stood at Gettysburg and heard the president recite some of the words I'd written so many years ago. Had I inspired Mr. Lincoln to write the most famous speech in history? No, that wasn't possible. The terms he'd used were common for the time, and while there may have been some similarities, I was not the source. So, where had I obtained the hubris to think this?

For this year's speech, I wrote, "We, as a nation and a people, still grieve the death of our president. It is a bittersweet time in our history. I feel such pain in my heart that now, as we rebuild the destruction suffered in our great struggle, we come together as a nation once again. We will, someday, have the wherewithal to realize that while we may disagree with each other, we should never again find ourselves at the opposite ends of weapons of death. Let this time of reflection and contemplation help us find common ground on the ideas that have always brought us together, love of the land, home, and family."

How was that, Father? I hope that I will be able to call upon the example you gave me with your life. I hope that your vision of the future and the hard work you did to make it happen will guide me. My only wish was that my brother might find a resting place here next to you, as I'm sure I will someday.

I turned and watched the sun fall through the limbs of the oak. The tangle of shadows reminding me of that night as my mother told me she loved me.

In the end, I still hope.

Chapter 82

July 4, 1913

I'm running behind today. I almost missed the train from Boston to Harrisburg. I had a hard time covering the shifts at the telegraph office, even though traffic there was waning. Soon, even this most advanced technology will be replaced with the telephone. Still, the office should stay open a bit longer.

I've read that President Wilson will address the attendees at the ceremony. It's hard for me to believe that fifty years have passed. Where does the time go?

I've made reservations at a hotel, knowing that I would not be accommodated at the official campsites. My secret service to the country would stay a secret. My sacrifice continues to affect my life in so many ways. While I married, my doctor found that after trying for years, I was unable to conceive. It seems the wound I suffered in my abdomen damaged something, he explained, but I could not understand.

So, with the death of Henry, my husband, last year, my identity has changed again, from wife to widow.

I'm not even sure why I'm going to this ceremony. I have mixed feelings now about the defense of the Union. Was it all worth it? So many lives were lost. So much destruction, of which we, as a country, are still recovering.

At seventy-two, I find myself slowing down and asking for help in some instances to accomplish the tasks that, in the past, were simple. For example, I will hire a buggy to attend the president's speech and have the driver wait to return me to the train station.

It is a long, bumpy ride to the battlefield. The day is hot, and I'm glad that I have dressed appropriately. My broad-brimmed hat shields me from the glare of the sun, and I'm thankful that my eyesight still works well while my ears do not.

I arrive and am astonished at the size of the gathering. I walk toward the platform and realize that a reunion of sorts is going on near a presentation of the American flag. The group squeezes into what I found out later is called "the angle." It is where I witnessed much carnage and where a cannonball took away much of my hearing. Finally, I see the flag being raised. Today, the former Union soldiers, men from both sides, approached from the North and the Confederate soldiers from the South. Instead of rifles, this time, they are open-handed, and when they reach the stone wall, they stretch their arms across the rocks and they shake hands. Where the wall has fallen, they breach the stones and fall into each other's arms, embracing and crying into shirt and jacket shoulders. Eventually, there are smiles all around. Flasks are passed from one to the other, and the joy of living is celebrated.

I felt I had no right to be there. Why did I survive when so many of my fellow soldiers lost their lives?

I looked at row upon row of graves of the men who had died. The grass had grown over many, but there were a few who still were bare. I looked at the sky and saw billowy clouds. Would this be the day the rain would come that would fill those blank spots? I felt like one of those dusty places.

But I fought too. I looked at the faces and remembered the heat of the burning grass and the smell of gunpowder. When would these memories fade? In my heart, I knew that would never likely happen. The images were too vivid, and the need to honor the fallen was too strong.

So, I decided to soldier on. I vowed to make the rest of my life a tribute to the lives that had been lost and the men, no, the friends, who had died.

I knew that, in time, I would even find a way to forgive my brother. While he had taken up arms, I knew now that he believed in what he was doing and that while it was wrong, it was his decision. I grieved that he'd lost his life, but I knew that I would someday be in heaven with him, and we would have a long talk about his last words and the story of how he'd come to his decision to join the Rebs.

I also felt the urge to visit the final resting place of my beloved Junebug. Was there ever a more valued and loyal animal? I had had dogs growing up, but Junebug outshone them all. She had served me and, at times, seemed to put her life in jeopardy for mine. I remembered how she loved me to scratch her nose and make her ears twitch. I would give anything to do that once more for her. But, yes, she needed new flowers to be planted on her grave.

And what of my dear President Lincoln? It was a devastating loss, but I feel in my heart that he will surely be remembered as one of America's best. Who could deny that his mind and determination to save the Union wasn't the greatest feat in this country's history?

I remembered a conversation we had in the war room. He had maps spread over a huge table. There were groups of toy soldiers massed on a line, facing the opposing force. A river ran through the middle of the map. This waterway was too deep to navigate for the soldiers, so there was a stalemate.

The president looked at the situation and remarked, "Look here. Brothers and fathers stand within shouting distance of each other, rifles and cannon at the ready, but too far from each other to be effective. Imagine, so close and yet so far away. Imagine how the anger would drain away, and the realization of the foolishness of war would seep into their hearts. Would they remember the times they would be together as a family and yearn for one last embrace before death? This war, this horror, will end soon, but, for some, that moment will have to last an eternity."

I make my way through the crowd, brandishing my ear trumpet. While some people complain about being passed by this old lady, I find myself at the same spot where I heard President Lincoln make his most heartfelt and historic address.

My hat, thankfully, shields my eyes as I follow the dignitaries as they take the stage. There are perfunctory speeches by the director of the cemetery, local government officials, and others. Their droning on tired my one good ear, but I kept my attention on them as best I could. A young man offered me a chair at one point, and I gladly accepted.

When the president was introduced, I realized that it was the first time I'd ever seen the man in person. Newspaper photos didn't do him justice. President Wilson was tall and thin. He had a long nose and bushy eyebrows, which allowed his animated speech to affect people deep into the crowd.

He began his talk by thanking the other dignitaries in attendance and the veterans who had fought for their country. At one point, he said, "We have found one another again as brothers and comrades in arms, enemies no longer, generous friends rather, our battles long past, the quarrel was forgotten—except that we shall not forget the valor."

I glanced across the field, and to my amazement, I saw Mordecai. I knew it was him by the way he stood, and while he had aged, as had I, I moved toward him through the crowd and touched him on the arm.

His shoulders were rolled forward a bit, and his hair had receded to a thin, white fringe around his head. He breathed heavily, and his chest moved with labor. I remembered how much I loved his hands, and I noticed they were still strong, and his fingers were well-shaped.

He turned slightly, and I looked at him. There was a question in his eyes as to my identity. I was confused at times when people would approach, and I couldn't quite place them. I had become bold in my old age and sometimes asked them how I knew them and their names. I could see Mordecai was also struggling to place me.

"Mordecai, it's me, Eloise," I said.

His eyes continued to register questions. Finally, smiling, he grabbed me by the shoulders.

"Edward, oh, Eloise, oh, my," he said. He moved forward as if he might hug me but quickly took a step back. "I am so glad to see you."

"As I you. It's been so long. Fifty years. And yet," I said, "time passes like a twinkle of the eye."

He took a deep breath, and his shoulders sagged. "There are so many nights I lie awake thinkin' about what happened with your brother. I am so sorry."

I touched his hand and nodded. "He chose the life of a soldier and met the same end that so many suffered."

Mordecai nodded. "I know. But still—"

I shook my head, and he stopped. I know it was rude to interrupt him, but I believed he would forgive me. We had shared so much together, and, over time, I had worked through the emotions of the incident that had taken my brother's life. I didn't need to forgive Mordecai because I knew he was only doing what every soldier was supposed to do.

Changing the subject, I asked. "How has your life turned out? Did you return to your music? Did you get married?"

"I was married to a wonderful woman for 44 years. She was a singer, and we had a daughter. I wish she were here to meet you," he said. His eyes shone with a light of pride and love when he talked about his child.

"What's her name?" I asked.

"Abbie," he said, smiling. "We named her after Mr. Lincoln."

I returned his smile. "Yes, that's a good name. You honor a great man."

"I still play music, just not as good as I used to."

I nodded and smiled. From the tone of his voice, I could tell that he was sincere in his interest, and I felt his genuine affection for me.

While the decades had passed, the reconstruction of the South was still lagging. I believed the plan President Lincoln had in mind was not followed. I think he would have led the Congress to complete recognition and reconciliation, but President Johnson was not Lincoln. Instead, the Northern congressmen and senators wanted revenge and made a point of punishing the South whenever possible.

Mordecai took my hand for a moment as the crowd dispersed around us.

"You know, I go by my African name now. It's Adebowale," he said.

I tried to copy his pronunciation but failed miserably.

"Adebowale. I can understand that, but I'm not sure I'll ever be able to say it correctly."

We both laughed. He took my hand and said, with a gravelly tone in his voice, "We were such good friends. What about you? How did your life turn out?"

"I, too, was married. I couldn't have children of my own, but I took in orphans from time to time and sold the telegraph office to Western Union last year. I'm officially retired now, and I do what I want."

We both laughed, reminding us of the good times we'd had and how lucky we were to have survived.

"Let's go back to town and see if we can rustle up some grub," he said, grinning. It was a phrase he'd said countless times when we were on duty or just wasting time waiting for orders.

Again we laughed.

"I have a buggy right over there if you need a ride."

"My, my, Eloise," he said the name with such deliberation and affection that I was embarrassed. I could feel my cheeks burning.

The recognition of the anniversary put me in a nostalgic mood. I had never told anyone about an incident that, in the history books, meant nothing.

"I was part of the protection troop assigned to Mr. Lincoln just two days before his death," I said. Adebowale seemed genuinely interested and looked at me intently.

"We were visiting the ruined city of Richmond, Virginia. I was just a few steps behind him. He was sitting on a horse. It was of average size, but his legs dangled almost to the ground. It looked most comical. It was moments like that that made me love the man even more than I thought possible.

"The streets were filled with former slaves, and many took out handkerchiefs and waved them at the impromptu parade. Some of the women carried flowers and offered them to the president.

"One young boy ran up, and several of the other soldiers became visibly nervous. How could they adequately protect the president if just about anyone could rush up to him and shake his hand?"

"He said, 'Massa Lincoln, I just wanna say we appreciate everything you done for us.'

"The president said, 'You have no master anymore, other than the Lord Himself. You are a free person with all the rights of every American.'

"The boy stood there, shocked at his newly acknowledged freedom. He didn't know what to say or do. He would never be the same after that day.

"I've felt that way for years. The war was so disruptive, so damaging. How could I not be changed forever?"

Adebowale said, "All of us who survived were changed. Some for the better and some for the worse."

I nodded in agreement.

A word from President Wilson's speech stuck in my head. "Valor," I whispered, but Adebowale didn't hear or didn't understand me with the noise of the horse and buggy.

I thought about the nature of valor and wondered if there might be a quote from Marcus Aurelius that would bring focus to the fight, the cause, and the outcome. Unfortunately, for the life of me, I couldn't remember one. But I did remember, "Death smiles at us all; all a man can do is smile back."

I had seen so much death and destruction. How heavy was the price of peace?

"This is pretty, Eloise," Adebowale said. He glanced at the ribbon on my lapel.

"It's nothin'," I said.

"It's somethin'," he said.

It's called the Civil War Campaign Medal. It was given to both Union and Confederate soldiers. It means they all served with honor, duty, and pride. I had forgotten I'd pinned it to my coat that morning. It was just a slip of blue and gray cloth and a small medallion. President Lincoln's face was on one side of the medal encircled with the words "With malice toward none, with charity for all." The opposite side read "The Civil War 1861-1865."

It had been pinned on my uniform on my last day of service. It was like Father's, and for some reason, it made me think about him and how he never talked about his service in the war. Would he be proud of what I'd done, or would he be disappointed in his little girl?

"*What does it mean?*" I thought. The sergeant had pinned it to my lapel and patted me on the shoulder.

"Good job," he said. And he moved down the row to ten other soldiers.

I had survived, and I had killed in the name of the Union, and now I was to return to my life before the war. Now, fifty years later, that had proven to be impossible.

Adebowale gazed at me with love and pride in his eyes. I could feel him eyeing the pin, and he suddenly reached out and touched it.

"I seen other people's," Adebowale said.

Memories flooded my mind of all the faces of the men and women, living and dead I'd come to know and love during the war. Then, Mr. Lincoln's face came to me. He was smiling and looked at me with pride in his gaze. There was no one else like him, and I would always cherish the hours I spent with him. I realized that I was truly blessed, and I said a small prayer of thanks.

"Why hadn't Adebowale received one?" I asked myself. Was it because he was a Negro soldier? He had mustered out before me, and I didn't see him before his last day of service. On the other hand, maybe it was just an oversight.

"Didn't they give you one of these?"

"No," Adebowale said softly.

I unpinned the medal from my lapel and handed it to him. "Here."

"Naw, I can't take that from you." His eyes grew watery, and he frowned.

"It's not a gift. It's recognition of your service. You deserve it."

He took the medal and held it in the hollow of his hand. "I'll wear it with honor."

I nodded and smiled. "As Marcus Aurelius said, 'It is not death that a man should fear, but he should fear never beginning to live.'"

Adebowale smiled and nodded. "And we have lived."

"Yes," I said, "in so many ways, we have lived."

As we approached the station, I felt my eyes grow heavy. There was a dull throbbing in my chest, and my left arm ached a bit as if I'd been chopping wood. I looked at Adebowale and said his name, but I couldn't hear his response.

I felt his hand on mine as I dropped the reins. The horse picked up her pace and swerved toward the ditch. He took the reins and brought the buggy to a stop on the side of the road.

"Eloise," he said, the horse and buggy were finally quiet, but his voice was drifting farther and farther away. "Eloise."

What is happening to me? I asked. What is happeni—?

THE END